Red Fork Roots

TULSA SERIES SEQUEL

NORMA JEAN LUTZ

NUWS LINK, INC. PUBLISHING

ISBN: 978-1-947397-03-3 Print / Paperback

ISBN: 978-1-947397-04-0 Digital

I love to hear from my readers. You may contact me here:

https://www.normajeanlutz.com

normajean@BeANovelist.com

http://www.beanovelist.com

https://www.cleanteenreads.net

Contents

Introduction

The Tulsa Series

Readers of the original four titles in the *Tulsa Series* will instantly recognize the names of characters from those stories. Namely: Tessa (Jurgen) and Gaven MacIntyre, Clarette (Fortier), and Erik Torsten

If you've not read the *Tulsa Series* books, this is the perfect time to do so. *Red Fork Roots* will hold a deeper, clearer meaning once you're aware of the background of these fascinating characters.

{See list on the last pages.}

Disclaimer

As any fiction author might do, I took the liberty of altering the history of Red Fork to create a substantial foundation for the story line. Actually, Red Fork was brought into the Tulsa city limits October 16, 1927. Engulfed by Tulsa, it maintained its identity solely in the heart and minds of those whose roots were already sunk deep into the community.

The juxtaposition of the rich girl from Tulsa, attempting to become accepted as a member of this close-knit community is not an easy task. Thus, the basis for the story.

The town name of Red Fork has always fascinated me. It was the juncture where the reddish fork of the Arkansas River joined the normally blue-green Verdigris River that caught the attention of early explorers, thus resulting in the name Red Fork. When casting about for a setting for the sequel to my 4-title Tulsa Series, it turned out to be the perfect fit. As you read Lucie's story, I trust you will agree.

Prologue

MAY 1930

T he streets of Tulsa were deserted giving it a dejected appearance. Dawn was still a few hours off. Sadella Patton steered her red Stutz Roadster slowly toward Riverside Drive.

She'd chosen a meandering route from Kiefer, trying to take as much time as possible, dreading to go home. Merry Mae's, the Choc Joint outside Kiefer, had at one time in the not-too-distant past, been a lively place where she could go to dance, drink, and have a little fun. Now everything felt different. For a time, she assumed it was just her imagination. But that assumption had fled. People were angry. Upset. No one even wanted to dance with her.

Mae, the buxom owner, fitted out her jukebox with the best ever dance selections. But Sadella had sat all evening in a corner booth, behind a haze of smoke, and drank the god-awful choc beer. She knew how to drink it and how to hold it. She'd had plenty of practice. And she seemed to be the only one dropping coins into the slot to bring the gaily-lit jukebox to life. But even the best songs were depressing tonight.

The regulars—both black and white—by midnight were normally whooping it up and dancing all over that sawdust-coated floor in the center of the room. But not tonight.

The stock market chaos last fall had drastically changed everything. It sure as heck changed everything in the Patton family.

With each passing day, her longing to leave Tulsa for Hollywood grew stronger inside of her. Wesley could fly her there. She still had a little money tucked away. And heckfire, Wesley had more money than all of them, what with flying all those rich oil people crisscrossing the country. He had enough to loan her some dough *and* fly her out there.

She'd asked him last year, but he just laughed at her. "Sis, I know you think you're beautiful and all, but you'd starve out there in Hollywood within two weeks."

That was before. Back when they were still among the rich and elite of Tulsa. Before the nose dive.

Wesley was right on one thing. Sadella didn't just think she was beautiful—she *knew* she was beautiful. She's been told so by many men. Even some of her father's oil tycoon buddies. Well, use-to-be buddies. She wasn't sure he had any friends by this point. He'd gone begging to most of them for help when everything hit the skids. Needless to say, with no positive results.

But most especially, Shelby Harland had never ceased to tell her how beautiful he thought she was. Her shoulders slumped at the thought of Shel. It'd been almost ten years since he died. And his death had been mostly her fault. What would her life have been like had he lived and she'd become his wife?

Strangely, Shelby's father, E.V. Harland, head of the massive Harland Oil Company, did not lose all his holdings in the crash. He'd been clever enough to not sink his oil money in the stock market. Henry Patton had not been that clever.

The effect of the booze on Sadella was, as usual, evolving from the giddy to the slump. Where she cried easily and hated the world.

The refineries along Riverside Drive shimmered in their usual glow. Flames of natural gas flickered in the night sky. Electric lights lit them up like metal Christmas trees, with the reflections sparkling in the waters of the Arkansas River. The site used to thrill her, knowing that that black gold had created their wealth. Now the lights only taunted her.

The Patton house sat on the crest of a hill above Riverside Drive. As she approached, she could see it was mostly dark. So depressing. Recently, she'd been sleeping in the apartment above the garage in back of the house, just to get away from the noisy arguments of her parents.

Sadella had to laugh at the thought that her mother had that very afternoon, taken the train to Kansas City for a shopping trip. Trevalene Patton still could not believe the money had run out. Poor Trevalene. She'd become addicted to being rich. Sadella's mother was another one who scoffed at her dreams of being a movie star. She had no one who believed in her.

Maybe Sadella could get Lucie to go to bat for her. Lucie and Wesley had always been tight. Chances were good that Lucie could persuade Wesley to fly her out to Hollywood. But first, she'd have to think of a way to con Lucie. Not an easy task. Younger sister, Lucie, was a sharp one.

Henry Patton stood at the window of his upstairs office in the Patton mansion and gazed across Riverside Drive, and across the Arkansas River, to the massive refineries glowing there. Those refineries, once his submissive, obliging mistress, now his cunning enemy. Everything that had once been real and vibrant, was now a vapor. Overnight. All lost.

It was never about the money. Henry Patton had repeatedly told himself that all through the years. It was true—for the most part.

It had especially been true in the early days. Red Fork had been a wild, untamed place. The speculation. The hunt. The thrill of the chase. He had feasted on it all. It made his blood run hot. The negotiations. The deals. Many of those million-dollar deals took place in the lobby of the Tulsa Hotel.

He and E.V. learned to saunter in like they owned the place—even though the two of them must have looked like babies to the veteran oilmen. Several of those oilmen had come all the way from Pennsylvania where they'd been working the wells for years.

Those Yankees may have known about oil, but what they didn't know was Indian Territory and how to deal with the Territorial regulations. Head rights. Mineral rights. And they had no idea who was the final authority with the say-so of who could drill where and not be shut down by the officials.

E.V. Harland knew more people in Red Fork than most anyone in the territory. And he knew the details about that parcel of land in the area the big boys were salivating over. And, best of all, he knew that the landowner's wife's father was Chief Leovy.

E.V., only a few years older than Henry, seemed to have an intuitive sense about the oil business. The two met shortly after E.V. arrived in Tulsa. He came into Patton Hardware, located on Denver Avenue, asking Henry about where to find the best drilling equipment company.

"You fixing to get into wildcatting? They don't joke when they call it wild."

E.V., who hated his name Elmore Vince, and felt that initials sounded distinguished, took off his hat and leaned his elbows onto Henry's front counter.

"I left Indian Territory a few years ago chasing oil. I been to Pennsylvania, Illinois, Indiana, even down to Texas. Now everybody and their dog is talking about this place. So, I'm back. I'm sensing something big is about to blow."

Henry's hardware store was located right in the middle of town and so he heard lots of oilfield gossip. But none of it had interested him. But now as E.V. talked, Henry felt his heart racing. He put the "Out to Lunch" sign on the door and personally walked E.V. over to the Brennan Brothers oil field equipment warehouse.

Within a week, the two of them formed a loosely configured partnership. So began a long friendship. Then came the strike. The gusher. The money. More money than he'd ever seen in his young life.

The boredom came later. For a time, it was unrecognizable. But the truth was, being disgustingly wealthy had never lit his fire. Unlike Trevalene who learned to wear the wealth like a mink stole. She loved the prestige and her place in Tulsa society. Even the Garden Club, as dull as that was to Henry, moved her to great animation. She'd been president for more years that Henry cared to count. Then there was the Literary Club, and the Ladies' Society Group. She could even hold sway at city council meetings, sitting right by Henry's side.

Henry stepped back to his desk, picked up his gold cigarette case, flipped up the lid, took out a cigarette and lit it with the matching gold lighter. He'd bought the set at a quaint shop in Paris during their last European holiday.

Blowing a cloud of blue smoke in the air, he thought back to that night in 1905, when he first laid eyes on Trevalene. It had been lightly raining. Strange for the Indian Territory where rain most always came in sideways and with a vengeance.

He and E.V. were whiling away the night in a Negro Choc Joint just outside Greenwood, drinking and talking business. A pastime that consumed most of their waking hours. The rain pattered against the tin roof mixing with the sounds of the raucous music played by a few Negro musicians seated on a raised platform. Couples were dancing in a space in the center of the room where tables had been cleared. Dark-skinned bodies glistened with sweat in the dim light, as they danced with electric energy.

All of Indian Territory was dry, which meant the Choc Joints were among the few places where a man could sit down a get a decent drink.

Because the place was crowded, the two men had chosen a table near the back door. Suddenly, the door opened a bit and a Negro boy stuck his head in and looked around. Spying Henry and E.V., he quietly closed the door and approached them. His young face was clouded with fear.

"Can you help us?" His soft little voice could barely be heard above the music and the rain.

Henry was closer to him and heard his words. "Help? How? What's wrong?"

"They's a white girl at my Grandma Teppy's house. She need help. Befo' she gets us all in a heap o' trouble."

Henry looked over at his friend. "Did you hear what he said?" E.V. shook his head. Henry then leaned over and whispered in E.V.'s ear.

E.V. scowled. "No sir. Not me. I don't wanna get messed up in that kind of stuff."

Henry turned back to the boy. "What kind of help?"

"She done had a baby. We finds her in our barn. Mos' close to being dead."

Henry drained the last of his beer, flipped a few coins onto the table, and stood to his feet. "Come on, E.V. Let's get this taken care of."

With a deep sigh to express his reluctance, E.V. grabbed his hat and mashed it on his head.

As quietly as the boy had slipped in, the three of them slipped out into the rain.

"Is it far? My buckboard's here." E.V. pointed to his wagon among about a dozen others.

The boy shook his head. "This way." And he took off running. The two men had a devil of a time keeping up.

It was a small but neat little house, actually quite a way from the Choc Joint. The boy jumped up on the porch and slammed through the front door. "I'se found help," he hollered. "They's white."From the kitchen they heard a woman's voice say, "For the sake of all that's good, chile. Keep your voice down. She's sleeping."

Into the tiny living room a Negro woman appeared, dressed in a cotton dress covered with a flower-patterned, ruffled apron. Henry was sure he'd seen her before in his hardware store.

"Charlie, now you git on over to Aunt Hazel's. You done good. I'se mighty proud of you." She stepped over and hugged the boy and then gave him a little push. He sped past the men who nearly filled the living room, and out the front door back out into the rain.

"That's my grandbaby." She nodded toward the door. "They calls me Teppy. I thank y'all for coming. We don't know what to do. Don't want nobody blaming us for doing something wrong." She smoothed her hands down her apron. Henry could tell she was edgy about having them in her house.

"Where is she?" he asked.

Teppy pointed to door on the other side of the room. "The back bedroom."

"Your grandson said there's a baby. Did you deliver the baby?"

She lowered her head. A little catch sounded in her voice as she answered. "She was bleeding awful bad. So we gots our doctor."

Now E.V. who had been hanging back close to the door spoke up. "A Nigra doctor?" He couldn't keep the shock out of his voice.

Teppy nodded very slightly.

Henry waved his hand to dismiss E.V. misgivings. "Don't matter. He probably saved her life. And the kid's." Stepping toward the doorway, he turned back to E.V. "You coming?"

E.V. shook his head. "I'll just wait out on the porch." And he was gone.

Even after all she'd suffered, when Henry first laid eyes on her, he thought Trevalene was the most beautiful girl he'd ever seen. Her skin was a soft ivory and her hair as black as a raven's. Her black lashes lay in stark contrast against her pale cheeks. In her arms lay a snuggled, sleeping baby wrapped in a clean blanket. There was no evidence of the bleeding they mentioned. They had taken good care of this girl.

Teppy stood at the door to the bedroom. "Will y'all take her? She gots to leave here."

"Have you tried to get hold of the father?"

"She say they's nobody. A hired man at their farm hurt her and her folks done put her out."

Henry wondered where she'd been all these months leading up to the birth. What a sad state of affairs.

"We'll get our wagon."

Teppy stepped out of the way as he moved out of the bedroom.

"We'll need more blankets," he told her on his way out.

"We gots plenty. And canvas from our old wagon."

Within hours Trevalene was safe in Henry's small house behind the hardware store. And within a few days he'd become a husband and a father. When he offered her his home and his life, she had said yes. They were married in the house with a local preacher officiating and E.V. and his fiancé, Flora, as witnesses.

The early years were bliss. Even though their daughter, Sadella, was a headstrong, difficult child, Henry loved her like his own. He was thrilled beyond words when son, Wesley, arrived. Then sweet Lucie came on the scene. But after Lucie was born, Trevalene began to change, choosing to leave their bed for her own bed and her own bedroom. Her own *suite* she called it. By then, they were ensconced in the Patton mansion. Devasted was an understatement for how it affected Henry. He desperately missed their intimate times.

From his office pinnacle in his mansion, the forlorn moaning of a train whistle sounded in the distance, and drew him down a dark corridor of the past. Back in the day, freight cars filled with giant culverts for Patton oil wells raced along the rails. Freight cars filled with countless pieces of equipment, headed in all four points of the compass making deliveries to the Patton refineries. And many were the occasions he, as the successful oil baron, rented a private train car in which his family traveled around the country.

Now he crushed out the half-smoked cigarette in the etched, lead-glass ashtray, yet another purchase from their European tour two years ago. From off the desk he picked up the framed photograph showing the two of them a year or so before Wesley was born. He stared at it for a few moments. Even then, Trevalene's beauty made men turn their heads wherever they went.

Within the same year of their marriage, the Red Fork well came in. Because E.V. knew the Osage Chief, and because of his finesse and ability to smooth talk and finagle a deal, they brought in partners who had the capital to build the rig and start the drilling. It all came to pass and never once raised the eyebrows of the Indian agents. Agents—those men who worked for the government to *protect* the poor Indians. Yeah. What a joke that was. Many other hopeful wildcatters were forced out of the picture for a year or so. The competition had been squelched.

They were both on the scene the night the well came in. As they slept in their open wagon near the rig, Henry felt it first. Just a slight rumbling and vibration. The other workers were asleep in the shack a few yards away.

Henry gave E.V.'s shoulder a rough shake. "Wake up! Can you feel that?"

E.V. sat straight up, paused for a few seconds, then said, "Hey! I do. Come on!"

Leaping out of the wagon they ran toward the rig and stepped up on the platform. The vibration got louder. Stronger. It became a bubbling, rumbling sound, then a whoosh. Black gold gushed up over the top of the derrick. The other workers were now awake and running their direction. Such yelling, shouting, and carrying on. No one had been drinking, but they were all intoxicated with excitement, plus a smidgeon of bewilderment.

When you work and work and work. And pray. And hope. And watch. And wait. When it finally happens, it's beyond belief.

From that day forward, life was never the same.

And now, once again, life would never be the same.

He stepped across the room to where three massive waist-high Chinese vases stood. He guessed they were called vases. Or urns. Or some stupid name. He hated those things with a passion. Two more were stationed in the front entryway to the house. Never a day went by that he didn't regret ever taking Trevalene to the Orient. She practically bought the place out. He hated it all, and especially hated those blue-patterned, hideous monstrosities that she insisted be placed in his office. She rattled on and on about Ming dynasty nonsense.

Then there was one smaller one that she kept in the safe in the dressing room closet in her suite. That one, she told him was Qing Dynasty. Rarer than all the others. Priceless.

If that weren't enough, the sunroom was overflowing in rattan that she'd insisted on purchasing and bringing home. Rattan furniture, wall coverings. Even rattan on the floor.

"Why?" he'd asked. "We have a heck of a lot better stuff in the good old U.S. of A."

He quickly learned not to ask why—about much of anything. Now it didn't matter anyway. The auction, scheduled for day after tomorrow, would close the chapter. Then where would he go? What would he do? If only he'd stayed in oil—stayed with what he knew—and kept out of the stock market... If only. Several people close to him tried to warn him. He refused to listen.

Too late now.

That morning, after putting his wife on the train to Kansas City, he was suddenly hit with a realization. That Qing Dynasty vase was still in Trevalene's wall safe. Who knew what it was worth? Priceless was how she once described it. He hurried back into the house and ran up the stairs and into the dressing room, removed a heavy, gold-framed painting off the wall. With shaking fingers, he turned the dial on the combination lock. She'd also kept some of her better jewelry in the safe as well. This could be the answer. Starting over twice, he continued to turn the dial until the door finally opened. Peering in, he viewed a dark, empty safe. Nothing. He stood there in front of the small cavern unable to move. Had she sold everything off without his knowledge? She had developed such a hunger for things. Her many furs alone attested to that fact. Not to mention her countless pieces of uniquely-designed jewelry.

In disbelief, he even reached his hand inside, feeling around. A silly gesture, but that's what desperation does to a person. This cache had been his last hope.

That had taken place early that morning. Now it was dark. Late. Trevalene wouldn't be home until the next day. He looked over at the pearl-handled derringer lying on his desk and wondered how much that historic piece might bring at auction.

Sadella nosed her Stutz up close to the garage in the back of the house. She looked over at her mother's elaborate rose garden, which like everything else at the Patton's these days, was in a sorry state of neglect. At one time there had been a team of trained gardeners who never let one little weed show its head. Now not only had the weeds taken over, the rose bushes were dying. There'd been no spring rains.

She had just placed her hand on the car door handle to open it when she heard the gunshot ring out. She froze in place. Slowly, she shifted into neutral and let the car roll back down the drive, and out onto street. The Pattons had always prided themselves that there were no close neighbors on this hill. They owned the hill. Tonight, it worked in her favor. Starting the coupe, she drove out to Standpipe Hill at the edge of town, stopped the car, and just sat there. It sure as heck wasn't going to be her that discovered a bloody body. Let him rot for all she cared.

Chapter 1

RED FORK, OKLAHOMA, MAY 1933

L ucie still felt like a stranger, an interloper, when she walked into the Red Fork Baptist Church. People still greeted her with suspicion. She felt the stares.

Miss Cordell seated primly at the piano on the platform played a mixture of hymns. Her Sunday hat, purple in color with the flowers blooming off the side, was different than the grey felt that she wore when shopping in town.

Pastor Levinson seated, not primly but very stoically, in his chair behind the pulpit, surveyed his small congregation. His loose-fitting tan suit was a bit more rumpled each week. No one bought new suits these days—over three years into what the newscasters and politicians were calling the Great Depression.

Lucie hadn't seen Pastor Levinson smile much. What his problem was, she wasn't aware. But she did wish he were a little more cheerful about his walk with the Lord.

When she and Wesley first set up shop—as Wesley liked to say—in Red Fork, she attempted to attend Sunday School. While she enjoyed the Bible studies, she couldn't abide the lack of companionship among those in the class. The teacher, Wade Nichols the town barber, offered at least a friendly smile to her when she came in. As did his wife, Sarah. They even chatted with her after service. But they were among the few. Lucie guessed that being the daughter of a formerly wealthy oilman, and being from Tulsa, set her apart. She wasn't sure what they thought. But even after over a year, she still held out hope she could win them over.

She'd taken to sitting near the back on the left side. A bit out of everyone's way. That position lent a safer feeling. When Wesley was with her, he of course, barged right down to the front. But of late, he'd been flying businessmen here and there, and seemed to be away more than she liked.

The purchase of the filling station and store, and their subsequent move to Red Fork had all been his idea. Well, his and Gaven MacIntyre's. Together they'd been watching the auctions. It was actually Gaven who found the listing. He said that the purchase would help someone who was desperate and would keep them from bankruptcy.

"It's a great deal," Wesley had said to her. "We can be part of a small community and be a service. This poor fellow needs out, and I seem to be one of the few people in Tulsa County with even a penny in my pocket."

When Wesley got excited, he resembled a puppy dog whose tail wagged him. The animation. The way his voice went up and up. Both in level and in tone. Rarely could she resist that excitement. He had a way of making everything sound so grand.

And he was right. His plane and his piloting skills were much in demand, as businessmen—especially those in the oil and gas industry—were racing about trying to locate new leases and salvage what they could after the crash. So yes, he did have a penny in his pocket. And more than that. Quite a lot was stuffed into the coffee tin at the top of the kitchen cupboard.

When she first saw the filling station, and the little store situated back of the driveway from where the tall, skinny red pumps stood, she lost any enthusiasm she might have mustered at hearing his story. It looked decrepit, neglected, and a bit dismal. Like everything else since the bottom fell out of the world in '29.

Reading her thoughts, he put his arm around her shoulders and gave her a little shake. "Aw Sis, I know it doesn't look like much, but it's a money maker.

We're right here on Route 66, and think about it. Who doesn't need a tank of gas?"

"If anyone will still have a car," she shot back at him.

"But of course people will have cars. This is America."

Shaking his arm off her shoulder, she said, "Wesley James Patton, I have no idea how to pump gas." She stepped over and tapped one of the sinister-looking metal gas pumps.

"We might have to hire someone to take care of that. Your place will be in the store. Ordering merchandise and stocking shelves. Taking care of customers."

She shook her head. "I don't know anything about that either. That subject seemed to have been missing in our curriculum at *Blakemore's Finishing School for Girls*."

True to form, Wesley laughed uproariously at her jab at humor. "Lucie, you're so quick. You'll learn it all in no time. And I know you'll have creative ideas of your own how to make the store turn a profit."

And he was right. Well, partially right. Actually, when they put their heads together, several ideas came to the surface.

Everyone in the congregation was standing for the first hymn and Lucie had missed hearing the page number. She stood, opened the hymn book, and pretended. Then realized she didn't need to pretend. She knew every stanza of "Love Lifted Me" by heart.

Of all subjects, Pastor Levinson's sermon this particular Sunday centered on forgiveness.

"I'm taking for my text today," the pastor began, clearing his throat a little too loud, "the passage in Colossians 3:13 that tells us, *Forbearing one another, and forgiving one another, if any man have a quarrel against any: even as Christ forgave you, so also do ye.*"

Gracious mercy, how she struggled with that one. She still wasn't sure she'd forgiven her father for making his convenient exit from this world, and leaving them all in a calamitous turmoil of endless details to sort through. She didn't have a quarrel with him, since he was no longer around. But in a way, she did.

She seemed to argue and rail at him in her thoughts way too much of the time. What a selfish thing for him to do.

He was the one who ran his business with an iron fist. Always in the right. Telling others how things should be done. Overseeing a multi-million-dollar oil company with wells, leases, pipelines, then even the refineries. He oversaw it all. Had it been a sham?

Shortly after Henry Patton's funeral, she remembered her dear friend, Tessa MacIntyre, saying something like, "We can never know what another person is going through, Lucie. Your father may have been struggling with demons you knew nothing about."

Tessa may have been right, but her kind words did little to settle the storm raging inside Lucie.

As Lucie turned in her Bible to the book of Colossians, she once again looked at the presentation page in the front. There in Tessa's flowing script, she'd penned the words:

May the power of the Word of God always be your lodestar. You will always be in my heart and in my prayers. Love, Tessa

Tessa MacIntyre, for a short time, had served as governess for her and Wesley. That was right around the time of the uprising that resulted in the decimation of the black community of Greenwood—Tulsa's Black Wall Street. Even though Tessa had disappeared from out of their lives for a time, she was now a close, trusted friend.

The pastor's voice droned on, and Lucie realized she hadn't been listening.

How am I going to learn about forgiveness if I won't even listen?

For May, it was already warm and most everyone in the congregation made use of the cardboard fans with the wooden handles supplied by Hogle's Funeral Home. She, too, pulled one out of the hymnal rack and made an attempt to move air.

For a moment she studied the sweet picture on the fan of Jesus holding a lamb. She loved that picture. In a strange way, it lent peace to her soul, if even for a few moments.

It was just as Pastor Levinson gave the benediction that the roar sounded outside.

Oh Wesley. Please. Not now.

Yes now. Several people turned to look at her and smile. They'd gotten used to the Blue Bolt flying over their heads and making a roar. Wesley had a habit of flying once over Red Fork, banking, zooming over a second time, and then off to the airport at Jenks.

Interesting to Lucie that people only paid attention to her when Wesley was involved. Everyone loved Wesley Patton. Sometimes she wished he were not so doggone good looking.

He'd be home soon and she needed to get his dinner ready. Before the last stanza of the closing hymn, she slipped out, stepped into the spring sunshine, and headed toward the house.

Their two-story stone house, located at the far west edge of town, known as Cairn Cottage by the local residents, was rather an iconic feature of Red Fork. Ever since she and Wesley bought it at foreclosure auction, they'd heard several stories of its past history.

Strange that it came tied to the filling station. Or the filling station was tied to the house. Lucie was never sure which.

Her walk home took her right by their business venture. From the outset, they'd vowed it would be the cleanest, neatest filling station in the area. Not like some they'd seen in Tulsa.

"It won't be an oily, greasy, trashy garage," Wesley had stated. "It's a filling station and supply store. That's it."

As she approached, Lucie paused and looked up at their sign, *Okesa Oil and Gasoline Station,* painted in bright cobalt blue letters, with the bold *Okesa OK* logo also in dark blue. Below in black script their motto proclaimed: *This is the day to trust OK – Okesa.* Their logo—a winged sparkplug—was becoming a familiar icon as Okesa increased their marketing.

Hearing the whistle of mid-day train arriving, she glanced back down Main Street to where the tracks intersected the town. It had been a long while since she'd enjoyed a long train trip. As a child, a family train excursion was a highlight in her life. Trains were her favorite. Ocean liners she logged way down on her list, because inevitably bouts of sea sickness ruined everything.

The train would be making only a brief stop at Red Fork to drop off the mail bags. Rarely did any passengers disembarked their small town. Unlike the oil boom days when the trains offered the most readily available transportation for the hundreds of people who flooded the streets of Red Fork looking for an easy dollar. From teamsters, to roustabouts, tank builders, pipe layers, storekeepers, lawyers, speculators, and of course the gamblers and prostitutes. She remembered her father and E.V. described it like a *carnival*. A *dirty, filthy carnival*.

The rattling, clanking, scraping, and hissing of the train carried through the hot, still air as the Frisco moved on toward its next destination.

Lucie's attention returned to their filling station. This venture occasioned one of the few times she and Wesley had a disagreement. It concerned which company to align with for their filling station. She much preferred to stay with Harland Oil, because of their long association with E.V. But Wesley had been spending time with the Okesa founder and CEO, Trent Calvert, and Trent had won him over. Plus, ever since the death of E.V.'s son, Shelby, the two families seemed to have parted ways. Wesley brought that up as well.

He also pointed out that Okesa Oil and Gas Company sponsored the Saturday morning children's radio program, *Spaceboy Sparkie,* which was hugely popular with almost every kid in America.

"Why would an oil company sponsor a children's program?" Lucie had asked when she first heard about it. "That's ridiculous. All the kids' radio shows I know about are sponsored by breakfast cereals."

She soon learned how little she knew. Trent was an endless fountain of marketing ideas. Secret code rings, plastic ray guns, and maps of the Sparkie Galaxy were just a few of the giveaways that brought customers to their location.

She'd met Trent only once. The day he came to check on their place, and complimented them on having the best-looking station in all of Oklahoma. A tall, muscular man with an open, jovial face, he appeared nearly always in his shirtsleeves. No coat or tie for this CEO. Pipe always in hand, with wisps of smoke curling around his head. Lucie liked him immediately.

Although outwardly he appeared to be all-business, he talked with her and Wesley as equals, cracking jokes all the while. He was willing to pour his marketing knowledge into them and assist in the success of their new business venture.

Shaking off the reverie, she hurried on home to get dinner on the table for her brother whose appetite was ravenous.

Chapter 2

RED FORK, OKLAHOMA, MAY 1933

T he Blue Bolt banked over Red Fork causing residents to shield their eyes as they gazed skyward. Wesley kept it higher than usual. A glance at his watch let him know church may still be going on. The Oklahoma mid-day sun reflected off the silver body of the most stunningly beautiful plane ever to fly. At least that was his opinion. And at this moment that was the only opinion that mattered.

Sometimes he wished he could watch it from the ground. To see that luminous bird gliding effortlessly through the air. But then, it was much more fun to be the one at the controls. Feeling it obey his commands. Responding to his directions.

Actually, he *had* seen it in the sky. Once. The day it was delivered to Artie's Airport almost a year ago. The very sight of it flying overhead sucked all the breath out of him. He felt faint and stepped over to lean against the door of the hangar. From the ground he could see the *Spartan NC 176616*. It was the blue lightning bolt on the side, contrasting against the silver fuselage, that sparked his idea for the name *Blue Bolt*. Only God knew that it would echo the logo of *Okesa Oil*. Trent was sure God had done it just for Wesley.

Even Artie was unable to hide his emotion the very first time he watched it come in for a smooth landing. "It's so beautiful," he had said with a catch in his voice. "It's classic. Pure classic. Wesley Patton, you are one lucky pilot."

While Wesley didn't counter the comment, he knew full well that luck had nothing to do with it. He'd been taking careful, calculated steps ever since the '29 crash. And even before. It was his father, Henry, who played the game with luck. And look where it got him.

Now the Blue Bolt headed south from Red Fork to Artie's Airport at Jenks. Wesley's and Artie's friendship had begun the day Gaven MacIntyre took the young boy Wesley for a visit to appease his interest in planes. Gaven's wife, Tessa, had been his and Lucie's governess for a short time, back when the two of them were still in grammar school. And even back then, Gaven had been kind enough to share books about planes with Wesley.

What a blessing Gaven had been during the years when Henry was going full throttle building his Patton oil empire. Wesley and Lucie rarely saw their father during those years. Gaven seemed to sense Wesley's need for a father-figure.

And then there was Artie. He immediately connected Wesley's love for planes with his innate ability to take to the air—his fascination for machines, his grasp of the basics of how a plane operated, and his understanding of all the moving parts of the plane. Artie gave Wesley his first flying lessons, but he wasn't the one who gave him his first plane ride. That happened on his thirteenth birthday. His father had driven him to Chickasha to watch a one-eyed pilot named Wiley Post, star in a barn-storming show. It was the only time Wesley ever remembered his father paying any attention to him. Or showing an interest in his fascination with planes and flying.

Wesley often mulled over the events of that day. Years later, he would always mark the day as a line of demarcation.

A crowd of onlookers filled the pasture. His father had parked behind the many rows of cars and not a few wagons with the horses still hitched. Wesley could see the airplane sitting in the middle of that pasture. It was all he could do to keep from taking off running toward it. It was the first airplane he'd ever seen. Other than the pictures in the books Gaven had given him.

His father tried to hold back, but Wesley pushed through the standing crowd to be right at the front. Henry had no choice but to follow his son. Spellbound, Wesley watched as the airplane took off and executed a series of loops, banks, and flips. Gasps and oohs and ahhs came from the crowd, but Wesley made not a sound. How could a machine do that? Pure magic. It was just like magic. Wesley wanted to know everything about it. How could a machine stay up in the air and defy gravity in such a grand manner? How could one man make it behave up there in the clouds?

When the plane landed, Wiley Post and his flying partner began offering rides for five dollars—a mammoth sum for most Oklahoma ranchers and farmers in 1926, but a mere pittance for a wealthy oil tycoon like Henry Patton.

Years later, Wesley would wonder. Was Wiley Post looking just for him? How did he pick him out of the crowd? Did he sense something? Before he realized what was happening, Wiley walked straight toward him.

"Young man, you'd like a ride in my machine, wouldn't you."

It was a statement. Not a question.

Henry Patton took that moment to step between them. "Those contraptions are death traps. Not sure I want my son risking his life."

Henry Patton stood several inches taller than Mr. Post, but was no match for the aviator's imposing demeanor. Wesley remembered looking up at Wiley Post, studying that eye patch and thinking, *If he can fly an airplane with one eye, then anybody can do it.*

"This boy is practically boiling over with eagerness to get in this *contraption* and meet the clouds." He looked square at Wesley. "Aren't you boy?"

Wesley, still unable to speak, could only nod.

To Henry, he said, "When will he ever get this chance again? Every day we live is a risk." He touched the eye patch. "When I arrived at an oil rig one morning, I had no idea I was about to risk my eye. But I did. And I'm still here. Who's to say what's a risk, and what's not?"

To that logic, Henry had no answer. He reached for his gold money clip and from the wad of bills, pulled out a five spot and handed it over.

That was the event that transformed Wesley's life. He felt no fear. And as Wiley told him later, he was one of very few who didn't get sick. Donning a pair of goggles, he felt the wind whipping by them as they slipped through the air. For a brief time, Wiley even allowed him to take the controls. The ecstasy of that moment never faded.

But there was yet another facet to the experience that day. As he looked down from their lofty position, as he saw his father, the great and mighty oil baron Henry Patton, standing there at the edge of the pasture blending in with all the other miniature people, a disconnect happened. Almost like an audible snap. Nothing Wesley could have ever described. But nothing he could ever deny.

Henry never stopped nagging at his son to come and join the Patton Oil Company and leave the *death traps* behind. A common occurrence at the breakfast table was when his father shoved the morning paper under Wesley's face, pointing out the lurid details of yet another airplane crash.

Out of respect for his father, Wesley resisted pointing out the many oil field, and oil rig accidents—some fatal. Not to mention the massive fires that broke out most anywhere there were pockets of natural gas. Such incidents became so common, they never even made the news. Plus, no reporter was on the premises to write the story.

The year preceding the stock market crash, his father took him to New York, where Henry introduced his son to many of his high-roller stock investor buddies. It was yet another attempt to take Wesley's mind off of being an aviator. Such irony that it turned out to be the very day of the homecoming, and tribute, to Amelia Earhart and her crew in a tickertape parade down Fifth Avenue. Amelia had become the first woman to fly across the Atlantic. She wasn't the pilot, but certainly would be in later flights.

Wesley ignored those to whom he was introduced by his father, and instead watching from a skyscraper window, he was totally mesmerized by the returning aviators. Long-distance flying was becoming almost an everyday event. His future in aviation was never so clear as it had been on that day.

As he brought the Blue Bolt over small town of Jenks, the words *Artie's Air Service,* emblazoned on the roof of the hangar came into view. Since it was Sunday, Artie's was pretty quiet. The Schneider's house, barns, and gardens, were spread out at the far end of the airport, on the other side of the hangar, nearly hidden in a thick grove of trees. Artie's Model A chugged along raising dust on the dirt road leading to their house. Their two sons, Ralph and Harold, were riding in the rumble seat. Probably coming home from church.

As Wesley came in for a smooth landing, shut her down, and jumped to the ground, he was attacked by two boys who raced to see who would get to him first. Pushing and shoving one another they nearly knocked Wesley over.

"Uncle Wesley, can we have a ride? Can we, huh? Can we please?"

That from Ralph the elder, the more boisterous and vocal of the two. Harold, a bit quieter—but not much—echoed the pleas. Now at nine and seven years old, both were showing greater interest in all that went on behind the scenes in their father's hangar and repair shop.

Since Wesley had known the boys pretty much all their lives, early on he'd become *uncle.* It wasn't often he could give them rides. Fuel was a precious commodity these days.

Reaching down and pulling them close, he said, "Not today boys. I know Lucie has my dinner ready and I'm hungry as a bear just coming out of hibernation." He sniffed the air like the said bear. "Oh boy. I think I can smell her cooking from here."

"Aw that's silly," Harold scoffed. "You can't smell anything from all the way in Red Fork. You're smelling Ma's cooking. A big pot of venison stew."

"Yeah," Ralph agreed. "So why don't you stay and just eat with us?"

"What?" Wesley mimed a shocked expression, making both boys laugh. "And leave Lucie sitting there at the kitchen table all by herself? Poor Lucie." Now he wiped a fake tear away bringing more laughter. "What kind of cad would I be?"

"Boys, stop hanging all over Uncle Wesley." Artie approached to join their little group. Patsy had gone to the house with a big shout and a wave in his direction. "The poor man's exhausted from flying this gorgeous bird through the air and making a pile of money," Artie added.

Now it was Wesley's turn to laugh. Artie was right, except for the exhausted part. At times, he felt he could fly forever. Getting paid for it was like a double blessing.

"Boys, you get on in the house now. Wash up for dinner."

"Aw daddy," Ralph said, "we want to stay out here with Uncle Wesley."

"He's leaving in just a few minutes." Artie took his elder son by the shoulder, turned him and gave him a pop on the behind. "Now get on like I told you."

Like a detonator, it set the two on a dead run to the house.

"Okay. Let's get her into the hangar," Artie said. "How was the trip? Who this time?"

"Skelly and two of his guys."

"Ha. Now that you can carry three passengers rather than two like the Red Robin. More cash, eh?"

The Curtiss Robin had been his first enclosed cabin plane. That meant his paying customers rode in comfort rather than being blown by headwinds. He had dearly loved his Red Robin and secretly wished he'd been able to keep it and still buy the Blue Bolt. But that was way out of his reach.

Artie opened the large hangar doors and together they pulled the Blue Bolt into the cave-like structure. Above the doors boasted the painted words: *Air Taxi. Passenger Carrying. Flying Instructions.*

Forward-looking Artie Schneider had sunk a fortune into his Air Service business back in the twenties. He often kidded that he'd been like the Jenks' version of Noah building his ark. People certainly laughed at him. The large structure seemed very out of place rising up just outside the town's city limits.

No one laughed these days. Artie not only bought and sold planes, and gave them a place to park, he had become a much-sought-after airplane mechanic. Wesley trusted him explicitly. And he and Wesley had a nice carrier business going between them. Oilmen like Bill Skelly played their cards close to the vest, and had come through the crash limping, but still standing. And had a great need to get from one lease to another, and from one refinery to another, as fast as possible. Only an airplane would do.

Once the Blue Bolt was secure in the hangar, Wesley said his goodbyes, jumped into his Hudson, and headed to Red Fork.

Pulling up into the drive beside Cairn Cottage where he and Lucie now lived, he paused for a minute and looked it over. It seemed impossible that they'd been able to make the purchase—along with the filling station. But it seemed more impossible that they were no longer the children of one of the most well-known and celebrated oil magnates in Tulsa. Life was so crazy sometimes.

He remembered the first time they came to look at the house. While it wasn't as big as the Patton mansion on Riverside Drive in Tulsa, still and yet, it was a large, very solid-looking, two-story stone house. The front sported a wide porch extending all the way from one side to the other. On the second story a screened-in porch extended the same length. Chimneys at both ends of the house indicated large fireplaces were in place. Thinking of the mild Oklahoma winters, Wesley couldn't imagine using them much. But still, it would be fun to have a roaring fire on one of those rare snowy days.

The forward-thinking original builders had planted a veritable forest in the front yard of oak, sweetgum, maples, and even a few smaller dogwood. The shade cast on the front of the house was a blessing as it warded off the worst of the Oklahoma heat.

There was only one outbuilding on the property and Wesley wondered as he studied it now, if it could be a money-maker somehow. He was always thinking of how to build their income. Even though they had the filling station, there was no space at that location for a car repair garage, and a filling station and a garage would fit together perfectly. Maybe that outbuilding could be refurbished and made into a garage. It would need the front opened and sliding doors mounted.

"Wesley Patton! Get yourself in here. I just lifted the chicken and it's getting cold."

Still donning her Sunday best, Lucie was standing on the front porch with her hands on her hips. Wesley laughed. "I'ma comin' ma'am. Be right there," in his deepest Okie accent, which their mother had always despised and never let them use.

He could smell the fried chicken before he hit the door. At the kitchen sink he grabbed the Lava bar and lathered up his hands. Flicking water on his sister, he grabbed the dish towel off her shoulder and dried his hands.

"Whatever were you doing out there? Just sitting there."

"Oh, and just standing there too. I was standing for a little while."

She grabbed the towel back and snapped it at him. "You were thinking about the outbuilding again, right?"

"I was."

After blessing the food, Lucie said, "Well? Have you come to a decision?"

As he was mowing through the fried chicken and mashed potatoes and gravy, he said, "I'm torn. I think it could easily be a car repair shop, but..."

"But? What?"

"Just not sure I want a car repair shop in my back yard. There'd be men working here and I wouldn't always be around."

Pouring him more iced tea, she said, "I agree with the latter."

"Plus, I was thinking about turning it into a chicken house."

She punched him in the arm. "Now stop it."

"How about a cow? Plenty of room in there for Miss Bossy and you could learn to..."

"No chickens. No cows. I'm doing good with just the garden."

Ever since they'd lived there, he threatened to make her keep chickens. "They're so easy," he'd say. "They just scratch around and eat bugs and lay eggs. Free food."

Lucie had absolutely no desire to mess with dirty chickens. Or mean roosters. Or a silly cow. Even the thought of milking a cow made her shudder. She'd much rather buy chickens, already dressed, from their neighbors. And the eggs and milk as well.

She was bringing the cherry pie to the table when he said, "And speaking of which..."

"Speaking of what? Chickens?" Cutting him a wide piece, she set it in front of him. Her brother had a weakness for pie, so she'd gone to great lengths to learn to bake them. Tessa was a great teacher. She was the one who had also taught her all about gardening—something about which she'd had no clue. The Pattons had always hired full-time gardeners. For the flower gardens, that is. Never a vegetable garden.

Wesley shook his head, because his mouth was full. Then, "No. Not chickens. About men."

"Men? Where'd that come in?"

"Weren't you listening? I just said I wasn't too keen on having men working in a garage so close to the house."

"Oh. Okay."

It wasn't always easy following Wesley's line of thinking.

"The hobo jungle is getting pretty entrenched about a mile west of town. Down there by the creek. Being so close to the tracks, and plus the water supply from the creek makes it a perfect spot." Finished eating, he pushed back his chair. "Now Lucie, these guys are just down on their luck. On the road hunting for work. For the most part, they're not bad people. So, if they come asking for food, feed them, but don't ever let them in the house."

Carrying dishes to the sink, she nodded. He'd told her this before, but she knew he worried about her when he was away. She'd learned to shoot, and they kept the shotgun loaded with rock-salt shells and leaning against the icebox. "Just point that thing at some guy who gets a little overbearing," he'd told her, "and I guarantee you, he'll run."

"Hate to change this quite delightful conversation, but are we going to go see mother today?"

Wesley stood to his feet and stretched. "Aw Lucie. I'm beat. Can we just skip today? I'll help clean up here then I need a long nap." He wouldn't say that he just told Artie a bit earlier that he wasn't tired. Maybe it was because he was now full and that made him sleepy.

She gave a sigh. She always felt guilty when they didn't get up to Vinita at least once a week.

"She never acknowledges us anyway," he said. Grabbing a clean cup towel he took a plate from the rinse water and commenced drying it.

"Still..."

"I know. I know. Just in case someday she'll snap out of it."

At one point they had actually made a joke of the fact that it was easier to go visit their father than their mother. Only between the two of them could they be so openly morbid.

Burying their father had been a painful experience. But placing Trevalene in the state mental hospital at Vinita was gut-wrenching. Upon discovering her husband with his head half blown off, she'd lost all sense of reality. Her mind had snapped like a dry twig. At first, raving like a lunatic, then deteriorating into a state of non-responsiveness. The doctors said she'd never be right again. But Lucie still hung onto the belief that her mother would be healed. Her faculties restored.

Changing the subject—Wesley never wanted to discuss their mother—he asked, "So, Sis, what was the sermon about this morning?"

She looked over at him. "Forgiveness."

"Yikes. How'd you hold up?"

She gave a short laugh. "We'll work on it together."

"Agreed."

He hung the towel on the rack above the sink. "Gonna grab that nap. Then we'll listen to Jack Benny tonight. Deal?"

"Deal."

Chapter 3

MAY 1931 —TWO YEARS EARLIER - TULSA, OKLAHOMA

Tessa lifted the lid on the pot of boiling potatoes, stuck a fork into one to check its doneness.

"Ah. Perfect," she whispered.

She had the house to herself as she prepared their company dinner. Stepping over to the icebox, she adjusted the small oscillating fan that was sitting on top, to blow more directly on her. Taking the potatoes from the stove, she drained the water into another pan, then grabbed the potato masher and went to work whipping them into a white fluffy mound. The saved water would be used for her potato bread later in the week. Eyeing the two skillets full of frying chicken, she hoped that would be enough. Tessa never ceased to marvel at Wesley's appetite. Not even Gaven could keep up with him.

The twins were down the street playing with the neighbor children, and Gaven had run out to grab a newspaper. For the past few weeks, Gaven and Wesley had been poring over the latest auctions to see what might be available for Wesley and Lucie as a place to live. Ever since the loss of their father and the massive Patton auction, the siblings had been living with Clarette and her husband Erik Torsten, Tessa's cousin.

At the back of the Torsten house was a small apartment which the two siblings rented for the time being. Coincidentally, that was where Clarette lived when she first came to Tulsa from New York. She and Erik had purchased the house soon after the couple decided to make Tulsa their home. That decision was after a short stint of living in Bartlesville where they owned a newspaper. Then back to Clarette's home town of New York City where Erik joined a leading newspaper as a star reporter. Unfortunate circumstances in the Big Apple had led them right back to Tulsa.

While the apartment served Wesley and Lucie for the present time, they all knew it was temporary. But where would they go? Wesley had talked about moving to Jenks where his plane, the Red Robin, was housed at Artie Schneider's hangar. Maybe he could go into business with Artie. Not that he'd even asked Artie, of course. Just dreaming. Weighing out all possibilities. And all ideas were batted about as he and Gaven scoured the auctions listed in the evening paper.

Tessa knew that poor Lucie had no idea where she fit. Nor what she was supposed to do. Having been brought up as a little rich girl in a privileged home, offspring of a privileged family, options were limited. *Cute* and *perky* were adjectives Gaven used to describe Lucie.

"It's like she bounces everywhere she goes," he would say. But Tessa knew he loved both Lucie and Wesley and would go to great lengths to help them in any way he could.

With the potatoes mashed, scooped into Tessa's best pink-rose flowered china bowl, and the yeast rolls taken from the oven, dinner was nearly ready. She relished their times with Lucie and Wesley. And was forever thankful that they had rekindled their relationship—even through all of life's disastrous events.

With a smile, Tessa thought again of the irony that Lucie and Clarette shared similar backgrounds. And that now they lived in the same house, both of them had related to Tessa that they discussed it endlessly. The big difference was that Clarette had willingly, gladly walked away from her prestigious, affluent New York family. Lucie, on the other hand, was forced out of hers. Strangely enough though, Lucie could say with all honesty, that she didn't miss any of it. And had said as much to Tessa many times in the past few months.

Between the tutelage of both Tessa and Clarette, Lucie was learning how to cook, sew, and even garden. What an education. "Better late than never," Tessa often said.

At that moment, Gaven came slamming in the back door. "I think I've found it, Tessa. Just take a look." As she was attempting to pour tea into the glasses, he grabbed her and planted a kiss on her cheek, all the while waving the newspaper.

"What? You haven't even had time to read it." But she could see the bulk of the paper was folded under his arm. As he'd walked home from the drug store, he had already pulled out the section where the auctions were found.

"Silly girl. Of course, I had time. I know right where to look." Tossing the excess paper onto the kitchen counter, he stuck the auctions page in front of her nose. So close she had to push it back so she could read it.

"Tell me you're joking."

"Not joking. This is perfect. A place to live and a business to operate. All in one. It's perfect."

The rattling sound of Wesley's Hudson pulling in the drive stopped the conversation.

"We'll see what they say," Tessa told him. "You'll see. It's not perfect. Not even close."

Lucie gazed through the dust-coated windshield of Wesley's old Hudson at the MacIntyre bungalow. With a sigh, she wondered if she would ever have a loving husband, a cozy little house, and a settled life like Tessa and Gaven enjoyed. She'd had the mansion and it was a cold, empty life. It'd be okay with her if she never had that lifestyle again. Ever.

"Oh my," Wesley said as he opened the creaking door, stepped out, and drew in a deep breath. "Boy oh boy. I can smell that good food clear out here. Yeast rolls. What do you bet?" He looked back in at his sister. "You coming or not?"

"Coming."

She had to push hard to open the rider's side door. Lucie had asked her brother more than once how he could have such a beautiful airplane and such a rickety automobile. His answer was always the same.

"An automobile is just a convenience. An airplane is an investment."

His logic was sound. Plus, he'd bought the faded green Hudson for pennies on the dollar from a family headed to California. They had a truck for their belongings and didn't need the car. Just needed a few bucks. As usual, Wesley was in the right place at the right time. The guy was a wizard. Plus, he knew all about the mechanics to keep it running.

Wesley had also been correct about the yeast rolls. The aroma filled the house. After hugs and greetings, Tessa turned to Lucie. "Lucie, would you mind rounding up the twins. They're down at the vacant lot."

"Be glad to. Did you tell them we were coming?"

Tessa shook her head. "I thought I'd let you surprise them."

As Lucie walked down the tree-lined sidewalk, she could hear children's voices up ahead. How she wished she could have had a normal childhood like Babette and Elysia. Their days were filled with jump rope, sidewalk skating, games of tag, and even baseball in the vacant lot. The neighborhood was replete with children and there was no end to the fun they had.

Trevalene would have had a heart attack if Lucie ever got as dirty as the twins did. All her growing up years, Lucie never had one friend to play with. And even at *Blakemore's Finishing School for Girls*, known as Boston's finest, she was the odd one having come from the wild state of Oklahoma. Most of the other girls envisioned Tulsa as being filled with cowboys and Indians. One of the best results of the stock market crash was that she had to leave that horrendous school which she hated with a passion.

Squeals of joy sounded the moment the eight-year-old twins saw her coming. They left the pack of kids and made a beeline for her, smothering her with hugs.

Babette was the "few-minutes-older" twin who mercilessly lorded it over Elysia. But Elysia, being the more mild-mannered of the two, never let it bother her. Babette favored her daddy with her dark hair and brown eyes. Elysia not only looked like Tessa with white-blond hair and sky-blue eyes, but also with Tessa's gentle temperament.

Grabbing one under each arm, Lucie said, "C'mon you two renegades. Time for dinner."

All through dinner, Gaven seemed to have a smirk on his face. But if he was harboring news, he kept it to himself. Instead, they talked about local goings on and which of the oil companies were thriving and which were being quickly and easily bought out.

Wesley said, not for the first time, that he was pretty sure E.V. Harland had come in and taken over most of Patton Oil. He was also pretty sure E.V. still blamed Henry Patton for the death of his son, Shelby. It had been, after all, Sadella's idea for her and Shelby to take a wild ride into the black community of Greenwood that cold winter night. The grieving community, still in the throes of the devastation of the riot the previous May, lived mostly in tents. Sleet-coated streets contributed to the horrific wreck when Shelby's car slammed into an electric pole. He was killed instantly. Sadella, who had hoped to marry Shelby and become part of the Harland oil family, was inconsolable.

In his thriving business of transporting oil men in his Red Robin, Wesley heard lots of scuttlebutt. And had made many influential friends. The one oil baron who had never used his transport services, was E.V. Harland. Lucie was convinced that was no oversight. She and Wesley also suspected that E.V. had given Henry damaging advice when it came to playing the stock market game. No proof, but highly suspect.

Once dinner was finished, mugs of hot coffee all around, the table cleared, and the girls playing in the back yard, Gaven, still smirking, pulled out the newspaper.

"Here we go Mr. and Miss Patton. I have found the perfect answer for your situation."

Wesley pushed back his chair and stretched out his long legs. "I thought you had something on your mind. I could read it in your face."

Tessa laughed. "He never was very good at keeping secrets."

Shaking out the paper, Gaven made a grand production of reading the notice describing the upcoming auction of a filling station and a two-story stone house in Red Fork. "It's called Cairn Cottage. The two come together."

Wesley sat up straight so fast he almost dropped his coffee mug. "Red Fork? Good Lord, man. What are you thinking? Who wants to live in Red Fork? It's dying on the vine. There's barely a town there."

Gaven waved his hand. "Now now. Calm down. Just listen. You two need to get out of Tulsa. There's nothing here for you but bad memories."

Lucie spoke up. "You're right about that."

"The filling station is right on Highway 66. Constant traffic. Besides gasoline, you'll be selling things like oil, tires, belts, spark plugs. It's a sure bet to make a profit."

Lucie could tell Tessa was deep in thought. "Travelers also need a cold Nehi, and maybe a few groceries." She looked over at her husband. "Maybe it would work."

He shrugged. "I tried to tell you."

"When's the auction?" Wesley wanted to know.

"Next week."

"When can we go see it?"

Gaven folded the paper. "How about tomorrow."

"Think we can afford it?"

"We'll cross that bridge when we get to it." Gaven stood up, walked over to the sideboard and pulled out two packs of playing cards. "Now Wesley, let's show the girls who rules in canasta."

Chapter 4

MAY 1931 —TWO YEARS EARLIER - TULSA, OKLAHOMA

The screen dimmed; the curtains glided to a close with a soft whoosh. The theater lights came on, forcing Sadella to squint against their brightness. How she hated for a movie to end. Or today—movies. As in two. A double feature. The movie theater was the only place where she could go to forget her miserable existence. She preferred the matinees since the crowd was smaller than the evening showings. Plus, fewer people she knew attended the matinees.

Before reaching the lobby, she pulled her handkerchief from her purse to wipe her cheeks. She always cried during the love scenes. They brought back vivid memories of her time with Shelby Harland. They'd had such fun together. It was her own stupid fault that he died. It had been her idea.

"Let's go speed through Greenwood," she'd said. "Give 'em a scare."

Shel wasn't too keen on the idea. "I don't know, Sadella. Seems they've had enough scares to last a lifetime."

But she was insistent. "It'll be fun," she said. Sadella love wild adventures. "We won't hurt anybody."

He was such a softie. Always did whatever she asked. It was such a nasty night. Sleet. Rain. So cold. All the streets were slick. As they raced through the ravaged neighborhood, Shel revved up his little coupe to make more noise and blared the horn. But then the car was sliding. Out of control. She was screaming. She could see the electric pole coming as them as they careened off the street. Then it was over. Shel was dead. And she would have joined him. She tried. With a piece of glass from the broken car window. It was that little blond twit, Tessa, who stopped her. Tessa Jurgen, who'd befriended practically the whole black Greenwood community. Wouldn't you know she'd have been right there at the scene. Just another incident in Sadella's run of consistent bad luck.

Sadella had already hated Tessa. She hated her more after that.

If it hadn't been for Tessa Jurgen, she never would have made the accusation against Jasper and Strapper. Jasper was the son of their cook, Chloe, and Strapper was their landscaping help. She hated them because Tessa liked them. Tessa talked to the black folk just like she did whites. It was clear, as a backwoods hillbilly, she knew nothing about how things were done in Tulsa. Even after Sadella's parents tried to tell her. After all, Tessa had come from the sticks. Somewhere up in the Oklahoma hills. What did she know? Nothing evidently.

Sadella had been downtown shopping on a warm spring afternoon in 1921. She just happened to see Jasper and Strapper heading down an alleyway. It was obvious they were running an errand for the Pattons. All Negroes were required to go in the rear entrance to make a purchase. She followed them and yelled at them, calling them names. "What do you think you're doing in this part of town?" she yelled. "Get out of here."

They tried to explain, but she wouldn't let them speak. That's when she got the idea to accuse them of accosting her. How was she to know a mob would later ambush the jail, kidnap the boys, and lynch Cloe's son, Jasper? How was she to know the incident would ignite the spark that caused almost the entire black community of Greenwood to be destroyed? At times, she tried to remember the hate and anger that caused her to make the accusation. But she could not. To the present day, the whole thing haunted her. Secretly, she was relieved when she learned that Strapper had escaped.

She needed a cigarette and she was out. Getting in her car, she rummaged in her purse looking for loose change. Never in her entire life had she not had money. There had always been money. So much they couldn't even count it all. Trips abroad. Shopping excursions to New York and Paris. Lounging in the sunshine on the French Riviera. Dances and balls. Trevalene's attempts at finding Sadella a duke, or an earl, or some wealthy landowner in England. Such wild, fun days.

Now here she was—stuck in dreary Tulsa, with no money. She'd had enough to pay for the movie ticket, now she just needed a pack of cigarettes. Her one excuse to ask Wesley for money was that she was taking care of their mother, and kept Wesley appraised of Trevalene's needs. Like new underwear. Or a pair of nylons. Or the prescription for the medication to keep her calmed down. The prescription which Sadella had forged several times. Wesley never asked for receipts. That then became her spending money. Now she seemed to be short—again. She never realized how fast money could disappear.

She heaved deep sigh and pressed her head against the steering wheel. For a while during the past year she'd locate old friends and borrow money from them. But they wised up in a hurry. Everyone in Tulsa knew she was broke. Plus, the fact that most of the kids she'd known in high school were married with families. She was the lone old maid. Essentially, she had no friends.

"That's fine with me," she said to no one. "Who cares what they think? When they see me on the silver screen, they'll all be sorry. They'll be green with envy. Absolutely green. And I'll be rich. All the stars in Hollywood are rich."

The first thing she planned to do when she arrived in Hollywood would be to peroxide her hair like Jean Harlowe. It'd be fun to do that now, but that would not fit in this little one-horse burg. She didn't want to waste the effort around people who had no level of understanding about the movies.

Actually, she needed a pack of cigarette *and* the latest copy of *Screen Play* magazine. She loved spending hours fanning through the movie magazines on the rack at the drug store, but the owner had started watching her and giving her hateful looks. *Screen Play* had become her favorite, but *Screen Book* was a close second. All the stars and the stories of their exciting lives jumped off the pages. When they talked about their screen tests, she knew exactly how she would handle her first screen test. She practiced at home every day in front of the mirror.

At boarding school, she'd enrolled in drama, but she and her friend Clarice Jarvis were busy joining forces to cause enough trouble to get themselves kicked out. Because of their antics, she hadn't been in the class long, but long enough to know she had what it takes to be an actress. And a darn good one. Even her instructor said so.

On a whim, she opened the glove box and rummaged around. To her ever-lasting surprise, there was a quarter underneath a pile of junk. She grabbed it and squeezed it. Ten cents for cigarettes and ten cents for her magazine. And a nickel left over. Putting the coupe in gear she headed to the drug store.

But first, she swung by the MacIntyre's house out on 21st Street—over by Lee School where both Gaven and Tessa taught. She didn't drive down their street, but slowly crossed the intersection a block away. Her suspicion had been correct. In their driveway sat Wesley's green Hudson. She supposed the four of them were having a gay old time together. Probably talking gossip about her. Or groveling over what a bad job she was doing caring for their mother.

"Well, just let them come and take a try at corralling a crazy woman," she growled. "See how they'd handle it." Grinding the gears, she sped out of the despised neighborhood, and away from the despised people.

The humiliation of living in the small apartment above the garage behind the Patton mansion knew no bounds for Sadella. It was in this apartment where their hired female help had boarded. The white help, that is. Like Tessa when she was their governess. Which only added to Sadella's agony and shame.

On the other hand, it mattered not to Trevalene where she lived. She barely knew what day it was. Sadella kept a bottle of hooch hidden in her dresser and simply gave her mother a small glass before bedtime. That, plus a tablespoon of Konjola, seemed to keep the wild outbursts to a minimum. Why she should be the one to babysit their crazy mother, was beyond her.

Wesley kept telling her that as soon as he and Lucie found a place to buy, their mother would be taken off her hands. That day couldn't come soon enough. That would be the day she would leave for California.

She decided at the outset that she would let her mother have the one lone bedroom so she could close the door and keep the crazy woman isolated. Sadella had brought in a small bed and slept in the living room. Such as it was. Her closet in the mansion was larger and more spacious than this little hovel.

After getting Trevalene into bed, Sadella changed into her nightgown, poured herself a little of the hooch, and settled into bed with her movie magazine.

"What a life," she mumbled as she punched the pillows up to make a back rest. "Leaving this hellhole can't come soon enough."

She fell asleep with the magazine open on her stomach, but then the nightmare came again. Jasper was being dragged away by men—lots of men—in white hooded robes. Jasper was screaming her name and begging for mercy. Begging for her to help. But she was frozen and could not move. The scene changed, as it always did in the recurring dream, and she saw his body dangling from a noose, his face purple with his eyes bulging out.

She sat straight up in bed in a cold sweat. The tremors shook her body. She dragged herself out of bed, walked to the postage-stamp-sized kitchen and filled a glass with water from the tap. Her hand shook so that she could hardly drink.

When would she ever be free?

Chapter 5

JUNE 1933, RED FORK, OKLAHOMA

L ucie was pleased that Rand had turned out to be a reliable employee. At age thirteen he was all arms and legs, with the cuffs of his overalls above his ankles, a testimony of his recent growth spurt. The only article of clothing that really seemed to fit was his gray-tweed newsboy's hat.

Randall Nussbaum, his full name, had come to them asking if he could sweep out the store. That's how it started. Then she needed his help cutting back the thick honeysuckle vines that had nearly taken over the front porch pillars. Now here he was helping her with the garden, which was situated in the wide clearing between the back of the house and the stand of trees that ran along the creek bed. The charming spring-fed creek ran through the woods flowing toward the Arkansas River. Lucie certainly never grew up having access to trees, grass, flowers, streams, and wildlife. And now here she was loving every minute of it. She often wished she had more time to just sit by the creek and listen to the water gurgling over the rocks.

The sun was blazing this day, and there'd been so little rain, but Rand never complained. Wesley had salvaged a water hose which he hooked up to the tap on the back porch where Lucie did the laundry. Between the two of them,

Lucie and Rand had worked hard using the hose to water and get the seedlings underway. Now they had a fairly healthy-looking garden.

Rand's mother, Oney, a widow who clerked at the five-and-ten, needed all the help she could get as Rand was the oldest of four. They had a houseful, which meant a lot of mouths to feed. Wesley and Lucie couldn't afford to pay him a lot, but every penny was appreciated by the Nussbaums.

Lucie enjoyed Rand's company. His curiosity seemed endless. Once he discovered she'd traveled abroad, he wanted to know every detail. Especially the Louvre, which had bored her to tears when she was ten years old. After she told him about it, he looked it up in the encyclopedia in the Red Fork school library to learn more.

They were watering their fledgling plants the day the three men stopped by. There'd been more hoboes stopping by recently. Usually they came by one at a time. But this day there were three.

Lucie wanted to help all of them. Some looked so beaten down. Lost. Discouraged. Tessa had suggested to her that she keep a pot of beans in the warming oven along with a pan of cornbread.

"But it's so hot out," she'd protested when Tessa first gave her that advice.

Tessa just shook her head. "Doesn't matter, Lucie. Cook a ham bone in with those beans. Not a lot, just enough for a nice flavor. Beans and cornbread will stick to their ribs and keep them filled up. They'll be so grateful." Then she added, "Pie too if you can. For a man on the road, pie is like a love note from home."

It was a great idea. Now when hungry men showed up at her doorstep, she never had to wonder what to feed them.

Wesley was agreeable to the plan. With his usual quirky humor, he said, "I've heard of soup kitchens. Never a bean kitchen."

"Well, I guess this will be a first."

But then in more serious tone, he added, "Please Lucie, just don't be going over to the hobo jungle to feed all of them."

She had to laugh. He knew how they pulled on her heart. To think they were catching rides in those empty freight trains in search of work. She couldn't imagine a more risk-filled, lonely life.

The church missionary ladies had decided that if someone drove by the jungle, and saw that there was a family with children, they would take food to them. Otherwise, as long as there were only hoboes of the male species, they'd leave them to their own devices. Lucie didn't completely agree with that reasoning, but she wasn't on that committee. Or any other committee for that matter.

Rand had turned off the water and was coiling up the hose, placing it carefully by the back-porch steps when the men approached them. Lucie wasn't sure if they'd come out of the woods or from the road. All of a sudden, they were just there.

Two were a little on the greasy side, probably having been on the road for a longer spell than the third. They were also a little older than the third. All three were polite and introduced themselves before asking if she had any food to spare.

"Of course." To Rand she said, "Get the quilt and spread it under the King Oak. Then come help me." There were several oaks in their yard, but the one she loved the most she started calling the King Oak. Wesley teased her. "Who but my sister would name a tree?"

On a bench near the back-porch door, sat a white enamel basin filled with water, and next to it a bar of Lava soap. Rand pointed them in that direction. As each in turn lathered up to their elbows, Lucie heard one remark, "Feels mighty good to have clean hands." The two older men removed their hats. The younger one was bare-headed, his unkempt dark curls much in need of a trim.

Once the men were seated in the shade, she and Rand brought out a large tray with the bowls of beans, and slabs of buttered cornbread alongside. Also, a pot of coffee and tin cups.

Rand then dragged over their metal outdoor chairs, and as the men sat on the quilt and ate, Rand and Lucie settled into the chairs and chatted with them to learn their stories. Lucie had been correct in her assumption that the two older men had been riding the rails for quite some time, getting work as they could find it along the way.

Warren and Gilbert had been friends in a small town in Ohio where they worked in a factory. Once the factory closed, the town folded.

"We hated leaving family behind," Warren said around a mouthful of cornbread.

"That's the hardest part of being on the road," Gilbert added. "We try to send a little money home often as we can."

The younger man had introduced himself as Nathan Anderson. His dark curly hair, swarthy complexion, and soft hazel eyes reminded Lucie of men she'd met in Paris. He was obviously of French descent.

She'd traveled abroad with her family on many occasions. In some of the countries, her parents instructed her to keep her eyes down. "Do not make eye contact with the men," they said. As any young person would, she disobeyed a few times. When she did, she immediately knew what her parents meant. Frightening. But this young man's eyes were not like that. And she caught him looking at her.

Nodding in Nathan's direction, Rand asked, "And what about you?"

Warren and Gilbert both laughed. "We picked up the babe in the St. Louis rail yard after rescuing him from the yard bull."

Nathan joined in the laughter. "I had no idea they were so mean. I didn't know a whole lot about hopping a freight."

"Oh, them boys is paid to be mean," Warren said with a shake of his head.

"They'll bash your head in without a second thought," Gilbert agreed. "Or shoot you. They're all armed."

By this time, having fed other drifters like these three, Lucie had heard similar of stories many times over. When they learned she also had black-berry pie, their eyes lit up. After being served slices of pie, they continued with the accounts of their travels.

The jobs they'd held down ranged from shoveling and loading coal, to cutting wood, picking cotton, harvesting wheat, mucking stables, and digging ditches.

They told about the different hobo jungles in the various cities. The good ones and the not-so-good ones. About the mulligan stew at each one.

"What kind of stew?" Rand was all ears. "Mulligan? Never heard of that."

"Whatever each man has in his possession goes in the stew," Gilbert explained. "We all share. An onion, a bit of dried beef, a potato or two, corn stolen from a farmer's field, maybe an egg, dandelions, sour dock..."

"...tobacco," Nathan added, wrinkling his nose. "It's what you might call an acquired taste."

"Each man has his own pan, or empty can, or a tin cup. Ladle up your own. That's how it works." This from Gilbert as he pressed his fork on the plate to get up every crumb of pie crust. "The sharing. The trust. The camaraderie. People who aren't there can never understand."

"But the bad guys," Rand put in. "Sure nuf, I bet there's some real bad men out there." Rand had watched a few too many gangster movies.

Nathan looked up from his pie. Lucie noticed his gentle expression. He'd not been on the road long enough to get the hardened look that she'd seen so often. "The jungles are like a telegraph network," he told Rand. "If anyone comes in and tries to hurt, or steal, or take over, he'll wish he'd never thought of it. He's marked and blackballed."

Rand's eye widened at that. "All this time I thought *law of the jungle* was just a saying."

His remark made the men smile. Lucie wondered if perhaps Warren or Gilbert might have left behind a son Rand's age. She was glad Rand was there to join in this conversation.

After the three men left, she thought about Nathan. He wasn't like the other two. He was quiet and had no stories to regale. Other than the story of his rescue in St. Louis, he didn't even tell where he was from. While Warren and Gilbert carried their belongings in mattress sacking, Nathan had a leather satchel with gold clasps that hadn't seen a lot of wear. Not yet, at least.

Later in the afternoon, she heard the whistle of the Frisco coming through town. She thought about Warren, Gilbert, and Nathan and said a quick prayer for their safety.

Wesley had been in South Texas for two days. By the time he arrived back home, Sadella had made attempts to place collect calls from California four different times. Wesley had strictly ordered Lucie to never accept them. "I'll handle it," he told her. "She'll just wheedle you out of more money."

Lucie waited until after he'd had his supper, was situated in his wingback chair and reading one of his many aircraft magazines, before she told him about the calls.

"I so wish you'd never helped her get out there," Lucie said as she fiddled with the radio dials. "You knew it would end in disaster."

Their Crosley radio-phonograph was among the items Wesley had been insistent on their keeping out if the auction. As she dialed in the *Kraft Music Hall* show, she was ever so thankful. Not just for the radio but the photograph as well. In his travels, Wesley continually brought home new record albums. Their collection grew by a few new ones every month.

Now he looked up from his magazine and commented, "I gave her the cash because I didn't want her to land in jail on charges of a bank heist." This his weak stab at humor.

But they both agreed Sadella had been getting desperate. Almost as soon as they were settled in Cairn Cottage, with Trevalene in the upstairs bedroom, she began badgering Wesley relentlessly to fly her to Hollywood. "I know you go to California all the time. Why can't you take me?"

"I have paying customers, Sis." He called her that because he knew she hated being called *Sis*. "In case you weren't aware, airplane fuel costs money. My passengers pay their own way."

A friend of Sadella's from boarding school named Clarice, was already in California living in a rooming house called Jarrell House in Hollywood. Close to the studios from what Sadella told them. "She says I can share a room with her in the house. She's at the studio every day and she's sure we'll both be in line for starring roles."

Neither Wesley nor Lucie bought into the story. But what could they do? In the end, Wesley had handed over enough money for a train ticket. That way, as he reasoned to Lucie, "I gave her money. What she did with it was none of my concern."

Lucie supposed he said that to ease his conscience. But they both worried about their older sister. She was wild with anger when she learned they had placed their mother in the hospital at Vinita. The language that came over the line could have burned down every telephone pole between Hollywood and Red Fork.

"Then you come back here and try to handle her," Wesley said, struggling to get a word in during the heated telephone conversation.

"I did handle her. You pushed her off on me. I took care of her. But as soon as my back is turned, you ship her off to live with crazy people."

Both Lucie and Wesley were well aware that Sadella had kept Trevalene sedated, not only with bootleg whiskey, but various medicines. They couldn't blame her, because when Trevalene was awake and aware, she was screaming and clawing and fighting the world.

In the months since that conversation, however, Sadella rarely mentioned it. And rarely, if ever, asked after her mother. It was as if Trevalene had ceased to exist. Instead, Sadella was focused on building her acting career, which didn't seem to be going so well.

Every time she called to ask for money, she told them she was sure a walk-on role was hers in the next upcoming movie.

"It's coming. I can feel it in my bones," she said. "Myron likes me. He talks to me on the set. He's told me many times that he's saving me for the *just right* role."

The Myron she kept talking about referred to Myron Reznick, head of *Starline Productions,* a logo that appeared on the movie screen with a loud whoosh, followed by a blinding explosion of bright flying stars at the beginning of many movies they'd seen.

It was nearly bedtime when the call came through that evening. Of course, it was two hours earlier in California. Wesley was kind, but firm. Lucie was thankful he'd insisted on being there and taking the call.

"In case you haven't heard there a depression in the land," Wesley said, after what Lucie had to assume was Sadella's request for money. She stayed in her place on the sofa and didn't go near the telephone which was on the desk in Wesley's office across the hall. But she certainly heard his side of the conversation.

"Yes, I'm still carrying passengers, but about half of what I had before twenty-nine. I know. It's tight for everybody." After another pause, he answered, "The filling station is making a profit, but barely. Lots of overhead in running a business." After yet another pause, Wesley said, "You could get a job, Sadella. I'm sure you could work at a five-and-dime. Or maybe the telephone office? They always need operators." Then, "I know you have to be at the studio, but do you have to be there twenty-four hours a day? Telephone operators work at night."

The loud swear words were clearly audible all the way from his office to the living room, and Wesley was holding the earpiece away from his ear with a crazy expression on his face. Lucie couldn't help but laugh.

In her head, she was saying, "*Yes, Sadella, the rest of us have to work, you can too.*"

After hanging up, Wesley went to the kitchen. She heard him chipping ice from the block in the icebox. "Want a glass of cold water?" he called to her.

"Sounds delightful."

Returning to the living room with two glasses of ice water, he handed her one, then settled into his chair and went back to his aviator magazine. Presently, he mumbled, "First I'm supposed to fund her travels, then I'm supposed to support her search for stardom." He put down the magazine and looked over at her. "What does she think we are? First National Bank?"

"I know it's hard, but think about it. Sadella was spoon-fed all her life. She knows nothing any different."

"Was she raised any differently than we were?"

She knew he was right. "I guess not."

"And you work harder than three people. I'd love to see her maintain a home, and keep a store, plus raise a garden..."

"Okay. Okay."

"If we keep doling out, she'll just keep draining us dry. No more. Not one penny more. And especially if she keeps swearing at me."

Her easy-going, cool-headed brother rarely got upset, but she could tell he was angry. "Sadella Patton has the power to bring out the worst in me."

"Well, don't think you're anything special. I think she has that effect on most people. Unless she feels the need to impress them."

She heard him chuckle behind his magazine. That made her feel better. Then he said, "Did you know Wiley Post is planning a round-the-world flight?"

Now he was back in his own world.

"Another one? Why?" It bewildered Lucie that anyone would want to brave such an undertaking.

"Solo this time." He laid down the magazine and finished draining his ice water.

"What? Alone? How could anyone do that? Hours and hours all alone."

"Wiley Post can."

It was obvious Wesley idolized Wiley Post and often bragged to people that he'd flown with the famous aviator before anyone even knew who Post was. Now the whole world knew of him.

"I know you'll be charting that trip," she said.

"Every single mile!"

Chapter 6

JUNE 1933, HOLLYWOOD, CALIFORNIA

C larice's alarm clock was clanging, making Sadella jump and causing her heart to pound erratically. Never before in her entire life had she ever awakened to an alarm clock. Even when the Patton family was leaving to board an ocean liner to travel abroad, her mother came into her room to gently awaken her. And the short time she spent at boarding school, before being expelled, there were bells. Not a clanging alarm clock.

"Oh, how I hate that thing," she growled.

Clarice turned over making the springs in the sagging bed complain. "If it weren't for my clock, you'd sleep the entire day."

"That's a lie and you know it," Sadella retorted reaching for her robe and struggling to climb out of the sagging bed.

She might have hated the small garage apartment in Tulsa, but it was a castle compared to this dump known as Jarrell House. They lived in a room. A room. One room. The bathroom was down the hall. Never in her worst nightmares would she have thought she would have to live in one small room. And with no privacy, but to share living space and a bed with another human being.

Water stains decorated the ceiling, the rug was ratty, the curtains dingy, and the bathroom always soiled. Clarice, bless her heart, had taken to scrubbing the toilet every Saturday.

"Why would you do that?" Sadella asked, wrinkling up her nose at the very thought of cleaning someone else's filth.

"Because it needs doing," was Clarice's reply.

The answer baffled Sadella even more than the actions. Clarice wasn't near as much fun as she'd been back at boarding school in Boston.

All of it made Sadella recoil. She was learning to shut down her senses. Shut down her emotions. At the outset, she was sure living at the Jarrell House would be for only a few months. But now it had *been* a few months, plus some, and the stardom she dreamed of seemed no closer.

Every young hopeful in Hollywood knew about the *Hollywood Studio Club*, a chaperoned dormitory where many of the now-famous stars had lived. Sadella had read all about it in one of the movie magazines. Disappointment heaped upon disappointment when she learned that, first of all, it was full up with a waiting list. Next, she learned even if there were available space, it was twice the cost of what she could now barely afford.

Only females were allowed to live in the Jarrell House, which was named for the owner and landlady, Opal Jarrell. A not-so-pleasant woman who ruled over her rooming house with an iron fist.

The white, three-story house with pointy dormer windows, a wide wraparound front porch, dark green shutters, and a plethora of lattice woodwork, was situated on the bus line that took them right to the front gate of Starline Production Studios. That worked well if and when they had bus money—otherwise they walked.

At the studio, the two of them spent their days working with costumes, moving sets, and anything else that needed doing. It was crucial to be on hand if they needed *extras* for a crowd scene. Or a walk-on. Either one or both. Although there were no speaking parts or credit, walk-on roles did pay a few bucks. And it put them in front of the camera.

Sadella kept an eagle eye on the job boards to see what might come up, but most were positions for men, such as grips and gaffers. She considered applying as a driver of one of the buses that transported the crews to locations. But that was iffy. She wasn't all that keen on driving, plus she wanted to stay around the studios as much as possible.

And with thoughts of driving, she never stopped kicking herself for selling her roadster. She could have driven out to California and then had her own way to get around the place. But back in Tulsa, that thought never occurred to her. In her mind, she would already be making enough money to buy an even nicer model. That hadn't happened. And she still didn't know what happened to the money she got from the sale. Money just seemed to disappear.

Every day at the studio, Sadella grew bolder, striking up conversations with actors and actresses. Especially the ones she recognized. It seems they always needed something, and running errands netted her a few extra dollars. Her highest goal was to actually talk to Mr. Reznick. Once she could finagle into position, get him to notice her, she knew beyond the shadow of a doubt she could impress him.

Clarice wasn't as bold. In fact, contrary to what she'd seemed to be back in their boarding-school days, she was rather shy and awkward. Sadella was fairly sure her friend would never get a movie role, let alone become a star. But for now, splitting the rent helped immensely. That's what mattered for the time being.

Chapter 7

JUNE 1933, TULSA, OKLAHOMA

"Siegrid is at loose ends this summer."

Tessa said this to no one in particular, but Lucie saw the concern on her friend's face. Gaven was busy scooping up the playing cards and boxing them. They'd just finished three hilarious games of canasta and, as usual, Erik turned out to be the sore loser in the group. They teased him mercilessly.

The group of them filled Tessa and Gaven's dining room as Erik and Clarette Torsten had joined them for supper and an evening get together. When Erik was there, the big Swede seemed to make the room shrink. Through the open windows, laughter and squeals floated in on the warm air as the children played out in the yard, some crazy chase game they'd made up. Tessa's twins doted over the Torsten's little Jacie. And Ernest filled his role as elder brother watching over all of them.

"What about Siegrid?" Clarette wanted to know. "What's going on?"

"Nothing's going on. That's the problem." Tessa brought the percolator from the hot plate on the sideboard and refilled empty coffee mugs. Replacing the percolator, she sat back at the table and continued. "She finished out her year of teaching at Glenpool and now she's just... Well, like I said, at loose ends."

"That's where you were teaching before you came to us in Tulsa, wasn't it?" Wesley asked.

Tessa nodded. "But everything's so different now. Pastor Stedman passed away last winter. That's where she'd been staying. His wife, Edith, is living with one of their children and their family. The Stedman's house has sold, and now with mama gone as well, there's really nothing there for her."

"Where's Vega?" Lucie asked, referring to Tessa's youngest sister.

"I guess I hadn't told you. She married a young man a few months ago and they're living in Colorado."

"Ah," Erik said with a long sigh. "Colorado. Mountains. Cool air. And here we sit in the Oklahoma oven. Whatever are we thinking?"

"She has a husband who has a job?" Clarette said between sips of coffee. "How'd she manage that? Who in the world has a job these days? What does he do?"

"Mail carrier," Tessa replied. "He was visiting some cousin there in Glenpool, they met, and as you might guess..." She looked around at them and smiled. "They fell head over heels in love."

"But she's only sixteen," Lucie said, doing the math in her head, to which Tessa was nodding.

"Tessa was only a few years older than that when we fell head over heels in love," Gaven said reaching over to take Tessa's hand, making her smile.

"Still," Tessa said, "we had so little time to get to know him." Shaking her head, she added, "I so wish Mama were still alive. Or Pastor Stedman. Or both." Looking over at her husband, she went on, "Gaven seemed to approve of him."

Gaven nodded. "I did. He seemed to be of solid character. And hey, a man with a steady job in this mess can't be too bad."

"But back to Siegrid," Clarette put in, bringing them back to the first conversation. "What does she want to do?"

Tessa shrugged. "I'm not sure. Right now, I think it's just to get out of Glenpool."

Lucie's mind was churning as they were talking. "Why not have her come stay with us?"

Almost before the words were out of her mouth, Wesley countered. "Lucie! What're you thinking? We're barely making it now. We can't afford..."

"I'm not talking about hired help. Goodness, Wesley. But she could just stay with us for a while and see..."

"She probably wouldn't like Red Fork anyway," he went on. "It's not much different than Glenpool. Just a bit bigger."

Wesley was rarely argumentative. They usually agreed on most everything. But Lucie felt this was a good idea. The thought of having another female around, especially one her age, seemed absolutely delightful.

"But..." Lucie wanted to push the discussion.

"We'll talk about it later," Wesley said firmly.

"I sure don't want to get in the middle of this discussion," Tessa said, "but I think Siegrid would be thrilled to be part of your little family. Even if just for a few weeks. Until she gets her direction figured out." Looking over at Wesley, she said, "But I respect your decision, Wesley. Think about it and let us know."

He nodded, looking a wee bit sullen, which wasn't like him at all. As Lucie well knew, her brother was a risk-taker in his Blue Bolt, but on the ground, at home, he had his routine and didn't much like change.

Just then, Erik broke the tension. "Wesley Patton, what do you know about Red Fork history?"

Wesley looked at him like he'd just woke up. "History?"

"History. Yes. History. The beginnings. The first Oklahoma oil strike was in Red Fork. Granted, it was soon overshadowed by the Glenn Pool, but it was the first."

Shaking his head, Wesley said, "Not much. Dad was there. But he never talked much about it."

"Would there be documents he might have kept? Journals? Photos? It was an historical event, you know."

Wesley was stymied. He'd never thought about such things. The idea of Henry Patton chronicling anything seemed totally remote. That wasn't like his father at all.

"We went through his things before the auction. Not much there other than dull business papers and documents."

"Lucie?" Erik said. "Your thoughts."

She shook her head. "I don't remember seeing old photos of the early days. I wish we'd found some. I think it would be fascinating to know more."

"What about Red Fork old-timers?" Erik asked.

Now Wesley was drawn in. Brightening a bit, he said, "Oh, there're plenty of them. They gather at the barber shop and at Annie's Café, and trade stories almost every day. Each one with a bigger story than the other. Why?"

"When this big-time editor gets hold of an idea, he like a dog with a bone. He can't let go," Clarette said, jabbing a thumb at her husband. "And of course, since he has a free-lance writer to hop to his bidding, he's off and running."

Tessa said, "He's wanting you to write an article for the magazine? I thought you were finishing up your novel."

Clarette gave a big smile. "Finished it last week. It's in the mail to my agent." A statement which brought cheers all around the table. They were Clarette's biggest fans.

The royalties from Clarette's books garnered nearly as much income as Erik's position as editor of the *Oil and Gas Reporter*. But he could care less. He loved his work and had brought the periodical out of a slump to being one of the premier industry publications in the nation.

"So," Wesley wanted to know, "in this day and age, who cares anything about Red Fork?"

Erik tipped his chair on the two back legs and stretched. Through a wide yawn, he said, "The country is going through a tough time right now."

"Well now, there's an understatement if I ever heard one." This from Gaven. The two of them loved to verbal-spar. They'd been pals since the war days when they served in the ambulance core together in France.

Erik shooed away the remark with a wave of his hand. "My thought is when things are tough, it's good to look back and remember where we came from."

"History matters," Tessa said in agreement. This from the school teacher who loved history.

"Thanks, Tessa, for that note of encouragement."

She nodded. The two of them, being cousins with the same Swedish genes, were blessed with open, out-spoken, frank points of view. They were also each blessed with golden, white-blond hair which glowed in the soft light of the MacIntyre's living room.

"I'm guessing," Tessa ventured, "you want to do a story on the beginnings of the oil boom that started in Red Fork. And you're sending your best investigative journalist, the famous newspaper reporter, and now even more famous novelist, Clarette Fortier-Torsten, to research and write it. And she comes free of charge."

Erik's chair banged down on all four legs. Laughing, he pointed at Lucie and pronounced with all authority, "My dear cousin, you are incredibly perceptive. Yes, that's *exactly* what I'm doing. And not just an article, but an entire book."

"And," Clarette added, directing her attention back to Wesley and Lucie, "we wondered if you two might lay a little groundwork for us. Maybe find a couple of men who were there. Who would remember what it was like during the boom days."

"I have a few memories myself." Wesley was now all in—the conversation regarding Siegrid seemingly forgotten. At least for the moment. "Not so much in Red Fork, although Dad did have leases all through the area, but I remember the few times he took me to Kiefer and Cleveland. What a stampede of people. The noise. The dust. I was terrified."

Clarette and Erik exchanged glances. "We want that as well," Erik said. "From a child's perspective."

"So why didn't you go into the oil and gas business?" Clarette asked, suddenly changing the subject. "You could have been in on the ground floor. What an open opportunity."

"Because his head was in the clouds," Lucie answered for her brother.

"She's right. Dad begged. Sometimes threatened. Flying was all I ever wanted to do." After a moment, he added, "From today's perspective, I believe I made the right decision."

On the drive home to Red Fork, her brother was all chatter about who they might ask to be interviewed by Clarette for the magazine article. He was even going on about his own memories. Lucie only half listened. She was still thinking about how great it would be to have company in their big house while Wesley was off flying his paying customers to their many oil leases and refineries.

She let the subject die down until a few days later when he was packing to leave. They were outside by his car, and as he loaded his suitcase in the backseat, she said, "I've been thinking..."

"Uh oh. Good or bad?"

He always asked that because she'd come up with some darn good ideas about items to stock in the store that turned out to be high-selling items.

"Good. Very good, in fact,"

He turned around and leaned against the car. "Let's have it."

"While you're gone on this trip, I want to invite Siegrid Jurgen to come and visit. Just to see..."

He was already shaking his head. "I told you how I felt about having a stranger come and live with us, Lucie. I'm not in favor of the idea. At all."

She took a step closer to get right in his face. "You won't be here. Remember? Don't you think I get a little lonely? No one in this little burg seems to want to be friends with me because I'm the alien from Tulsa who used to be a rich kid."

She could tell he was taken back a bit by her intensity.

"Rand's here," Wesley countered. "He's company."

"Oh sure. Rand's here." She hadn't meant for her tone to be mocking, but mocking it was. "Rand's a little kid. He's my helper. I pay him. And he goes home."

She could tell by his expression he was softening.

"I thought we were partners in this deal, Wesley. I work hard. While you're gone, I keep up the store, and the house, and the garden, and the laundry, and..."

At that point, he threw up both hands. "Okay. Stop. Stop, already."

She stopped. And waited. She knew she'd won. That's all the space she needed. She knew what was coming next... *Just this once...*

"Okay. Just this once. For a short visit. While I'm gone on this gig. And that's it. Then she goes back to Glenpool. Or to Tessa's and Gaven's. Or wherever."

Lucie smiled. "Thank you, dear brother. I knew you'd agree once you saw the light."

He reached over and mussed her hair which was loose and flying that morning. "You are a mess."

She stepped over and gave him a hug. "Please be careful. And as always I'll be praying for your safety the whole time."

"In the car or in the plane?"

"Both. Silly boy."

The car was barely out of the drive when she ran inside to telephone Tessa and tell her the news.

.

Chapter 8

JUNE 1933, RED FORK, OKLAHOMA

E ver since the '29 crash, Lucie and Tessa had restored their friendship from years prior and had become close confidants. However, she'd never been around either of Tessa's younger sisters. After convincing her brother to allow her to invite Siegrid, she began to have second thoughts. The girl was a total stranger. The two of them had very little in common. Completely opposite backgrounds. Well, she'd forced Wesley to state—*just this once*. A visit. That's what it was.

She and Rand were in the store when Tessa delivered Siegrid to Red Fork. Rand was on the rolling ladder putting canned goods up on the higher shelves, when Lucie heard him let out a loud, "Whoa."

She'd been filling the candy jars on the shelves in front of the counter. She looked up at Rand. He was looking out the front window. Then she saw. Siegrid was getting out of Tessa's car, and Rand's expression became quite evident.

From childhood, Lucie always admired Tessa's beauty, but her younger sister was even more beautiful. She stood taller than Tessa, more willowy and graceful in her movements as she stepped out of the car and started toward the store.

"Who's that with Tessa?" Rand wanted to know. His tone was almost breathless. "Is that a movie star?"

Now Lucie had to laugh. "No Rand. That's Tessa's sister Siegrid. She's come for a visit."

Lucie poured the last of the candies into the jar, replaced the lid and hurried out to meet her guest.

What she anticipated would be so awkward, wasn't at all. Siegrid, who was as lovely as a Dresden doll, was warm, friendly, and completely unassuming. There were hugs all round as Tessa introduced the two.

"Lucie, I've heard stories about you for years, and now we finally get to meet. I can't tell you how grateful I am for your invitation."

Tessa was beaming. "And I've wanted you two to meet for ever so long. This is so perfect."

Rand was now down off the ladder, but was so bug-eyed and stammering, he could hardly speak. He did collect himself enough to shake Siegrid's hand as Lucie introduced him and say, "Glad t'meet'cha." All the time his ears turning bright red.

Tessa couldn't stay. She'd left the twins at a neighbor's house and had to get back to Tulsa.

"What should I do with her suitcases?" Tessa wanted to know,

"I don't have the car, so could you take them to the house? Just set them inside the back porch. They'll be safe there. We'll be here till closing time."

Rand was perfectly capable of watching the store, and pumping gas, so Lucie invited her guest down the street to Annie's for lunch. And there the friendship began to blossom.

As it turned out, Siegrid had for two years attended a small teacher's college in Kansas, and lived in a dorm setting. Which wasn't all that different from Lucie's experiences at boarding school. By the time they'd finished their stew and biscuits, they were sharing laughter over the escapades they remembered.

The townspeople, as happens in small towns, were all agog, wondering who this bedazzling young stranger was who just appeared with Lucie Patton. But no one asked.

After closing the store at five o'clock, the two walked to Cairn Cottage together. Talking the whole time. Lucie explained about the fixing up they'd done to the house before moving in. Creating an upstairs bathroom. Repairing the wood floors. Adding the furnace.

Upon seeing it, Siegrid caught her breath. "Oh my. Lucie, it's like a castle."

"Well not quite," Lucie said, having not only lived in a mansion, but had seen castles all over Europe. "But we've made it a home."

"Much more fancy that the small house I've been living in."

"I hope you'll be comfortable."

"If I can't be comfortable in this house, I'd be plum loco."

Arriving at the house, they took Siegrid's suitcases to the room that Lucie had fixed up for her guest. She didn't know much about hostess-ing, but she was ready to give it her best shot.

"It's so pretty." Siegrid walked over to the four-poster bed and ran her hand gently over the pale blue chenille bedspread. "How could I not be comfortable here?"

Lucie opened the chifforobe. "Lots of hangars here." She waved to the chest of drawers. "All your other things can go in there."

This particular bedroom faced the back of the house, overlooking vegetable garden, the outbuilding, and the wooded acreage and creek past that.

Stepping to the window, with excitement in her voice, Siegrid said, "Oh my. Is that your property too? The woods?"

"Some of it. Several acres. I forget the number."

"I love the woods."

"There's a creek, too. I like to walk along the creek. Sometime I just sit and listen to the water."

"I've missed that. Once we moved to town, my times alone in the woods ended."

"Tomorrow evening we'll go for a long walk. Tonight, I have to buckle down and take care of the books."

"Books?"

"Accounting." Lucie wrinkled up her nose. Of all the tasks that came with owning a business—two businesses really because she kept the books for Wesley's flying business as well—the bookkeeping was the one she despised the most.

"I took an accounting class in college. Maybe I can lend a hand."

"No joke? I might take you up on that offer." Going out the door, Lucie added, "I'll be downstairs whipping up something to eat. Take your time. Rest if you want."

She laughed. "Won't take me long. Not much in those suitcases. And I'm not tired." Her laughter was lilting. Musical. Making Lucie smile.

After a supper of ham sandwiches and home-canned peaches, they spread the accounting books out on the kitchen table. The radio was surrounding them with soft orchestra music in the background.

Siegrid had earlier looked through the record albums, exclaiming joy over each one. "Jazz. I love jazz. Never heard it much till college, and there all the girls were playing it. I fell in love with it."

It was decided after the books were put to bed, they'd retire to the living room and listen to records.

Lucie was surprised how much help Siegrid offered. She couldn't have imagined working together with another person doing accounting, all of which was such an enigma to her. *Double entry? Assets? Credit and debit?* Some of it was just common sense. The income and the outgo. But there was nothing about it that she liked. Siegrid, on the other hand, seemed to love it all. They were finished in no time. They stayed up late afterward, listening to records and talking.

The next evening after supper, they were outside heading out to the woods, but Siegrid stopped to admire the garden.

"Is this your work?" she wanted to know.

Lucie had to laugh. "Such as it is. If it weren't for your sister, I wouldn't know a tomato plant from a radish."

"It's looking mighty fine. And with so little rain."

"Wesley fixed a hose. Hooked it up to the tap inside." She pointed to where it was coiled up against the house. "Rand and I use that to water."

"Rand. That's the boy at the store?"

"The one who went googly-eyed over you."

Her lilting laugher sounded again. "He helps you?"

"Yeah. He's great. He's willing and ready to do most any chore we ask of him."

Their chatter continued as they walked into the woods, with Lucie telling the story of how they came to buy the property. The temperature among the trees always seemed to be at least ten degrees cooler.

Siegrid hurried down to the edge of the creek, knelt down and plunged both hands in. "So pretty and clear. And cool. I bet there are fish." She looked back up at Lucie. "You catch any?"

"I'm not much on fishing. Wesley either. But I have seen fish in there."

"And frogs?"

"Lots of frogs."

"Got a fishing pole?"

"There were fishing poles left in the outbuilding."

"How about frog gigs?"

Lucie shook her head. "I wouldn't know a frog gig if I saw one. But there's still quite a lot of junk in there."

Continuing their walk, Siegrid peered into the water. "Catfish in there for sure. Fried catfish. Good eatin'."

Just then a cottontail jumped out of the bushes startling both of them.

"Do you have guns? Rabbit stew is delicious."

Lucie was beginning to wonder how far this conversation might go.

"I have a shotgun loaded with salt shot. I've never had the need to fire it. Wesley wants me to use it if I need to scare someone off."

"That would riddle a rabbit. Got a .22?"

"What's that?"

"A .22 rifle. That's what you'd use to kill a rabbit."

"Oh." She couldn't even imagine killing a rabbit. Even if she did, she had no idea what she'd do with it. "Wesley has a gun cabinet."

"Is it locked?"

Lucie shrugged. "Have no idea. I've never opened it."

The evening Wesley arrived home, he could smell dinner before he even stepped out of his car. What was that aroma? His stomach started growling before he hit the front porch steps.

His fly-over had heralded his homecoming. After which, Lucie explained to Siegrid exactly how much time they had to get dinner on the table. Rabbit stew with biscuits. Wilted lettuce from the garden. Lucie had never even heard of wilted lettuce before Siegrid introduced it. Deep dish cherry cobbler, made from the cherries Lucie and Tessa had canned last summer. And to add to the allure, a platter of fried frog legs. It was a banquet.

Wesley was duly impressed, which was all Lucie had hoped for.

He, of course, was firing questions like a gatling gun. "You opened my gun case? You loaded and shot the .22?"

"I hoped you wouldn't mind. I was careful with it." This from Siegrid in her soft voice.

Wesley stammered a bit. "No. Fine. Not at all. Since you're experienced. Know what you're doing." Taking another bite of stew, he added, "And when it winds up in the cooking pot and comes out tasting like this."

"She's a crack shot," Lucie put in, continuing her ongoing hope that this would clinch Siegrid's welcome in their home. "And," Lucie just had to add, "you should see her handle a frog gig."

"Um. A frog what?"

Lucie had to laugh. "Gig. A frog gig." She knew he had no idea on earth about a frog gig. No more than she did. "You gig them in the head, then cut off their legs," Lucie explained.

"And, pray tell, how did you come across a frog gig? Are they just lying around?"

"The outbuilding. Lots of stuff still in there. We found fishing rods, reels, tackle box, wire baskets, waders..." Lucie said, unable to keep the excitement out of her voice.

"And frog gigs."

"Yeah. Looks kind of like a fork with barbed tongs." Lucie passed the plate of biscuits to him. He took two. "I'll show you after dinner."

Wesley nodded. The look of disbelief on his face was priceless and Lucie was enjoying every minute. She also noticed how, every once in a while, he would look over at their guest. Lucie was sure he was bewildered that such talent could reside within such beauty.

The day Tessa was slated to come and fetch Siegrid, Gaven happened to be working on their car, so she was unable to make the trip. After another few days, another time was scheduled, and something else had come up. Lucie was never sure if Tessa and Gaven were conniving, but before they all realized what had happened Siegrid had become a permanent resident of Cairn Cottage.

Chapter 9

June 1933, Oklahoma City, Oklahoma

Hopping a freight was tricky, but being young, athletic, and nimble, Nathan quickly learned. At first, he was terrified. A train is a massively huge, noisy, and fast machine. Surprisingly, he faced down the fear and just did it. Others did it, and he convinced himself he could as well. Another surprise was how the men who were already aboard were willing to reach out a hand and pull you into the boxcar. You learned to grab for the wrist. Grabbing wrists lent more stability to the grab. Hands could slip. Soon, Nathan was the guy extending his hand out to pull others up and in.

The key was timing. Rather like a dance where one slips in at the precise moment. He'd only seen one accident where the man waited too long and the train had built up too much momentum. He fell away and rolled down into the ditch. Nathan tried to look back to see if the man was hurt, but he'd already disappeared from sight. Accidents, horrific accidents, were a common subject of conversation on the boxcars and around the campfires. Some were pretty gruesome.

Next popular subject was the trainyard bulls. The older veteran riders of the rails could tell you which yards were the most dangerous, which ones were a little more friendly. Many of the men had been apprehended and jailed. Nearly all said they were released the next day. It was mostly a scare tactic. That seemed ridiculous to Nathan. Which would be more terrifying—jumping on and off a moving train, or spending a night in the clink? It was a tossup.

A night spent in a filthy jail cell could never stem the tide. Thousands out of work. Men leaving their wives and children. Children leaving parents. All on a desperate search for a way to make a few bucks. Buy food. Or steal food. And keep going.

The jungle on the east side of Oklahoma City was well established. By all appearances, it was much used. Fruit crates to sit on. Hay for beds. A few tents even. Blankets hanging from ropes stretched between trees. A washtub hung from a nail driven into a tree, beneath which leaned a washboard with a bar of soap balanced on top.

It was early evening, still light when Nathan and a few others approached the site. A Dutch oven, coffee pot, and skillet sat on the grillwork placed over the fire. The aromas pulled them in. Introductions were made.

Nathan dropped his satchel by a tree and sat down, leaning against it. It had served as a pillow many nights. He had a small paper bag containing coffee. He'd purchased it from the store behind the Okesa filling station in Red Fork. Purchased it with the little loose change he'd had in his pocket. He wasn't quite broke, but getting close. That was the same town where the cute, petite gal had fed him and his two fellow hoboes, beans and cornbread. And the best pie he'd ever tasted.

The group around the fire that night was larger than most that he'd been in. This seemed to be the best place give over his coffee stash. It was much appreciated, making him a welcome addition to the tribe. What coffee was presently in the pot, they said, was pretty weak.

Turtle soup was cooking in the Dutch oven and dandelion greens in the skillet. An older man sporting a scruffy beard offered a loaf of bread. Purchased or stolen—no one asked. No one ever did. The bread was passed around, each man taking a slice, while the soup and greens were dished up. Bread was quite a treat. Helped to soak up the soup broth.

There always seemed to be a musician and a storyteller at every stop. With their stomachs at least not *eating their backbone,* as the hoboes were fond of saying, but still not really full, they were lulled into a sense of temporary contentment. No rocking of the boxcar, no loud threats from the bulls, no baking sun beating down. They watched in contentment as the setting sun transformed the western sky from bright copper into soft lilac.

The storyteller was the older man who brought the loaf of bread. Bernie was his name. He'd built oil rigs during the Oklahoma oil rush years earlier.

"We couldn't build 'em fast enough," he told them. "Some of them oil patches had rigs every few yards. You'd look across the prairie and the derricks out there thicker'n trees in a pecan grove." Pulling a packet of papers from his pocket and a small cloth bag of tobacco, he proceeded to roll a cigarette. Once finished, he used his teeth to pull the string on the bag tight and crammed it back in his shirt pocket, then lit the cigarette with a stick pulled from the fire.

Nathan, who never smoked and never wanted to, was amazed at how hoboes seemed to always have tobacco even when they had no food.

"Sapulpa, Cleveland, Kieffer, Cushing, Red Fork, Drumright, Mounds...," Bernie was saying.

Nathan, half-sitting, half-lying down, and half-asleep, sat up at the sound of those town names. The names stirred up a memory from way back in his childhood years. He couldn't quite recollect clearly.

"Glenpool?" someone in the group asked. "Were you at Glenpool? That was the big one. Wasn't it?"

After a long drag on the cigarette pinched between fingers that looked to be permanently dirty, he remarked, "Big? That'd be a mighty under-statement. It t'wern't Glenpool back then. It was *the Glenn Pool.* Coulda even been called the Glenn *Lake.* So much dern oil, it just ran all over the place. Hadda build dikes to hold it all of it." He chuckled. "We turned them little towns of hundreds into thousands in a few short days. Like the California gold rush—it was the oil rush. Speculators, investors, gamblers, loose women, all converged chasing the almighty dollar."

"But they was a lot of men made a lot of money in those places, didn't they?" someone ventured. "Like Skelly, Philips, Getty, Sinclair...?"

"A few," Bernie agreed. "Big mansions they got back there in Tulsey Town."

"And then," came another voice from the group, "wham, bam, alakazam—lost it all in the crash."

That remark brought laughter all round.

"Maybe one of 'em's right here in the jungle," came another comment.

More laughter.

"Pride goes before a fall, it says in the Good Book. And did they ever fall."

"I think my father was there," Nathan said, not realizing he'd said it out loud.

"What say? Speak up boy."

Now he leaned forward. Without meaning to, he'd caught the attention of the group. Other than offering the coffee, he'd contented himself with being an observer. A listener. He enjoyed listening to the endless stories.

He cleared his throat. "I said, I think my father was there."

"There? Where?" Bernie asked, his cigarette making a waving arc of a small glow as darkness closed in around them. He added, "You think? Not sure?"

Digging for the memories in the back of his mind made it difficult to put thoughts together, let alone sentences. "Those town names. I was just a little kid. He was hurt in a bad fire."

"Plenty of those," Bernie said. "They just let the natural gas go anywhere and everywhere. Explosions and fires happened even just in the low places around the creek beds. They's too dumb to know the value of natural gas."

"Ah, Bernie," said another older man sitting beside him, "you wouldn't have knowed either. You don't know what you don't know. They hadda learn it."

"So, Sonny," said Bernie, returning attention to Nathan, "how is it you don't recall?"

Gazing at the glowing embers of the dying fire, Nathan said, "After the bad burns, my father was never again in his right mind. He died a few years ago.

"When I was about seven, he had me come down from Indiana on the train for a visit to the sites. And we have his letters and postcards that he wrote to us describing the sites and towns. The throngs of people. The dust and the mud, the noise and the confusion. And those town names. I hadn't thought about them for years."

It was true. And even when making the quick stop in Red Fork for food, it failed to dawn on him. When you're on the road, riding the rails, one town blends in with another. But now the name came rushing back. As a small child, he kept picturing a *red fork*. A confusing mind-picture for a youngster.

He thought about the many postcards and letters that came in the mail while his father was working in the oil fields. Now he wondered if his mother might have kept them. And if so, where they might be. They'd moved out of the big house after his father died. It was only the two of them and his mother couldn't afford to keep up the house. A strong business woman, she opened a photography studio on main street and the two of them lived in the upstairs apartment. It took a few months after the crash for her business begin to dwindle and that's when Nathan took to the road. By then she'd also opened her home to her ailing Uncle Sacha.

"What was your Pa's name?" Bernie wanted to know. "Maybe I knowed him."

"Donly Anderson, but he was always called *Andy*."

Bernie shook his head. "Andy Anderson. Don't sound familiar. So many men. So much work." He inhaled deeply, blew a cloud of smoke in the air and flicked the butt into the fire. With a sigh, he repeated, "So much work. Payday for everyone. Every week. And most of us throwed it away on gambling, booze, and women. We was a bunch of empty-headed fools." With that he unrolled a makeshift bedroll and stretched out on it.

The rest of the men followed suit and quiet fell over the camp, except for one fellow who had pulled his harmonica from his pocket and commenced to play the saddest melody Nathan had ever heard.

He went to the pile of hay and strew armfuls there beside the tree. From his satchel he pulled out a folded blanket. It was thin, but it would keep the hay from poking through his shirt. As he lay down to sleep, he couldn't stop thinking of Red Fork. Something was drawing him back. Tomorrow instead of jumping a westbound freight, he'd be waiting for one eastbound.

Chapter 10

June 1933, Hollywood, California

The girls' rooms in the Jarrell House were on the second and third floors. Sadella was grateful their room was on second. Another flight of stairs to climb after a long day at the studio would have been unbearable.

The first floor housed the *Great Room* as they called it, where the girls gathered to chat, commiserate, and cheer one another on as they all hankered after stardom. The parlor, located in the rear reminded Sadella of the sunroom in their house in Tulsa. Large windows and plenty of light. This is where the girls were allowed to entertain guests. Usually of the male gender. The kitchen and dining room took up the rest of the ground floor.

The basement, with its concrete floor served as a practice area. Singing, dancing, script reading, whatever. The place reverberated with the sounds. Sadella's mother had attempted to talk Sadella into voice lessons, dance lessons, and even piano lessons. But the child, Sadella, rebelled. She never wanted to be told what to do, and that's what lessons were all about—being told what to do.

Now as she watched the girls tap dancing, listened to their trained voices, she experienced twinges of regret. Often the roles for extras required girls who had a song-and-dance routine. She had none of that. Even Clarice had a routine, which miffed Sadella to no end.

"Come listen," Clarice said to her on occasion. "I need an audience."

But Clarice soon learned not to ask. Sadella was never going to be an audience for her. Clarice began to feel that Sadella disliked her. They'd come on this adventure together, and because of that Clarice assumed they would be doing everything together. It wasn't turning out that way at all. Clarice loved the Great Room. She relished the friendships of the other girls. The camaraderie. Getting to know where the girls came from, their backgrounds, their reasons for coming to Hollywood. Sadella cared not an iota about any of them. She spent little or no time building friendships. Even at mealtimes when the conversation was lively and going nonstop, Sadella seldom if ever joined in. She ate quickly and went to her room. Or went for a walk—alone.

Lucie had taken to writing long newsy letters, which Sadella barely looked at. She glanced over the pages, folded them up and laid each one in a growing stack in her top bureau drawer. The most recent said that Clarette Torsten was making regular trips to Red Fork because she was writing a history of the first oil strike, which just happened to have been in Red Fork.

Sadella frowned deeply at even the mention of Clarette, remembering how her beloved Shel had romanced Clarette before she spurned him. Clarette with her big-city ways, her writing and photography skills which through the years had given her a little touch of fame and glory. Well, her fame and glory would be nothing compared to the fame and glory that Sadella would show on the big screen, and with her name emblazoned on the marquees and the movie billing.

A few photos fell out of one of the most recent letters. Sheer curiosity made Sadella stop and look. It was Lucie with a taller version of Tessa MacIntyre. Yet another name she detested. Reading the letter, she learned the girl was Siegrid Jurgen, Tessa's younger sister who was living with them in Red Fork. Even

Sadella couldn't deny that Siegrid was strikingly beautiful, with hair the color that Sadella had to manufacture with peroxide on her own hair.

"Well, isn't that just so cozy," she muttered in disgust.

The photos showed Lucie and Siegrid laughing, cutting up, being silly, out in the back yard of their place in Red Fork. On the back Lucie had penned the date and the note, *photographed by Clarette Torsten.*

Lucie always closed her letters with, *I hope you're doing well, and that all your dreams are coming true.*

"I just bet you do, little Miss Lucie. You're nothing but a child. A child living in a Podunk little burg playing house and pumping gas." At that she shoved the letter into the drawer and slammed it shut.

The next morning at the studio, Mr. Reznick called for her. This was it. Her moment. She ran to a dressing room, touched up her lipstick—well, Clarice's lipstick which she'd taken to borrowing—ran a brush through her peroxided hair, and hurried to his office on the third floor of the studio. In all these months, she'd never been on the third floor. Her heart felt like it was exploding out of her chest.

An efficient-looking receptionist sat at a paper-strewn desk, furiously typing. Looking up, she adjusted her glasses. "Name please?"

"I'm Sadella Patton. Mr. Reznick asked to see me."

She picked up what appeared to be an appointment book. "I don't see your name here."

Sadella stammered a bit. She'd never stammered in her entire life, but she felt she'd lost her voice. "That's because... It's because he just now did it."

That sounded dumb.

Flicking on the intercom, the receptionist leaned toward it. "Mr. Reznick. A Miss Patton is here."

His voice came booming over the box. "Oh yes. Send her in."

She waved a manicured hand toward the door. "Go on in," and returned to clicking the typewriter keys.

Sadella caught her breath when she walked into the expansive office. It'd been so long since she'd experienced such opulence. The massive mahogany desk, plush Oriental carpeting, leather upholstered chairs set about, glass shelves filled with trophies, photos, and other memorabilia. Mounted animal heads filled the higher reaches of the paneled walls. Book shelves stretched across the opposite wall. Tall, open windows allowed the sweet California breeze to waft in. For a moment she was off kilter, dizzy. This was what she should have. All this should be hers. And she'd been robbed. Stolen from. The unfairness of it all stunned her.

If the studio owner and CEO noticed her hesitancy, he covered it well. Obviously, he met with starstruck girls every day. Nothing would surprise him. Standing up from his desk, he stepped over to shake her hand. "Ah, Miss Patton. Thank you for meeting with me. This'll only take a few minutes." Releasing her hand, he waved her to a chair situated in front of his desk. "Come over here. Please sit down."

Instead of returning to his chair, he sat on the corner of his desk. He reached for a gold cigarette holder, opened it and extended it to her. "Cigarette?"

Sadella nodded. She used to own a gold case similar to this one. She couldn't remember what happened to it. Had she hocked it? Perhaps she had. One day when she was overwrought at her mother's behavior and had to get out of the apartment. Who knew?

She took the cigarette and allowed him to light it with the matching gold lighter.

"I'm sorry to bother you, Miss Patton. I know you help out in the studio some. And we appreciate it." He lit his own cigarette and blew a smoke cloud into the air. "You're usually with another gal. A dark-haired gal. Miss Jarvis, I believe?"

Sadella was taken aback. The man took more notice in his studio than she'd given him credit for. She nodded. "That would be Clarice Jarvis."

"But she's not here today."

"No. She stayed up late with one of our girls at the house who was sick in the night. She was exhausted this morning."

"Hm. We need a brunette walk-on with a few lines. I'd like to try her out. Please give her the message. And as soon as she's rested, have her come see me."

Sadella immediately sat up a little straighter in her chair. Reaching up and pulling at one of her permed, peroxided curls, she said, "Oh, no need to wait for Clarice. I can dye this and be ready in a few hours."

Standing to his feet, he said, "Please don't bother. Who knows? We may need a blonde walk-on at any moment."

It was clear the meeting was over. She stood as well. Mr. Reznick crushed out his half-smoked cigarette. Sadella remember back when she could afford to do that. No more. She should probably do the same, but she was desperate. She needed that cigarette in her hand more than she was willing to admit.

"Thank you for your time, Miss Patton." He walked toward the door and she obediently followed, hating that this man had such power over her. "I'll expect Miss Jarvis in my office soon."

Sadella could barely speak. "I'll let her know."

Reaching for the door to open it for her, he added, "Oh and one more thing. I want to put you and Miss Jarvis on a salary. Very small I'm afraid. Everything in the country is in a free-fall. Movie ticket sales are the lowest we've seen in years."

Small salary. Even a small salary was better than nothing. Which was exactly what she had at the present time. Especially now that her calls to her brother to loan her a few bucks had been ignored. The fiend.

The door was now open. "Thank you. Sir. Thank you, sir." How she wished she'd been taught some manners growing up as a rich kid.

"There'll be an envelope for you at the end of the week."

As she descended back down the steps to the melee, noise, action, and commotion of the studio proper, she realized that giving the message to Clarice would be one of the most difficult things she'd ever had to do. Other than asking her brother for money, that is.

Chapter 11

JUNE 1933, RED FORK, OKLAHOMA

Nathan had experienced only a couple of bad scares of losing his satchel as he went leaping on and off trains. All his sign-painting supplies were contained in that satchel—brushes, tape measure, charcoal sticks, pounce pad, pounce wheel, bottles of mineral oil, paint thinner—his precious stash. No way he could ever afford to replace his tools at this point in time. One incident was in St. Louis when he was being chased by the bulls and was rescued by Gilbert and Warren. He came so near to just throwing the satchel aside so he could run faster. Suddenly the two men were on either side of him, practically dragging him and helping him grab the rungs to be pulled into the empty boxcar. And then they were off and going.

"One thing about being nabbed," Gilbert had explained after they'd caught their breath, "those bulls'll pick a man clean as a plucked chicken. Even the poorest hobo hanging onto a few pennies, they gots them pennies in a heartbeat."

Nodding toward Nathan's satchel, Warren added, "Them old boys would purely hanker after yore nifty bag there."

Just hearing those words, gave Nathan prickles on the back of his neck. He could not lose his tools. Could *not*.

In one of the jungles, Gilbert found a length of dirty rope lying on the ground. Waving it in front of Nathan's face, he said, "Now this here's just what you been a'needin' boy."

Settling himself down by where food was cooking, he patted the ground beside him. "C'mon over here. And let's firm up that bag of your'n."

With that, Gilbert tied the rope to the handle and then created a knotted loop. The knots were firm. Secure. Holding it up, Gilbert said, "Hold out your arm."

Nathan did so, and thrust his arm through the loop. A perfect fit.

"Before you take off running, you best put your arm through here and hold the handle both. If you turn loose of the handle, you still got your bag."

Nathan was touched by this extension of kind-heartedness. Tears actually welled up hot in his eyes and he was glad it was dark. Time and again, he'd seen these gestures of compassion among the hoboes. He never remembered ever seeing a fight, or hearing a cross word. They were all in the same mess, and each one watched out for the other.

As for his sign painting, there'd been only one place so far where he'd asked for a job. And got paid fifty cents. Most towns where there was a soup kitchen and men selling pencils on the street corners, made him know that no one would actually *hire* a sign painter. But Red Fork didn't appear to be in too bad a shape.

Now as he walked down the Main Street, he looked at the signage in each window. The barber shop might be a good place to start. The wooden sign over the door looked as if it'd been hanging there since the oil rush days. Checking the change in his pocket, he would have to choose between a haircut or a shave. He chose the latter, stood a little straighter, and strode in as if he had dollars in his pocket instead of a few coins.

Of course, his leather satchel told that he was just passing through, but that couldn't be helped. An older gentleman was coming out and Nathan heard him say, "Thanks, Wade. See ya next week."

From the faded lettering in the window, Nathan noted the name *Wade,* but the last name was unreadable.

"Howdy, there, son. Come on in here. What's your preference today?" The greeting was friendly, something hoboes pick up on immediately. The place was now empty with the last customer having passed him as he came in.

Nathan rubbed the stubble on his chin. "A shave would be welcome."

"Get yourself on up here." Wade waved to the chair nearest the back. The shop looked like it'd just been scrubbed. Bright and shiny as a new penny. "You can set your bag right there by the back door."

At that moment it dawned on Nathan what had just happened. Wade placed him at the back of the shop so his precious satchel could be placed out of sight. A small, but much appreciated gesture. He was liking Red Fork more every minute.

As with all barbers, Wade chatted away, talking about the lack of rain, the ranchers' plight, the economy of the nation, all that Roosevelt was doing to turn things around, and on and on. His voice was soothing, as Nathan basked in the sensation of the hot towel, the clean shave, the splash of lotion.

"I know you didn't mention a haircut, son," Wade said, "but how about a quick shampoo. On the house. As a new customer bonus."

Nathan tried to mask his surprise. "That would be swell. Thanks."

As Wade's fingers worked a massage over his scalp, Nathan nearly melted into a puddle right there in the barber shop. He could barely remember the last time he'd had a barber shampoo.

Raising the chair back up, and turning Nathan around, Wade began combing. "Well now, we got it wet, let's just trim a little around the edges." And with that, the scissors were in his hand and he began clipping before Nathan could peep out a protest.

"Son, you got curls on top of curls here. You Italian?"

"French. My mother's pure French."

"Oh boy! Parlez-vous français?"

Nathan had to laugh. "Just a little." Thinking about his mother nearly brought him to tears. He missed her intensely.

"My brother was in France during the Great War. Came home with all kinds of wild tales."

Changing the subject, Wade said, "I see you got a little New Testament there in your pocket. You a preacher?"

"I share the Word some, to the guys in the hobo jungles. Lots of them have lost hope and just need a smidgeon of encouragement. But I'm not a preacher."

Nathan remembered it happened in one of the jungles in Missouri as the men were chatting, one young traveler said with a despondent sigh, "It's like God's just forgotten all of us. Just wrote us off and forgot us."

"It may feel that way," Nathan had offered, "but my Bible tells me different. In the book of Isaiah, it says that a nursing mothing might forget her baby, but God says, 'I will not forget thee.'

"Then it says in the next verse that He has engraved you on the palm of your hand. I don't know about you, but that feels personal to me."

No more conversation followed, but Nathan trusted a seed of hope had been planted.

Bringing Nathan back to the present, Wade asked, "Been traveling long?"

"About a year or so. Lost count."

And he had. He hadn't even thought about it until that moment. Time means nothing when you're catching a freight and hoping for food or a job at the next stop.

As Wade used his soft-bristled whisk to brush off the stray hairs, and removed the cape, Nathan was hatching an idea. "You've been more than kind. I'm a sign painter and I noticed the lettering in your window is faded. May I touch it up for you? In payment for the bonus shampoo and *trim*."

Wade looked over at the front window. "I been a-hating that ugly sign for a spell now. That'd be right nice to have it all spruced up." He reached out his hand. Nathan took it and they shook. "I accept that offer."

Nathan then reached in his pocket to pay for the shave and Wade touched his arm. Shaking his head, he said, "Naw. Keep it."

"But I can pay for the..."

"Seems to me like a new sign would more than pay for a shave *and* haircut."

Within the hour, Nathan was out front surrounded by his tools and his paints enjoying the feeling of exercising his talent. He already felt like a million dollars with the shave and haircut alone, and now this. But God wasn't done pouring out the blessings.

Nathan began by removing the original lettering, which quite clearly had been applied by a rank amateur. The fresh new lettering—*Wade Nichols, Proprietor*—was larger, easy to see, easy to read, and each dark blue letter was shadowed in red which made the letters stand out.

When Wade stood out on the sidewalk inspecting the finished work, he was quite clearly impressed. "Now that's what I call a real sign by a real sign painter. Goodness mercy me. Wait'll Sarah sees this. She's gonna love it."

The barber then looked up at the wooden sign above the door. Pointing up at the sign, he said, "What could you do with that thing?"

Nathan smiled. "Oh, I could do a lot with that. Those kinds of signs are my favorite."

"What would you need to get started on it?"

"A ladder, hammer, maybe new wood. I won't know that till it's down. And space to work on it."

At that moment a customer came to the door of the shop. Wade ushered the man inside. "Be there in a minute, Ron." Reaching into his pocket, he brought out a few coins. "Here's your advance. Take this and go down to Annie's and get you some dinner. Come back and we'll get to work on this."

Giving Nathan's shoulder a fatherly pat, he said, "The garage behind our house is empty. You can work in there." With a wink, he added, "I don't think it'd be too bad a place to sleep for a few days. We got a cot."

Chapter 12

JUNE 1933, VINITA, OKLAHOMA

When it came to visiting their mother, Lucie had become the conscience. Wesley dragged his feet and came up with every excuse imaginable. Lucie hurt for him. Of course, it was difficult for both of them, but it seemed to cut Wesley to the quick.

"She doesn't even know we're there," was his most oft-used reasoning.

"You don't know that," Lucie would reply, as gently as she could. "We have no idea what's going on in her head."

"Nothing. Obviously. Flat out nothing."

To a degree he was right. Trevalene never acknowledged their presence, staring off into space with vacant eyes. It was heartbreaking to say the least.

On this hot Sunday afternoon, she'd somehow guilted him into compliance. All windows were down, and dust roiled around and into the car till Lucie felt she could feel the grit in her teeth. The drive from Red Fork to Vinita—almost to the Kansas border—was not a pleasant one even in the best of conditions. Now with the ongoing drought, the dust was almost unbearable. Wesley, as Lucie well knew, would much prefer flying to driving. And he was fairly making the car fly.

She could have driven, but she dared not even suggest such a thing. Wesley's usually open, cheerful countenance was closed and stoic. Lucie assumed he was bracing himself for the visit. The Eastern Oklahoma Hospital as it was known, consisted of a vast complex of imposing-looking, three-story brick buildings. A ward for women, one for the men, administration building, dormitories for staff, and a medical hospital. Even a farm with gardens and a dairy. Essentially, the place was a self-contained city. To Lucie, it seemed totally out of place, spread out here on the outskirts of the small town of Vinita.

Their mother was in the women's ward located at the far west end. But first they had to go to the administration building and meet with the doctors. As a matter of course, they had telephoned ahead to make an appointment. This wasn't a place where you just dropped in for a casual visit. It was all business.

In the doctor's office, he filled them in on recent developments. As usual, there were none. This report set the mood for the visit. No changes. Little hope.

Trevalene had been brought into a visitation room which was filled with light streaming in from a bank of tall windows, some of which were open letting in the hot Oklahoma wind. Oscillating fans were set about the room, keeping the hot air moving. Lucie would have much preferred being out on the grounds under a shade tree. But then she reasoned that if they were uncomfortable, perhaps it would shorten the visit.

Other families scattered about the room, visiting with their loved ones in various stages of mental incompetence. As despondent a place as Lucie had ever seen in her life.

The two of them greeted their mother with as much cheeriness as could be mustered. Trevalene was seated in a wheeled chair with a tray fastened to the front much like a child's high chair. Lucie assumed the tray not only held food at meals, but also kept the patient from falling out of the chair. Trevalene rubbed the tray with her hands, back and forth, over and over again. As they both talked, Wesley wheeled his mother's chair over closer to an open window, then pulled two folding chairs over to face Trevalene.

Trevalene had lost weight and was no longer that portly, strong-willed woman who had ruled her family, her household, her household help, and the Tulsa community with an iron fist. Her eyes never seemed to focus on any one thing. Those vacant eyes apparently saw nothing.

The doctors had told them early on that the two intense shocks of her life, first losing their vast fortunes, and then discovering her husband's body after he'd taken his life, had short-circuited her brain. The mind, being unable to register such a nightmare, mercifully shut down, allowing her to live in a peaceful state. Albeit, a useless one.

"Will she ever begin to respond to us?" Lucie had asked during one of those early exchanges.

The doctor simply answered, "We have no way of knowing." Then he added, "But we never want to stop trying."

And so they did. They kept trying.

They talked about Sadella now living way out there in California. How she was dreaming of becoming a movie star. That they didn't hear from her very often, but, "she sends her love." Which was a lie. Sadella never asked about their mother.

"And," Lucie went on, "you should see our rock house. We call it Cairn Cottage, because Cairn means *stone pyramid*. We figured the stone part was close enough. And we like the sound of *Cairn*. It's in Red Fork. I know you remember Red Fork, where Daddy and E.V. hit their first oil strike."

"I wish you could see our filling station. It isn't really a filling station like some in Tulsa," Wesley continued, trying to fill the silence, "it's just two pumps in front of a small store." He reached out and touched his mother's arm when he said, "And you should see your younger daughter pump gas, check the oil, and wash windshields. You wouldn't believe it."

No response from Trevalene. Just swiping the tray, back and forth, back and forth in a maddening repetition.

"But I pretty much just mind the store," Lucie added. "We have a boy named Rand who loves automobiles. We let him tend to most of the outside chores."

"The CEO of the Okesa company really likes us and tells us he's proud of the way we run our business," was Wesley's input.

"And," Lucie put in, "Wesley's still flying. I wish you could see the Blue Bolt. It's not really blue, it's actually silver with blue lightning bolts on either side.

And when the sun shines on it, well, it's almost blinding. All of his clients love and trust him. Trust him with their lives, actually."

They couldn't keep it up. Eventually, they looked at one another and gave a sigh in unison. It was exhausting.

Lucie reached out and tried to pat her mother's hand, but the hand would not stop rubbing the wooden tray. So, she patted the arm instead. "We have to go now, Mother. It was so good to see you."

The two of them stood, and Wesley motioned to an attendant to come and take Trevalene back to her room. Lucie bent to kiss her mother's cheek. It was cool to the touch, making her recoil.

Both were silent as they walked back to the parking lot. In the car, Lucie reached into her purse and pulled out her comb to try to put back into order what the Oklahoma wind had mussed up. When she looked over at her brother, his head was resting on his hands on the steering wheel. His shoulders were shaking. It took a moment for her to realize that he was crying.

She was shocked. Never had she seen her brother cry. Not through all they'd recently endured together. Not at their father's funeral. Not when they were suddenly in charge of a mass auction, watching all their possessions being sold off piece by piece to the highest bidder. Not when their mother was out of her mind and they were unable to care for her. Not when they had to get others to assist in restraining Trevalene, forcing her into the car and admitting her to the hospital in Vinita. And now this.

"Wesley," she whispered, laying her hand on his shoulder. "Oh Wesley. It's okay. Everything's gonna be okay."

"I hated her, Lucie. I hated her," came the muffled words between sobs. "She was so cruel and cold. All my growing up years, I hated her and wished bad things on her. But now..."

"Wishing things on someone doesn't make it happen," Lucie offered. Rummaging in her purse she pulled out her handkerchief and pressed into his palm. He lifted his head then and wiped his eyes and blew his nose.

Looking at her with red-rimmed eyes, he said, "I would welcome that loud-mouth, bossy, cold-hearted mother over this any day of the week."

"I know that, Wesley. You were just a child. You didn't mean those things. God knows your heart."

Shoving her flowered handkerchief into his shirt pocket, he said, "I hope so. I've repented often enough. Especially during my hours in the sky, when I feel so close to God."

"Silly. It only takes one time. He heard you." Then she added, "We both would have much preferred a soft, gentle, huggable mother, but that's not what life handed us. She was fighting her own demons." She closed her purse and set it on the floorboards by her feet. "We will probably never know the struggles she endured deep within herself."

Wesley inhaled a deep, shaky breath, blew it out, and started the car. "You're right, sis. As usual. Thanks. We *will* get through this."

"As God shows us the way."

"Yes. As God shows us the way."

Chapter 13

July 1933, Red Fork, Oklahoma

In a town like Red Fork, one had no need of advertising. Just be on the good side of Wade Nichols. Nathan quickly learned that Wade was better than any advertisement.

"Your sign is pathetic," Wade had said to the owner of the hardware store. With that, Nathan was creating a new sign for the hardware store. After that Peterson's Grocery and then two others.

He spent a few nights in Wade's garage, but Wade and his wife, Irene, insisted he sit at their table for his dinner each evening. Her cooking was larapin good, as he'd heard the hoboes say. It was the first time he'd been full for more than one day at a time in months.

The cot was ten times more comfortable than the hard ground. They gave him a blanket and a pillow. In that garage, at the work bench that lined one side, he painted the perfect sign that was then placed above the door of the barber shop. True to his nature, Wade bragged about it to every customer who came in the shop. And to some folk who were just walking by.

After a few jobs, Nathan was flush enough to rent a room from Mrs. Dolores Powell. A room. A real room. A real bed with a rainbow-colored rag-rug spread out on the floor beside it. Clean sheets. A wash stand with a wash bowl and pitcher. Soap. A clean towel. How he wished Warren and Gilbert could see this.

Having no idea how long he'd be in Red Fork, he just paid for one week. The first night, lying in that soft bed, he felt surely he'd died and gone to heaven. Through the open window came the shrilling of insects in the trees. Off in the distance, over the still night air, came the nostalgic melody of a train whistle.

Having been on the go for seemingly endless days and nights, he was safe, even if just for a few days. He was well aware he would soon run out of business owners who needed fresh signs painted. After that, he'd have to move on. But for this moment, he could rest.

When it came to the Red Fork First National Bank, however, Nathan was in a dilemma. Bank president, Luther Cavanaugh, made it very clear he wanted the new sign on his front window painted in gold lettering. Nathan had no gold paint.

His initial meeting in the bank office with Mr. Cavanaugh had Nathan's gut tied in knots. Ma Powell, as she insisted he call her, had laundered his clothes and even starched and ironed his shirt. He kept reminding himself this was just to talk about painting a sign. He'd been a hobo, an outcast for so long, it proved a tricky mental adjustment to remember his old life where he was loved and valued by everyone in the small town of Ulen, Indiana.

But then came the stipulation about gold paint. The primary colors, he still had plenty of, but not gold. Nathan had a little money, but not enough to order paint, then pay for it to be shipped to Red Fork. If he'd had the courage, he would have asked for an advance. His current overriding sense of timidity simply wouldn't allow it.

After his conversation with Mr. Cavanaugh, Nathan stopped by the barber shop to see if Wade had any advice or ideas. He sat in one of the chairs placed against the far wall and waited patiently until the current customer was all spiffed up and sent on his way.

Wade went to the back room, filled two mugs with steaming coffee from the hot plate. Handing one to Nathan he seated himself in the chair beside him. "Something on your mind, son?"

Sipping the coffee and burning his lip, Nathan paused. "It's Mr. Cavanaugh."

"Did he insult you? I'll take him in hand..."

"Oh no." Nathan could hardly believe this man who'd already gone out of his way to lend a helping hand, was now ready to take on the bank president. "It's nothing like that. He wants me to paint his front window."

After another gulp of coffee, Wade said, "Well, I should certainly hope so. Looks like the one on there now was painted long before statehood."

Nathan laughed. He never would have mentioned the fact that when he first arrived in Red Fork, Wade's signage looked as bad or worse. "It is in pretty bad shape," he agreed.

"What the problem?"

"Gold paint. He wants it all in gold."

"It figures. His bank isn't all that secure at the present, but he wants it to look like it's worth its weight in gold." He chuckled at his own joke.

"But I have no gold paint. I can't afford to order it, plus it would be days before it arrives and..."

Wade jumped to his feet, drained the rest of his coffee and said, "No problem at all. I was gonna head in to Tulsey Town this very afternoon for some things I need." Taking Nathan's empty cup from his hand, he added, "You just as well ride along. We'll find a place that's got the paint you need."

"But you can't just close your shop."

"Guess I can. My shop. Do it all the time. Hang loose just a sec. Let me rinse these out."

And within the hour they were rattling toward Tulsa in Wade's red Model T. All the while, Wade was explaining how he'd bought it from a Tulsa man who'd lost his business in the crash. "Told me he bought it brand new in twenty-eight. Brand new. Can you believe that?" Shaking his head, he said, "Such a bad time for so many people. So much loss."

Nathan had nothing to add, thinking of how his mother lost her photography business and had to close down her store and studio. *Bad time* was such an understatement. At least now he could send a few dollars home to her. Made him feel like a king. Leaving her behind was one of the hardest things he'd ever done. But he had to find work. And he'd found it in Red Fork, of all places. Close to the oil field where his father nearly lost his life.

At the art supply shop, Wade insisted on footing the bill for the paints that Nathan needed. Hushing Nathan's protests, Wade assured him, "You'll have enough to pay me back when you're making more of a profit. Especially when that old windbag Cavanaugh pays you. Until then, keep your cash in your pocket."

Unsure of how he'd come upon such favor, Nathan made no more protests. Wade's supplies of razors, after-shave lotion, shaving soap, shampoo, beard balm, and such, were bagged up and carefully placed on the floorboards of the back seat. Nathan, on the other hand, kept his sack of bottles of paint in his lap. Feeling like a little kid with a new toy, he could hardly wait to begin painting that bank window.

As they crossed the Arkansas River bridge, Nathan thinking out loud said, "But there aren't that many more businesses in Red Fork who are gonna need my services."

"You like Red Fork?"

After a pause, "Yeah. Yeah I do."

Wade shook his head. "Not sure why an adventurous young man would choose such an uninteresting place as Red Fork, but that's your call." Then he said, "How about road signs."

"Like billboards?"

"That'd be too big. More like Burma-Shave signs."

"Like what? Burma-Shave?"

"You never seen Burma-Shave signs?"

Nathan gave a wry laugh. "Don't see many signs flying along inside an empty freight car."

"I guess that'd be true at that. Wanna see 'em?"

Nathan shrugged. "I guess so." He really wanted to get busy on that bank window. But Wade had been so kind, he couldn't say no.

"They're on the other side of town. Got a few minutes?"

"Sure."

Passing through the short Red Fork Main Street, heading toward Oklahoma City, Wade said, "They're right along here. Just a few miles... Ah. Right there." All they could see were the back sides. Wade turned the car around in a farmer's driveway. Heading back toward Red Fork he slowed down. There they were. Six signs in a row. Each one had a short line, and they all rhymed.

Shaving brush

Don't you cry,

You'll be a

Shoe dauber

By and by

Burma-Shave

Nathan was laughing. "So clever. Never saw these in Indiana."

"They're scattered all over the Midwest. Of course, you can't copy Burma-Shave, or their ideas, but I bet that filling station in town would like signs posted coming in and out of town. Travelers need to know where to get gas."

Nathan was listening.

"And other supplies for their automobiles. Oil. Tires. Batteries. Spark plugs. Grease. They got all that stuff."

It sounded as if Wade had already talked to the owner. When Nathan asked, Wade shook his head. "Naw. I was just thinking. I do that a lot you know." Then chuckled at his own joke.

"But are they making enough to pay for a sign-painting job? I mean most people don't have much money these days."

"This guy's a go-getter. He flies his own airplane. Gets paid to ferry oilmen around to their leases and refineries."

"His own airplane?" What a baffling thought.

"Been a-flying on his own since he was just a kid from what I hear tell. Name's Wesley. You two're about the same age. I bet you'd get along swell." Wade was turning into the driveway of his house located a block off Main Street. As the Model-T shuddered to a stop, he said, "Wesley'd sure enough have money to pay for signs. And I betcha he'd like the idea."

To Nathan's everlasting delight, Mr. Cavanaugh liked the sign. The money he earned was more than all the other signs he'd painted so far in Red Fork. First thing was to repay Wade for the loan for the paint. Then to the train station office to wire money to his mother, with the added note, "I'll write soon. I'm well."

Still unsure as to his future, Nathan made the decision to pay Ma Powell for a whole month's rent for the room. It was almost like a decision in direction. He felt good about it.

Wiping her hands on her apron, she took the money he handed her. Taking down a coffee can from the pantry shelf, she tucked the money inside. "This is mighty nice," she said giving a wide smile that showed a few missing teeth. "I'm mighty grateful to have such a fine young man in my spare room."

"It goes both ways. I'm mighty grateful to have such a fine lady to rent from." At that Nathan thought Ma Powell actually blushed. And he added, "Not to mention you're about the best cook ever."

"Aw pawsh. Just old-fashioned stuff I learned from my ma back on the farm."

"You learned it well."

Saturdays in Red Fork reminded Nathan of Saturdays back in Ulen. Farmers coming into town to buy their groceries. Some to sell milk, eggs, and vegetables. Get their week's supply of feed at the feed store. Let the kids see a moving picture.

Nathan's task this morning was to follow up on Wade's idea to talk to the fellow at the filling station about a roadside sign. Ma Powell's house was at the opposite end of town from the filling station, and so he maneuvered through the clusters of people on the street—men in overalls and their wives in worn print dresses—and strode to the opposite end of town. Past the welding shop, past the bank where he admired his work of art, past Annie's Café, past the drug store, and the watch repair shop.

Halfway down Main Street, he could see a crowd of children massed around the tall, red gasoline pumps, and filling the driveway where customers drove their cars up to have them serviced. No car could have pulled in there now. The excitement was palpable as the kids laughed, and talked, and milled about.

As he approached, Nathan saw a couple of adults at the front door. They'd just come out with boxes which they set beside the soda pop cooler on the front porch. At the sight of them, a cheer rose from the kids who started a bit of a shoving match to move toward the porch.

"What's going on?" Nathan asked a taller, older, towheaded boy.

"It's the day we get our Space Boy Sparkie flight-patrol badge and galaxy map."

Now it made sense. Everyone knew about the radio show starring *Space Boy Sparkie and his Space Dog Sport*, sponsored by Okesa Oil and Gas Company. Nathan marveled. What a great advertising and marketing idea.

"Hey," Nathan said to the towhead, taking him gently by the arm. "You look to me like a born leader. I bet just by singing that Sparkie space jingle, you could corral this gang and get them into an organized line."

The boy looked Nathan right in the eyes. "I bet you're right."

Stepping off to the side of the group, the boy raised his voice. "Hey. Looky here. Everyone who can sing the Space Boy Sparkie theme song, line up right here." He waved his hand to indicate the direction. "Don't worry, there'll be plenty of badges and maps for all of you. Come on now. The line starts here. You older boys, help the little ones to line up in front of you." Directing them further, he instructed, "Come this way, away from the pumps. Leave room for people to get gas."

He began to sing the ditty:

Spaceboy Sparkie and his Spacedog Sport
Zooming out to their Jupiter Port...

The voices were almost yelling as they joined in the chorus:

There goes Carina – careening through space

on a race to save the cosmos.

In a few short minutes an orderly line formed. Now standing on the bottom step of the store and facing the crowd of children, the boy instructed them over the sound of singing voices, "Once you have your badge and map, move over by the feed store. Wait for your siblings, or go find your parents."

Nathan was speechless. It was like he'd turned on a switch. The kid was a natural.

The children knew all the verses of the theme song, and obviously enjoyed singing them over and over.

The young man up on the porch handing out the cellophane-wrapped packages, Nathan surmised, must be Wesley. Who, Wade had said, was the owner of the place. Once this mayhem calmed down, that's who he needed to talk to.

Then a tall, dark-haired woman, very attractive in a cultured way, carrying a Graflex camera came out of the store. She stationed herself off to the side and began snapping photos. Nathan was stunned for a moment. His mother owned a Graflex identical to the one the woman was holding. No ordinary person on the street owned a press camera like that. Who could she be? And why did she have such a special camera?

By now, Nathan had removed himself from the center of the action, stepping over to lean against the corner of the feed store to wait. He could smell the good smell of grain and feed. He reached down and grabbed a long piece of straw from off the ground and chewed the end.

The vast lot behind the building is where farmers loaded their wagons and pickup trucks with feed and grain for their animals. An activity he could see as he stood there waiting. When he turned his attention back to the store a new figure had come outside. She was about the same size as some of the children in the crowd. Tiny. Her flowered dress swirled around her legs as the wind caught it. Soft brunette curls fluttered around her face. The energy she exuded could be felt all the way to where he was standing. He could hear her laugh. Hear her voice. In a split second, she looked his way, as if drawn to him. The instant look of recognition and surprise, as she recalled him sitting in her back yard under what she had called the King Oak, eating cornbread and beans. How he wished that her memory of him was not that of a hungry hobo. Then he wondered why did it even matter? She smiled at him, then quickly looked away, busy handing out the packages and talking to the children.

Seeing her made him feel shy and awkward. All the bravado he'd felt as he left his room that morning drained right out of him. Tossing down the piece of straw, he walked away. He'd go get a cup of coffee at Annie's. Maybe come back later. Once his courage returned. If it ever did.

She was about the cutest little gal he'd ever seen. She literally took his breath away.

So, she lived in the big rock house. And she worked in the store at the Okesa filling station. He wanted to know more. But not now. He was too flustered.

Chapter 14

July 1933, Red Fork, Oklahoma

L ucie pulled cold bottles of Nehi from the cooler. The iceman was due tomorrow. And just in time. The block in the cooler was going down fast.

Wesley, she knew wanted grape. Her favorite was the peach. Rand loved the cola. Wesley took his bottle and rolled it across his forehead before reaching over to the cooler to hook the bottle cap and open it. Then he took a long drink.

Morning was only about half over and it was already miserable hot.

"Clarette," Lucie asked, "what's your preference?" She stuck her hand back down into the cooler just to feel the coolness.

Clarette had seated herself in one of the wooden rocking chairs situated on the store's front porch. "Got a cola in there?"

"Well of course. What uptown store like this would not have a cola?"

They both had to laugh at that joke. Clarette, like Lucie, came from wealth and opulence. Hers, as she often joked, was *old money*. Her ancestors made a fortune in the silk industry dating back to the 1600s. "These oil upstarts are the *new money* people," she would say. "Mere babes in arms."

The two of them often bantered about wealth, but it was all in good fun. Because both had joined the ranks of the common folk. Clarette by choice. Lucie by default.

Clarette had turned her back on her family's fortune to try her hand at becoming a successful New York newspaper reporter. In fact, that's how she happened to wind up in Oklahoma. Her editor sent her *out west* to cover the *Negro Uprising* as they called it back then. She met and fell in love with Erik Torsten and here she was, living in Tulsa. Her novels continued to bring her fame and income.

She also wrote articles and worked in public relations for her husband's Oil and Gas publication of which he was the editor.

Her son, Everett, was inside the store talking it up with Rand. The two seemed to have hit it off in a matter of minutes.

Wesley opened the screen door. "Hey you two jokers. Come choose your soda pop."

At that they came barreling out the screen door on a dead run pushing and shoving to be the first to open the cooler and grab the cold bottles.

"Everett," Wesley said, "thanks so much for organizing the kids for us. I thought for a minute we were going to have a stampede."

Taking a long drink from his orange soda, he wiped his mouth with the back of his hand and shook his head. "I can't take a bit of credit. A fellow just walked up to me and said I looked like a leader. Then told me to get them singing and after that we lined them up. Presto. It worked."

Lucie felt a shiver in spite of the heat. She knew that fellow. He was standing by the feed store. She knew he was watching her. When she looked again, he had disappeared.

Clarette gave her son an admiring look. "Well of course you're a leader. Your father and I keep telling you that."

"So, Lucie," Wesley said, "what do you think? Was it a success?"

Where had Nathan gone? She wondered. And why had he left so quickly?

"Lucie?" He touched her arm. "Are you awake?"

"What? Sorry."

"Was it a success?"

"Not sure how to measure the success. I was hoping more parents would have come to the store as well. But I guess it was easier to just send the kids over. And since they'd heard it on the radio show, they all knew about it."

Just then a car pulled up to the pumps. Rand set his half-empty bottle on the cooler and flew down the porch steps two at a time and tended to the customer. Both Lucie and Wesley were pleased with how Rand had learned the ropes and made himself indispensable. His congeniality with the customers added to his value as their one and only employee. He pumped gas, cleaned the windshield, checked the tires, checked the oil. He was even great at making change. He made them look good.

"Is Trent coming today?" Wesley wanted to know.

"He telephoned yesterday and said he'd try his best to get over here," Lucie answered. "I have no idea how he'll check on all his locations in one day."

"Do we have any badges and maps left?"

Lucie looked in one of the boxes. "A few here."

Rand was back on the porch having made the sale and even sold a can of motor oil. "There's still one more box in the back."

"Another box?" Lucie was surprised. So many kids had swarmed the place, she assumed they were cleaned out of Spaceboy Sparkie prizes.

"A line is forming down at the picture show. Maybe the boys could hand them out to the kids there."

Lucie recognized that voice. She whirled around. There stood Nathan Anderson in the driveway near one of the pumps. He'd evidently overheard the conversation. There was that shiver again.

Wesley reacted immediately. "Hey there, stranger. That's a clever idea. I like it. If the kids don't come to us, we go to the kids. Rand, fetch that extra box. Take Everett and hand these out to the people at the movie house."

"Grownups too?" That from Everett.

"Well, we have the product. They're not doing any good just sitting here. Plus, they have our brand name all over them."

"And Spaceboy Sparkie's," Rand added. As if that was of prime importance. "I can't wait till they decide to give away a space ray-gun. That's what I'm waiting for."

"Hey Wesley," Everett said as he chunked his pop bottle into the wooden case, "that's the fellow who told me how to organize the kids."

Once the boys were gone, Wesley stepped down to where Nathan was standing and reached out his hand. "I guess we owe you thanks on two occasions now. Once for the idea of organizing the kids, and now the idea of taking the prizes to the movie house."

Nathan's soft voice betrayed his shyness. "No need for thanks. Just happened to be in the right place." Returning Wesley's handshake, he said, "You're Wesley, right?"

"Guilty as charged."

"Wade suggested I look you up."

"Oh, the barber? That guy should be the mayor. He knows everything that goes on here. If he'd been in control during the oil rush, I'm convinced Red Fork would have been the *Oil Capital,* rather than Tulsa."

The chuckle that Lucie heard from Nathan took her back to that afternoon in their back yard. She hadn't realized until this moment how that soft laugh had affected her.

"I have a business proposition to make."

Placing his hand on Nathan's shoulder, Wesley said, "Makes my little heart go pitty-pat. Nothing I love better than a business proposition."

Now they were both laughing.

"Annie's Café is the best place for business."

"I just came from there."

"What'd you have?"

"A cup of coffee."

Wesley wrinkled up his nose and shook his head. "Not the best."

"I've tasted a lot worse."

That's for sure, Lucie mused. *In all those hobo jungles.* She couldn't imagine what this man was doing here. Why'd he come back? And what business proposition could he possibly have in mind? How she wished she could tag along.

"This time around, we'll have iced tea and pie," Wesley suggested, as he guided Nathan away from the filling station in the direction of Annie's.

Back inside the store, Clarette was packing her camera into the case.

"Did you get some good shots?" Lucie asked her.

Clarette nodded. "If I didn't, I'm a complete failure as a photographer. The look on those kid's faces. Priceless."

Moving behind the counter, Lucie began straightening the merchandise. Their customers would be coming later in the afternoon and early evening. "These kids have so few toys. To be able to get one for free made it an extra special day for them."

"That was obvious from their clothing. Pants too short, shoes too small. Makes me want to cry."

"It's the drought," Lucie explained. "Crop failure means the farmer can't pay his loan at the bank. Or his taxes. We've already seen a few foreclosures."

Clarette took her camera case and tucked it in a corner behind the counter. "Do you think Trent will like the photos?"

"He'll be deliriously happy. I bet we're the only one of his stations today taking professional photos of the event."

"He likes you and Wesley. I could tell when I talked to him."

"We were such greenhorns, he had to take special care of the two of us. What we knew about running a business you could fill a thimble."

"Well you're no slouches now. You're making a profit, right?"

"We are. It's due to Trent's marketing. Sponsoring a kids' radio show is genius. Every kid knows Spaceboy Sparkie..."

"...and his Spacedog Sport," Clarette finished.

"And they know Okesa filling stations."

Clarette picked up one of the cellophane packages from off the counter and opened it. Pulling out the badge, she said, "These aren't junk. They're well made."

"Look at the *galaxy map*. That takes a lot of imagination. It cites all the locations mentioned in the radio show stories."

"Marketing, marketing, marketing."

"I have a few more crates in back to bring up and put out. They're not heavy. Come help."

As they filled candy jars and put condiments on the shelves, Clarette asked, "You're so close to Tulsa, how're you guiding potential customers to your filling station rather than Tulsa?"

"We've been talking about that. In fact, we're hoping Trent'll stay over for supper tonight. It's a subject that'll be brought up. We're searching for fresh ideas."

"Wish I could get to my dark room before then. I could show off my works of art."

"There'll be plenty of time for that. I'm betting he's going to want to run an ad in Erik's magazine and let Spaceboy Sparkie take the starring role."

"Erik would love that."

"And including your photos of course."

Clarette's laugh rang out. "Then I'll love it as well."

Chapter 15

JULY 1933, HOLLYWOOD, CALIFORNIA

When Sadella heard Myron asking about the photo he'd found on the floor of the studio, it frightened her. It was hers. Of course it was hers. It'd been in her skirt pocket. It must have fallen out when she pulled her handkerchief out earlier that morning. She was ashamed to admit she was even carrying it around. It was the photo of Siegrid and Lucie. On the back, in Lucie's handwriting, it simply said, "Siegrid and me acting silly."

Myron was waving it over his head. "Whose is this? Where'd this photo come from?" he said in a loud voice.

How was she to know if he was mad about it? Maybe he was upset that someone was cluttering up the studio floor. Just then one of the girls from Jarrell House, one of the *mouthy* girls at that, stepped right up to Myron Reznick and said in her loud, obnoxious voice, "It belongs to Sadella."

At that moment, Sadella had been standing back, away from the action, trying to make herself invisible. The girl, whose name was Gretchen, turned to scan the group behind her. Spying Sadella, who was inching toward the nearest exit, Gretchen said, "There she is. That girl there. That's Sadella. It's hers."

Sadella sent Gretchen the most hateful glare she could muster. To which, the girl was totally oblivious.

Mr. Reznick now had eye contact with her. "Sadella. Oh yes, Sadella Patton. Miss Patton, meet me in my office in ten minutes."

Ten minutes later, with stomach churning, Sadella was once again in that lavish office. And once again, he opened that gold cigarette case, offered her the cigarette and a light. She sat in the same chair. And he sat on the corner of his desk. In one hand he held a cigarette, in the other, the photo.

"First of all, Sadella, I never thanked you for connecting us with Clarice. She wasn't spectacular, but a fairly good walk-on. She could use a few acting lessons."

Trying to quell her nervousness, and calm her shaky voice, she managed a clear, "You're very welcome."

"Now about this photograph. Who is this?"

"Which one, sir? One is my younger sister. The other is just a friend of the family."

"The one with the flaxen hair."

"That's the friend."

"Do you know her well?"

Sadella shook her head. She loathed Tessa MacIntyre and anything or anyone who had anything to do with that woman. Including her younger sister, Siegrid, who was now living with Wesley and Lucie. Not only did she not know Siegrid Jurgen, she didn't *care* to know her. But, in this meeting she was unsure what she should say. She shrugged and said, "I know her. But not well."

The studio tycoon was now literally gazing at the photo. "Is she this beautiful in real life?"

Now the bile in Sadella's throat was rising up. She hated herself for her stupidity of having the picture in her pocket in the first place. Hating to admit it, she was simply admiring how grownup her younger sister looked. It was almost as if Lucie had matured overnight. She'd always been such a thorn in Sadella's side. Always the good little girl. Never disobeying. Never doing anything wrong. But now...

"Miss Patton? I asked a question."

She shook her head, "I've never been around her that much. So, I can't say for sure."

He placed the photograph on his desk and walked over to the windows that looked over his vast domain. "She might be just what we're looking for. Do you think she might want to be in pictures?"

Without thinking, Sadella answered, "Doesn't everybody?"

He turned around. "I'm afraid not." Blowing blue smoke into the room, he said, "Mary Pickford, the nation's innocent ingénue isn't so young any more. Jean Harlowe shows no innocence much at all. We're looking for the just-right combination of young, innocent, and beautiful. We have a couple of scripts ready to go." Then he added, "We're willing to pay for the discovery."

At that, Sadella sat up a little straighter. Pay? For a discovery? And she might have access to that just-right person that *Starline Productions Studios* was searching for? The conversation just changed for the better.

"How much?"

Myron was back at his desk, lost in thought, gazing at the photo again. She waited. A few hundred bucks in her pocket meant she could enhance her beleaguered wardrobe and begin attending the parties about town. Up to now, she'd been too embarrassed to go. She recalled, and not for the first time, the luxurious ball gowns that had once filled her closets. Because of her pride, she let them go to auction. She couldn't bear the thought of pulling them out, and dragging them up the stairs to the garage apartment. Even if she had, where would she have put them? There'd been no space for such luxuries.

"Would you have any persuasive powers in this situation?" Mr. Reznick asked.

If she were honest the answer would be no. No one back home would ever let her come within a country mile of Siegrid Jurgen. But where there was a will, there would always be a way. And she definitely had the will.

"This is my family. These are my friends," she answered with all the calm she could muster. She was, after all, an actress. "Naturally, I would have persuasive powers."

"We just need you to get her here. We do the rest. We'd take good care of her."

Sadella doubted that. No studio every really *took care* of their people. All they wanted was the money. The top stars did pull in a lot of cash at the box office and were amply rewarded. Perhaps she could help Siegrid get there. And contract for a percentage. Like a real agent.

She so wanted to ask *how much* again. But she knew he heard her. She contained herself and waited.

Finally, Mr. Reznick said, "It'd be worth a thousand to us."

It was all Sadella could do to remain sitting in the chair. All of the breath had gone out of her. One thousand dollars. She hadn't seen that much money since the '29 crash.

She nodded before she could speak. "The girl is quite mature for her age. And reasonable. She attended college for a couple of years and teaches school. I'm sure she'll agree to come."

"This won't be a binding contract, Sadella, but we will give you a couple hundred up front on good faith. The balance will be paid once the girl is here on the lot." And with that he pulled two one-hundred dollar bills from his money clip and handed them over to her.

And that very morning she hadn't had enough money for bus fare, or a pack of cigarettes.

That night, sleep was a long time coming for Sadella. She had to come up with a plan. A failsafe plan. She was dead-sure she could do it. Even if she had to hog-tie the girl and drag her all the way from Podunk, Oklahoma to star-studded Hollywood.

She had to have that thousand bucks.

Chapter 16

July 1933, Red Fork, Oklahoma

The dining room at Cairn Cottage overflowed with people. Lucie loved every minute of it. She loved having Trent with them. He'd definitely taken them under his wing to guide them and assist in every way he could to show them how to create a successful business. Even in the midst of a depression.

Siegrid's cooking would put any French chef to shame. And Lucie knew because she'd feasted at many a Paris restaurant in her childhood days. Of course, she'd never seen a platter of fried catfish and frog legs in Paris. She smiled to herself just thinking of the comparison. So much food on one table. Lucie wasn't sure how the girl did it. But she did it well. Siegrid had been busy in the kitchen while the rest of them had been at the filling station all day.

Artie Schneider, Patsy, and their boys had been invited. Erik and Clarette had driven out from Tulsa, bringing with them their precocious four-year-old, Jacie, and Everett of course.

Erik alone nearly filled the room, especially with his booming laughter. He had a lot to talk about with Trent, particularly about the possibility of Okesa running large advertisements in his magazine.

Conversation bantered around the table non-stop, as did the passing of plate after platter after dish of food. Boiled new potatoes from the garden. Lettuce and tomatoes from the garden. Fried okra from the garden. Lucie practically hung on Siegrid's side as she served up the stupendous meal, listening, learning, and soaking up all she could.

Once the eating had slowed, the pies cut and pie plates emptied, and the coffee served, the youngsters headed outdoors. The parents asked the boys to keep an eye on Jacie, who led them on a merry chase out through the timber and down by the creek. Their shouts and laughter floated in waves through the open windows, adding to the merriment of the evening.

Trent pretty much had the floor. These were his people. His boots-on-the-ground, as he liked to call them. He let it be known that he was duly impressed that Lucie and Wesley had thought to professionally photograph the Spaceboy Sparkie giveaway event. "That's going to make our PR go through the roof," he stated with pride in his voice.

Then there was Nathan Anderson. Lucie thought it so odd that he'd happened to be a part of the dinner company. But Wesley seemed to be quite impressed by him. He sat at the table opposite Lucie and every once in a while, there was a flash of eye contact, but each quickly looked away.

At a point of a lull in the conversation, Wesley waved to Nathan and remarked to Trent, "This fellow here is a sign painter, Trent, and he has what I think is a novel advertising idea using road signs."

Trent tamped a fresh pinch of tobacco into his pipe, then carefully lit it. "Road signs? Billboards?"

"Not billboards," Wesley answered. "More the size of Burma-Shave signs. Very brief messages. Tell him, Nathan."

Nathan's voice was quiet, steady, and sincere. "Actually, it wasn't an original idea with me."

Trent gave a friendly chuckle. Lucie believed it was to set Nathan at ease. "Ideas are like eggs, son. Once the chicken lays it, it belongs to anyone."

"That's the truth," Erik put in. "I love studying other magazines to pick up ideas."

"Go on," Trent said to Nathan.

"As Wesley said, I'm a professional sign painter..."

"You should see some of his work, Trent," Wesley interrupted. "He's been painting signs all over town."

Lucie noted just a hint of a blush. She couldn't remember the last time she'd met a man who was vulnerable enough to blush.

"Thanks Wesley." Turning back to Trent, he continued. "The idea is to have a sign—or signs—to alert travelers that there's an Okesa filling station coming up. Red Fork is rather small. They might think they have to drive all the way to Tulsa to fill up. Or get oil. Or a tire."

Taking a few puffs on his pipe, it was clear that Trent was thinking. Wesley had taken their father's etched, lead-glass ashtray from the sideboard and placed it in front of their guest on which he rested his pipe.

"Wouldn't need much verbiage on them," Trent said. "Right?"

"Right," Nathan agreed. Looking over at Erik, he said, "The magazine writer could help come up with clever words to grab attention."

Erik put his arm around Clarette's shoulders. "Oh now, that would require the talents of the author in the family."

To which Clarette added, "Sounds like a fun assignment. More fun than writing boring articles about oil and gas."

"Hey now," Trent said in a teasing tone. "That boring stuff keeps a lot of wheels turning in this country. And pays a lot of paychecks."

"I do agree," Clarette said, holding her own. "Nevertheless, writing about it is not nearly as delightful as penning my novels."

"I have to concede on that, Miss Clarette. Plus, I confess the two of you give Okesa plenty of ink on the pages. Boring or not." Turning back to Nathan, Trent said, "I definitely like the idea of the smaller signs. I'm beginning to wonder if people even look at billboards. But a smaller sign. It's right down in front of them."

Lucie had been watching Nathan's reaction to all of this. She was still the only one in the room who knew he'd been riding boxcars just a few weeks prior. The pleasure spreading across his face was unmistakable. She saw him reach up and touch the New Testament that seemed to always reside in his shirt pocket. As he did, he caught her watching him. He smiled. She rewarded him with a knowing smile.

Artie spoke up and asked Nathan if he'd ever done any painting on metal. Nathan shook his head. "I have not." Lucie noted the tone of respect as Nathan interacted with men several years his senior. "But," Nathan quickly added, "I'm always geared up to learn and improve my skills."

"People aren't exactly lining up to purchase airplanes these days," Artie said with a trace of humor. "However, this might be an opportunity for you."

Wesley, eager to jump into the conversation, agreed. "Oh yeah, Nathan. You haven't seen my Blue Bolt have you. Let's you and I drive out to Artie's one day next week. You can see my bird, study my logo branding, and go for a spin."

"Actually," Artie added, "I can introduce you to the fellow who painted Wesley's logo. Lives in Cushing. Let me know when you're coming and I'll have him come on over."

Erik, glancing over at Nathan said, "Hey friend, how about taking that little book from your pocket and sharing something with us."

Lucie caught Nathan's initial look of surprise. Then he calmly took the Bible from his pocket.

"Sure," he said. Flipping the well-worn pages, he began...

He that dwelleth in the secret place of the most High shall abide under the shadow of the Almighty.

I will say of the LORD, He is my refuge and my fortress: my God; in him will I trust.

Surely he shall deliver thee from the snare of the fowler, and from the noisome pestilence."

After Nathan finished reading all of Psalm 91, Erik said, "Great choice, Nathan. Gaven and I had that Psalm memorized when we were dodging exploding shells in France."

Gaven, gazing off into space, agreed. "Every word."

At that moment, wild wailing from outside broke into the conversation. The children tromped in all hot, sweaty, and dirty. Everett was carrying his sister who was putting up an awful cry. Her dress was wet, but otherwise seemed unharmed. No blood gushing.

"I falled in the ribber," she stammered between sobs.

Erik stifled a laugh. "Aw. You falled?"

"Uh huh. I falled and most drownded."

Everett carried his sister around and placed her into their mother's lap, where she snuggled down and buried her face in Clarette's shoulder.

Artie's two boys were wide-eyed, obviously wondering if they were in trouble. Ralph spoke up. "We tried to keep her away from the edge. Truly we did. She moves like a jackrabbit."

Now Erik was laughing. Softly of course. Not to spoil Jacie's moment of drama and agony. "That she does, Ralph. That she does."

Everett had her shoes, with the laces tied together, slung over his shoulder. Her anklets stuffed inside. "The rocks are slippery. It's shallow where we were," he said, handing the shoes over to his father, seemingly finished with his job of caregiver. "Her dress got wet, but she's fine. Just scared her."

Jacie raised up her head and rubbing her eyes with both little fists, reminded everyone, "I most drownded in the ribber."

Now everyone around the table struggled to hold back chuckles.

Standing up with her daughter in her arms, Clarette announced, "I think this day has come to a perfect close. And this little one needs her bed."

"I not sweepy."

"Of course not," Clarette said patting her daughter's small back and holding her close. "Of course not."

Erik was gathering Clarette's camera bag and meanwhile Artie and Patsy were also getting ready to leave.

To Lucie, Patsy said, "I hate to leave you with all these dishes to clean up."

Lucie patted her arm. "Not at all. I have Siegrid here now. And even Wesley isn't above drying dishes. You should see him wield a dish towel. Quite a spectacle!"

Lucie was watching to see when Nathan moved toward the hall tree to fetch his hat. Trent was there as well and they were still deep in conversation. She wanted to tell him good-bye and to thank him for coming, but she didn't want to be too forward. Then Wesley joined them and of course, he was blabbing on and on as her brother was want to do. Soon they were out the front door, standing in the drive and still talking.

She listened as car engines revved up. The Torstens left. The Schneiders left. Next Trent's canary-yellow Packard, sounding the smoothest, faded into the distance. Wesley came back in, letting the screen door go with a hefty slam.

As Lucie joined Siegrid in clearing the table, she pictured Nathan walking through the still night back to Ma Powell's house.

Summer nights in Oklahoma were not like summer nights in Indiana. At least back there it would cool down after sunset. Here there was no cool down. But Nathan didn't really care. He felt he could float back to his room on Third Street. He, Nathan Anderson, a few weeks this side of riding the rails and drinking out of a tin can, had just shared dinner with the owner and CEO of one of biggest Oil enterprises in the Midwest.

"Dear God," he whispered in a sincere prayer. "How can I ever thank you? You are so good to me."

Trent—he guessed it was okay to call the man by his first name—said they would set up a meeting in Tulsa to talk over ideas for the signs. And then Trent assured Nathan that Clarette would be there as well. Did he add that just to put Nathan at ease? Clarette had a mind like a steel trap, and yet was easy going and approachable. Now he knew why she owned a Graflex.

At some time in the future, he'd share with her about his mother's photography work. *In the future.* What a compelling concept. It hadn't been that long ago when he felt he had no future at all.

To top it all off, Wesley had invited him to Artie's airport to see the Blue Bolt. And learn about painting on metal. And possibly even go up in an airplane. Nathan had never even come close to an airplane let alone taken a ride. He'd heard of people who got sick and puked all over the plane. He prayed that would not be his fate.

But that would be in the *future*. For now, his heart was full.

"Oh, and Lord," he said softly as he let himself in through his entryway and down the darkened hallway to his room, "is it okay that I get a kick out of watching Lucie? I just can't seem to stop looking at her. I hope it wasn't too obvious."

That first morning at the filling station, Nathan had presumed Wesley was Lucie's husband. It was when he and Wesley sat together talking at Annie's, he learned they were siblings. Thinking back, he wondered if Wesley detected his deep sense of relief.

Chapter 17

JULY 1933, HOLLYWOOD, CALIFORNIA

Of all the times that Sadella hated The Jarrell House—and they were numerous—she hated dinner hour the most. If she weren't so darn hungry, and if the meal wasn't included in the rent payment, and if Miss Jarrell were not such a stickler about rules, Sadella would just grab food and go to her room. But that was definitely out of order for Jarrell House residents. Dinner served promptly at six, and late-comers were doomed to go without.

The way Miss Jarrell acted as though the place were some sort of silk-stocking palace grated on Sadella's already-frayed nerves. She had rubbed shoulders with the blue bloods of Europe. She'd been grandly escorted into palaces. Several palaces for that matter. And she knew a junky joint when she saw one. And she was having to *live* in this one.

It also grated on her nerves that she seemed to be the only dame in the whole place unable to either sing, tap dance, or play the piano or the accordion. It wasn't for the lack of Trevalene trying all through Sadella's growing-up years. For Sadella, each new series of lessons opened a new door for her to rebel against her mother's wishes.

Much as she hated to admit it, now she regretted her rebellion. Even at boarding school, opportunities abounded on every side and she had turned up her nose at the whole circus (as she referred to it at the time). She'd gone to great lengths to get kicked out. Those memories now only added to her regrets.

But she refused to let those small details drag her down. She could act. That was her shining hope. You never saw Katharine Hepburn singing or hoofing a silly dance. That woman was a heart-and-soul dramatic actress. Sadella knew she could do the same. She just had to be discovered.

As the food was being passed at dinner one evening the girls were laughing about Denby Baer. A couple of the girls always seemed to be making fun of someone. Sadella could have scoffed with the best of them if she'd chosen to. But she couldn't be bothered with these know-nothings. She only took note on this particular night because she'd met Denby and he'd been pleasant to her.

Denby wasn't like the suave Douglas Fairbanks. But not as empty-headed comedic as Charlie Chaplin. And it was common knowledge that Chaplin was brilliant. Smart enough to own his own studio along with Mary Pickford and Douglas Fairbanks. No, Denby Baer seemed to be in a class of his own—and simply hadn't been pegged yet.

"His legs look like he just came in off the range and dismounted his steed," one girl was saying in twittery, high nasal twang, causing the others to laugh their agreement. All but Sadella. She continued eating the dismal food that had been served, wanting to hurry and get out of earshot.

Another agreed that Denby's mannerisms were quirky and awkward. "Kinda like a monkey's," she said, causing more laughter.

Sadella could barely endure their shallow observations. They wouldn't know real acting if it slapped them square in the face. She was probably the only one in the room who knew that Denby had been on the Broadway stage. In major roles at that.

Sadella's first encounter with Denby was while the two of them were decked out from head to toe in costumes to be extras in the street scene of a Western. She in button-up shoes, bonnet, and long dress. He in shirt, vest, Levi's and a

Stetson. Standing about the lot, waiting for their call, they began to chat. That's when she learned more about him.

A couple of years prior, his agent had arranged for him make the trek from Broadway to Hollywood, just as many others had done. "Following the Barrymore family," he joked. Since he'd arrived, he'd snagged a few small speaking parts, he told her, but still waiting for the big break.

As they talked, Sadella kept the details of her past life to herself, sharing only that she'd grown up in Tulsa, Oklahoma. No one gave a hoot that her father had been an oil tycoon and at one time was worth millions. Nor that she'd traveled the world and was highly educated. Well, she *would* have been highly educated had she taken advantage of all that had been handed to her.

Their little chat that day had opened a small door. Casting a critical eye over the waiting group of extras, the director spied them and said they looked "good together." They were then selected to stroll together down the boardwalk on the dusty re-created Western street scene.

At first, they linked arms, but the director said no, because they were supposed to be a married couple not a courting couple, which brought laughter from others standing about. They were to act as though they were chatting, which was easy because that's exactly what they'd been doing for the past hour. They were to walk into the General Store and begin to shop. She was instructed to look at a bolt of cloth and Denby to stroll over to the where the bronze-colored bottles of liniment were lined up on the shelf. When gunshots sounded outside, they were to scurry to the front door along with two other extras who were also in the store. They carried it off in one take, and laughed together about it later.

Sadella didn't think him awkward, clumsy, or anything like a *monkey*. Oh, the silly, short-sighted, empty-headed wenches at the Jarrell House. Well, let them think what they wanted to think. She knew the truth.

Her partner and compatriot, Clarice, had deserted the cause by recently taking a clerk's position at the neighborhood Five & Dime. At first, Sadella was miffed. But then after a short time, realized this was just one more person out of her way.

"I'm tired of being broke," Clarice said after announcing her new employment. "This job doesn't pay much, but at least I have bus fare."

A lot of good that'll do you, Sadella thought when she heard the news. *Bus fare to where? If you're not on the sets, if you're not on the lots, you'll never be seen. You'll never be chosen. You'll never get the parts.*

She didn't even bother to share with Clarice about the extra part she'd played with Denby. However, the director's words continued to ring in her ears. Pointing the two of them out, he'd said, "These two look good together." Music to her ears. One step closer.

Meanwhile, she continued to mull over how she could deliver up Siegrid Jurgen to Mr. Reznick. She hadn't a single doubt that she could make it happen.

Chapter 18

JULY 1933, RED FORK, OKLAHOMA

D riving back to Tulsa from Red Fork, Trent's mind was on Henry Patton. The man had been a fool. Trent kept telling Henry that fact for months before the crash. Anyone with an ounce of sense could see things were getting rocky. Getty could see it. Skelly could see it. Frank Phillips and even E.V. Harland were tippy-toeing around. Trimming costs. Keeping an eagle eye on the bottom line. And above all, backing away from Wall Street.

All of them except for Henry. "Stocks," Henry had said to Trent in a gleeful tone, "Easiest money I've ever made. You just sit back and watch it grow."

Trent never stopped warning him to slow down. Henry tuned him out.

Early in twenty-nine, Trent was having dinner with E.V. at the Tulsa Hotel. Trent could remember back when Henry Patton and E.V. Harland had been thick as thieves. That seemed to be old history.

"You know Henry better than most," Trent had said, "you could warn him to back away from the crazy stock market. Taper off. Pay closer attention to his oil and gas businesses. Those refineries don't run themselves. As you well know."

Cutting into his thick steak, E.V. just shook his head. "Don't look at me. I'm not his nanny. He's a big boy."

"But lately he's been taking unnecessary risks. Big, scary risks."

E.V., now completely involved in enjoying the steak, again just shook his head. Between bites, hardly looking up, he said, "Henry's consumed with greed. It's overpowered any common sense he once had."

"But the two of you go way back. Way back. Surely, he'd listen to you."

Waving his fork in the air, E.V. replied, "I don't care whether he would or wouldn't listen. I've not spoken to Henry since his empty-headed slut of a daughter killed my son. He can go to hell for all I care."

Realizing his friend was getting heated, Trent quickly changed the subject. Everyone in Tulsa knew that Sadella Patton had been the reason Shelby was on that slick street in Greenwood that wintery night. But, to be completely honest, Shelby was a man of free will. The freak accident was just as much his fault as Sadella's. They'd been up to no good. They had no business even being in the area. But try telling that to a grieving father.

As Trent turned up Denver Street past the Patton Mansion—what was *once* the Patton Mansion—he thought about the roomful of enterprising, promising young folk he'd just left back there in Red Fork. Watching Wesley and Lucie, he was even more convinced that Henry had been a fool. But what the enemy had meant for evil, it was quite apparent, as the Bible promised, God was turning it all out for good.

He listened with amazement at how Wesley and Lucie were growing their business. Two kids who grew up having everything handed to them on a silver platter, and now here they were out on their own making their own way. And with great success.

It had pleased him as he looked around that dining room and took stock. Erik, not only using Okesa advertising in his national magazine, but having Clarette write articles that often gave Okesa the spotlight. Clarette taking professional photos of their giveaway event that day. There was Artie who exclusively used Okesa products at his hangar, not only for his own planes, but also for those that landed at the airport. Wesley, of course, used the products for his Blue Bolt. They were definitely his tribe and he wanted to watch over them and give them as much support as possible.

Then there was the quiet newcomer, Nathan. A sign painter. A sign painter with a willingness to put his talents to good use. Trent's mind was whirling a mile a minute. Roadside signs, yes. That would be a good start, but several other possibilities were coming to mind. He looked forward to getting to know the young man and learn more about him. He was curious. How had Nathan Anderson happened to just *show up* in Red Fork? Of all places.

A boy with an armload of flyers stopped by the store asking Lucie to post one in the window. It was midday which meant there were few customers. Theirs wasn't the place where the locals hung out. That was either Annie's. Or the barber shop.

Taking a copy from the top of his stack she said, "Sure." He turned to go, but she stopped him. "Why not leave a few more and I'll lay them here on the counter."

He grabbed more, laid them near the cash register, and was out the door. He was no doubt getting paid to hand them all out.

Coming over to look, Siegrid's eye lit up. "A dance? Now that sounds like fun." She held up one of the flyers and was reading aloud, "*Saturday night at the VFW hall.*"

Lucie had a long time ago lost interest in any of the male species of Red Fork. She too had been excited about the dances when she first arrived. "Every month," she explained. "Third Saturday night of the month."

Handing Siegrid a box of fan belts, she said, "Hang these up for me please."

It had been agreed that when Wesley was out of town, Siegrid would help at the store. Otherwise, she stayed at Cairn Cottage cooking and cleaning. Which she seemed to love; which baffled Lucie to no end. She'd never developed a love of either.

Siegrid took the box and crossed to the opposite side of the store. From the outset, Lucie had determined that all the auto supplies would be on the far side of the room. The canned goods, soap flakes, tooth powder, candies, tobacco, and such, would be stocked on the shelves behind the counter. "The two should not mix," she informed Wesley. "And please, no perishables. Leave those to the grocer and the butcher." Thankfully, Wesley had agreed.

"Do you go?" Siegrid asked as she hung each belt in its designated spot.

"Go?" Lucie had already dismissed any thought of the dance.

"The dance at the VFW. Do y'all go?"

Lucie paused a minute. "Usually. We try to be out in the public as much as possible. It's good for business."

"What kind of dancing? Do they play the phonograph?"

"Nope. No phonograph. Red Fork has its own band. They're pretty good, I have to say." She broke open a roll of pennies and placed them into the cash register. "Square dancing mostly. No jitterbugging."

"That's okay. I enjoy square dancing. I know practically every one that's ever been invented."

Lucie wanted to tell her that most of these farm boys were clods when it came to dancing. But she didn't want to break the girl's bubble. No sense spoiling her visions of a fun evening in the little burg of Red Fork. She'd learn the awful truth soon enough.

Nathan was convinced that Wesley could talk forever and never wind down. He seemed to be geared with some kind of relentless buoyancy. The two of them were driving from Red Fork to Artie's airport in Jenks. Wesley couldn't stop talking about Wiley Post's upcoming round-the-world venture starting on the 16th.

"This time he'll be all alone," Wesley explained.

Nathan, too, had been following the news as the drama unfolded. As was the whole world. It seemed they were keeping most details under wraps until the very day of takeoff. But he let Wesley talk on.

"In thirty-one Gatty was with him, but this time, he'll go solo." Wesley jerked the car to miss another deep rut forcing Nathan to hang on for dear life. "Hasn't rained in who knows how long," he muttered, "yet we still have hub-deep ruts."

Nathan was fascinated as well at the thought of a man flying alone, circling the globe. It seemed too far-fetched to even comprehend. "How can a person stay awake that long?"

"He'll make quick stops along the way to re-fuel. He'll sleep in short spurts. But heck, Wiley can do most anything. The man's a walking miracle. Not only does he do what no other man has done, it does it all with one eye."

"And he's an Okie."

Wesley nodded. "Yeah imagine that. My first plane ride was with Wiley."

"You don't say."

"I guess you could say, he's my hero."

"Naw," Nathan intoned. "You coulda fooled me. I was certain it was Spaceboy Sparkie."

Wesley let loose a loud peal of laughter. "And his Spacedog Sport," he sang on key.

In unison and on key: "*Zooming out to their Jupiter Port.*" Followed with more carefree laughter, like a couple of kids.

To Nathan, it's was the best feeling ever. Especially that it had been his joke, and that Wesley enjoyed it to the hilt.

It only took a few minutes before he was back on his favorite subject of Wiley's upcoming daring adventure. "He's using the latest and most update instruments. Ones that will guide him through the densest clouds, the fog, and the dark of night." Turning from watching the dusty road to glance at his passenger, he added, "One day I'll be flying a plane with those kinds of instruments. I'm sure of it."

Sounded pretty far-fetched to Nathan. But Wesley spoke with such confidence he lost all disbelief.

They were greeted at the airport by Artie, with his boys running out ahead, pushing and shoving to get close to Wesley, to walk by his side. Several planes sat about the wide-open field, but Nathan instantly knew which one was the

Blue Bolt. Blinding silver reflecting the summer sunshine, and of course the unmistakable blue lightning bolts. Observing it, he could begin to catch a sense of Wesley's fascination.

"Gassed up and ready to go," Artie told Wesley after shaking Nathan's hand and offering a warm greeting. Spending time together at dinner had sealed this new friendship.

"Are you going to fly the Blue Bolt, Mr. Anderson?" Howard wanted to know.

Nathan had to laugh. "That might be an invitation to wreck that gorgeous bird," he said. "No, I'm just a passenger." Then he added, "To tell you the truth—you do want to know the truth, right?"

Howard nodded. "Sure. Nothing but the truth so help you God."

"I've never even been close to an airplane before."

The boys, who had known nothing but airplanes their entire lives, were astonished. "Never?" Howard asked. "That's the saddest thing I ever heard."

"I thought the same thing. However," Wesley said, ruffling the boy's tangled mop of wind-blown hair, "we're going to change that. This very day. Come on, Nathan."

They were right beside the big bird now and the boys, eager to assist, were opening the doors. Wesley was inside in an instant, now moving over to the co-pilot side to give Nathan a hand up.

Nathan had thought the gleaming silver body was the most beautiful part. He was totally unprepared for the luxurious interior, with pearl-gray upholstered seats and navy-blue curtains at the windows, drawn back and secured with silken bands. He knew he was gawking, but he couldn't help it.

Finally, finding his voice, he said, "I had no idea the interior of a plane would be this..."

"Plush? Gorgeous? Luxurious? Deluxe? Comfortable? Go ahead. Pour it on. I can take it," Wesley said in a laughter-filled voice. Showing Nathan how to buckle in, he added, "Boy oh boy. You should have seen my very first bird. The thing was wide open. No closed cockpit back then. You got your teeth brushed and hair combed all at the same time."

Now Nathan was laughing as well, which helped to calm his nerves. He still held out hope he wouldn't puke all over this immaculate upholstery.

The motor roared to life; the plane began to move. Smoother than a car on a country road. Much smoother. The bird traveled to the far end of the runway before turning around, building up speed, and taking flight.

Magic. That was the only word Nathan could think of. Magic. How could this machine defy gravity? How could it happen? They were in the air. Houses, fields, cows, automobiles, trees, shrank into miniature forms.

"Well? What do you think?" Wesley asked.

Nathan couldn't stop staring out the side window. He shook his head. "No words. I'm baffled."

Wesley was beaming. He obviously loved introducing the ordinary earth-bound layman to his passion.

"How do you feel?"

"Fine." This surprised Nathan. He was so sure he'd be green around the gills. But not at all. "I feel great!"

"What would you like to see?"

"Um. Tulsa, I guess. And of course, Red Fork."

"At your service."

The plane banked and turned north with ease and power.

"And the oil fields."

"Which ones?"

Still staring out the windows, Nathan was quiet for a moment. "I'm trying to remember the names Dad talked about."

"Your father was here? In Oklahoma? Well, what do you know about that. In the oil fields?"

Nathan nodded. "Let's see. Funny names. Cush something-or-other."

"That'd be the Cushing-Drumright field."

"Sapa..."

"Sapulpa."

"That's not how he said it."

"Oh." Wesley laughed. "Sometimes known as *Sapalupa*."

Nathan brightened. "That was it. It wasn't always easy to make out what he was saying."

"No? Why not?"

"The burns. He was nearly killed in an oilfield fire. The burns affected not only his body and his speech, but his emotions. Sometimes he was out of his head. Raving and yelling."

"How is he now?"

"He passed on five years ago."

"I'm so sorry."

"It's okay. He was in such agony. No pain now. He was ready to be with his Lord and Savior."

"Which field?"

"What do you mean?"

"Do you know in which oil field the fire happened?"

"I remember him saying, *Polecat Creek*."

"Yeah. That would be somewhere around Sapulpa and the Glenn Pool. Fires flared up on creeks because of the natural gas that they had no idea how to contain or utilize. Many times, it simply exploded into flames."

"What's that over there? Are those oil fields?"

Nathan was looking at the massive tanks standing in orderly rows, with dozens of pumping rigs, all working away, doing what they were designed to do.

"Yep. You'll see them all around this region. You should have seen it when the derricks were thick as trees, as far as the eye could see."

"I did. I mean, I *did* see it. I wasn't but about eight or nine, but I was here. I saw it." The memories rushed back in a flood. "I came on the train, all by myself. Dad assured mother I would be safe. He wanted me to come and see. *So, you'll remember*, he told me. *This is history in the making.*"

"He was right about that. And he was smart to let you witness that history."

They had swung around a circle, over Sapulpa, Kiefer, Mounds, the Glenn Pool (which was now Glenpool), then up to Tulsa, even as far north as Bartlesville, with Wesley pointing out the oil fields, which, by now, Nathan could quite easily recognize.

"Now back over Red Fork," Wesley announced, "which is pretty much where it all started—thanks to my father."

"And that would be who?"

"Henry Patton and his partner, E.V. Harland. Both instrumental in the Red Fork gusher, which soon proved to be pretty paltry compared to the other strikes. But it all started right there in Red Fork."

Wesley glanced over at his partner whose face had gone white. So, all the banking and turning had done him in after all.

Chapter 19

JULY 1933, JENKS, OKLAHOMA; RED FORK, OKLAHOMA

At the look on his passenger's face, Wesley was about to help him locate to the barf bag.

"Henry and E.V.? That's too much. That's just too much." He was sort of mumbling to himself, still gazing out the side window.

"What's the matter, man? You sick?"

"You're a Patton? Your name is Patton?"

"Guilty as charged."

"Lucie's a Patton?"

"As my blood sibling, that would be correct."

"You're never going to believe this." Nathan stopped again, collecting his thoughts. "My father worked with Henry Patton and E.V. Harland on the Red Fork field, and other fields after. I have the postcards and letters he sent to us mentioning those very names."

They were banking over Red Fork. The citizens, who now apparently claimed the Blue Bolt as their very own, recognized the sound and stepped out of the stores on main street to wave. Wesley tipped a wing in reply.

Wesley shook his head in disbelief at the news he'd just heard. "That's just wild. Who would have ever thought...? How could that even happen? Is that why you came to Red Fork?"

"Not exactly."

The conversation was open now for Nathan to tell about his hobo days, and that he'd been a bum with nowhere to go. Just looking for his next meal, and hopefully a job. He told how he'd stopped at Cairn Cottage with his fellow hoboes, and how Lucie had fed them.

"The name of Red Fork sounded vaguely familiar to me," Nathan went on, "but it took a while to register. When it did, that's when I came back. I was in Oklahoma City. I parted company with my two friends and caught the first freight going East. And here I am."

"I know the Bible says God orders our steps. I never actually grasped the full meaning of that promise. Until now."

"But I'm confused. The Patton Oil and Gas Company... I thought..."

Wesley gave a little snort. "Oh yeah. That it was worth millions?"

Nathan nodded.

"And so why in the world are his children running a little filling station and living in Red Fork, Oklahoma?"

"Well, yeah. I mean, I suppose there's good reason. Not that there's anything wrong..." Now he was stammering a little, embarrassed that he'd waded in over his head.

"Hey, it's all right. You wouldn't know because you don't live around here. My father invested heavily, unwisely, in stocks. As things began to tumble, he was in a panic, borrowing to try to cover the margin calls. Before he knew it, there was not another penny he could come up with and lost it all."

"When Wade drove me to Tulsa, we passed by the Patton mansion. I remember he pointed it out to me."

Wesley heaved a deep sigh. "That where I grew up. That was our home with all the trappings. When he saw no way to move forward, he chose the easy way out and shot himself."

Nathan was stunned. He had no words. His new friend had also walked a tough road. Not riding freights, but tough nonetheless. Thankfully they were now circling over Artie's airport. Artie was at the end of the runway waving them in. Nathan steeled himself for the landing, but for nothing. The bird came down smooth as silk.

"I gotta take care of Blue Bolt here," Wesley said, "and I think you have an appointment with a painter of planes."

"Oh yeah. I almost forgot about that."

Wesley shook a finger at him in jest, "One must never forget about a possible money-maker." After they were out and on the ground, Wesley said, "You're having supper with us tonight, friend. We have a lot to talk about."

"Yeah, I guess we do."

For Lucie, it was always a great day when her friend Tessa, came for a visit. Today wasn't quite as happy. She had come to whisk her sister away for a couple of days. The three of them had had at least a couple of hours of gab time, drinking coffee on the back porch while the twins had the run of the timber.

As they walked out to the car, Lucie was realizing how much she was going to miss her new friend. Even if for a couple of days. A thick layer of brown dust coated the MacIntyre's black Chevy. These days, nothing much existed that avoided the dust coating. Lucie couldn't remember the last good rain. And the drought was pretty much all the farmers and ranchers talked about.

Tessa reached into the open car window and tapped on the horn. At hearing the sound, the twins came running, squealing and laughing, pushing and shoving. Obviously, they'd been playing in the creek and were wet, muddy, sweaty, and happy.

Tessa didn't want them getting mud on the seats of the Sedan, so before they could take another step, Lucie stopped them and rinsed off their legs and feet with the water hose as best she could. Tessa and Siegrid spread old towels across the back-seat upholstery as a failsafe. All the while the three adults chattered non-stop.

"How long are you keeping my slave labor?" Lucie wanted to know. She was joking of course. They were paying Siegrid more than most employers in town paid their hires. "I might have to scrub the kitchen floor myself." Pressing the back of her hand to her forehead, she said, "I think I feel a swoon coming on."

The twins laughed at her.

"We need her, too," Babette voiced with great authority. "But we don't make her scrub floors."

"No?" Lucie feigned shock. "Then whatever would you need her for?"

"For hugs and cuddles," Elysia said, nearly running her aunt over as they approached the car.

Babette followed suit, showing her agreement by hugging her aunt.

"Get in the car, girls," Tessa said. "You're getting mud all over auntie's dress."

"But she doesn't care," Babette said, "because she loves us."

Tessa shook her head. "I should have thought to bring them a change of clothes. I didn't think we'd stay this long."

Siegrid laughed. "When you two get to talking, time is forgotten."

It was true. Lucie could never get done tapping into the deep well of knowledge that both Tessa and Siegrid offered up when it came to gardening, cooking, and canning. And even sewing. She still had so much to learn.

"And to answer your question, Lucie, this is only for a couple of nights."

"We'll try to grin and bear it. But gosh, we've just gotten so used to having her here."

After climbing into the front seat, Siegrid feigned a show of being bashful and coy. "I'm in such demand, you know," waving her hand in her face in a fanning motion. "Wanted by so many of my fans."

"That's right," Elysia agreed reaching her arms around Siegrid's neck from the back seat. "You're pretty enough to be a movie star, with your picture in the movie magazines even."

"And with lots of fans," Babette agreed.

"I'd start your fan club," Elysia stated proudly.

"I'd be president," came Babette's retort.

"But if I start it, I'd be president."

"Don't fuss, girls. And please sit back. Give your aunt space to breathe." Tessa scooted her slight frame behind the steering wheel and started the motor. She looked at Lucie, who was standing beside the car, and rolled her eyes. "Auntie may be ready to come back in a day, just for peace and quiet."

Frantic waving and loud good-byes ensued from the back seat as Tessa guided the car out of the driveway and onto the road. Lucie waved back and returned to a quiet house. As she did, the telephone was ringing. She hurried to the Wesley's office to answer. It was her brother.

"Hey sis, got any food in the house? I'm bringing Nathan for dinner tonight."

Lucie sucked in her breath. "Oh gosh. Our cook just left the premises."

"Siegrid? Gone? Where'd she go?"

"To spend a couple days with the MacIntyres. The girls are crazy about her and want time with her."

"Aw."

Lucie heard disappointment in his voice. "Why? What's up?"

"Well, just throw something together. Maybe just bologna sandwiches. Doesn't matter."

"I can do that. I can make potato salad. Plus, we always have plenty of okra and tomatoes."

"Perfect. Keep it simple."

"Wesley, what's going on? You sound like you're about to bust." She knew him well enough to tell his moods. And right now, he was excited.

"I got something remarkable to tell you. You're not going to believe it."

"I guess it's good." She waited a minute to see if more was coming. "Any hints?"

"Nope. Just gotta wait'll we get there."

Once it had turned so hot, Wesley decided to buy a table for the front porch. At a foreclosure sale he'd found an aged round wooden table, then added five mismatched chairs. Lucie figured this would be the perfect night to eat outdoors. She spread one of her nicer tablecloths over the table and proceeded to bring out the dinnerware, making the settings as attractive as she could with her limited supply. Not a day went by that she didn't recollect the abundance in which she'd grown up. She never even knew how many sets of dinnerware and silverware the Pattons owned. Obviously, one for every entertaining occasion, from the most informal Garden Club luncheon, to the most formal dinner when government officials and other oil barons were entertained in the main dining room. Such extravagance they'd experienced. And for what? For nothing. Absolutely nothing.

She just shook her head as she steadily took the dishes of food from the kitchen, through the front room, out to the porch, and covered each with a clean cup towel. Chipped ice in each of the glasses and a pitcher of lemonade at the ready. Her timing was perfect as she had the entire dinner on the table when they drove into the driveway.

Lucie wanted to know all about Nathan's first experience in a plane. And to know all about what he'd learned about sign-painting airplanes. But that would have to wait. The two came bounding up the porch steps like puppy dogs, about to explode with excitement.

With not even a greeting, Wesley came up to her, took hold of her shoulders and gently sat her down in the nearest chair. "Sit here and listen, Lucie. You are just *not* going to believe this. You're not." He looked over his shoulder at Nathan. "Is she, Nathan?"

She looked over at their guest. He just shook his head. He seemed unable to speak from grinning so big.

Wesley grabbed another chair and dragged it over to face her. He picked up both her hands and looked right into her eyes. "Lucie, Nathan's father knew Dad and E.V. Back in the boom days. They worked together."

Lucie sat there stunned. She was quiet for a moment, letting the words sink in. "That's astonishing." Looking at Nathan, she said, "But are you sure? How can you be sure? It was so long ago."

Wesley, always the talker now squeezed her hands. "Lucie, his mother still has all the letters that his father wrote home naming them both. Both of them, Lucie. Both of them. Dad and E.V."

"Our fathers knew one another." It was almost a whisper. "What are the odds that that could ever be?" Then she looked at Nathan, "And that you would wind up here. Right here." Pulling her hand away from Wesley, she waved it to indicate all of Cairn Cottage. Then she added, "God surely does order our steps."

Wesley jumped up from where he was sitting. "That's what I said. Hey Nathan. Wasn't that exactly I said?"

Nathan nodded. "It was that," he answered quietly.

Slinging his arm over Nathan's shoulder, Wesley almost pushed his friend down the porch steps. "Let's just wash up out back. Then dig in. I'm starved."

Nathan had no choice but to comply.

Oh, the stories that flew across that dinner table. Lucie was content to listen and let them have a go at it. One would have thought the two of them had been the roustabouts working those derricks, rather than two little kids who were only hanging beside their fathers as onlookers, witnessing the action.

"Main Street in Kiefer is burned in my memory," Nathan offered. Between eating and Wesley's gift-of-gab, he had a bit of a challenge to squeeze a word in edgewise. Lucie enjoyed watching the animation in his features as he spoke. "I never saw so many people jammed into one place. The smells," he said, wrinkling up his nose. "And deafening noises. Horses, oxen, wagons, trucks, trains coming and going, and the yelling and shouting as they loaded equipment on wagons to take them out to the fields."

"The biggest team I saw was twenty oxen. Ten teams. Pulling a load of pipe."

Nathan nodded. "The oxen were the biggest animals I'd ever seen. They were gentle and obedient beasts, but no matter. They scared the dickens out of me."

Even though Nathan was too polite to ask for second helpings, Wesley kept passing bowls of food to him, and Nathan didn't hesitate to accept the offers.

"Did you ever hear the gunshots?" Wesley asked. "So many fights broke out every night. Probably a new murder or two on a daily basis."

"If I did, I would have begged Dad to put me on the next train bound for Indiana. I was already spooked by the oxen. Gunshots would have done me in for sure."

Lucie liked Nathan's laugh. A soft chuckle rising from deep in his chest.

Both men remembered climbing onto the derrick platforms. And both remembered seeing fields of derricks as far as the eye could see. Like a vast forest of wooden structures, they said.

"Which probably seemed even bigger when you were little boys," Lucie put in.

Nathan looked her way as though he just remembered she was there. "Were you ever out in the oil fields?" he wanted to know.

"Oh my goodness no. My mother would never have allowed that. I wasn't supposed to have a speck of dirt on me. Ever."

"And I got that privilege," Wesley said, "only because Dad insisted. He so desperately wanted me in the business. And," he added after emptying the last of the fried okra onto Nathan's plate, "he just happened to win that one argument—just to let me visit."

Lucie had to laugh at the memory. "Mother ruled the roost," she explained. "Our father ruled only when he was in his own territory—his oil fields, his refineries, and his offices. That was off limits to her."

The conversation turned then to their father's suicide. How Trevalene discovered her husband's body, and then went into shock—shock from which she had never recovered. Nathan had never heard of the hospital at Vinita. Understandable, since it was known mostly to native Oklahomans.

Nathan then shared bits and pieces about his own father's struggle of living with the terrible burns that had ravaged his body. "Mother always said that I was the one who could get through to him when he was at his worst." He was lost in thought for a few seconds. "Not sure why that was. I just accepted it. We were heartbroken to see him suffer. He'd been so strong and active before the accident."

Lucie's mind was whirling. "You said your mother has letters and cards from your father?"

Being pulled from the sobering memories, Nathan brightened. "Lots of letters. Dad was quite articulate in his writing. Colorful descriptions. So clear and detailed you could see the scenes."

Lucie looked over at her brother. "Are you thinking what I'm thinking?"

"Clarette?"

Lucie nodded. "Nathan, you remember meeting Clarette."

"The lady with the Graflex?"

"That's her. She's writing a book about Red Fork and about the oil boom. She's been driving out here and interviewing some of the old guys who still remember those days. I know she'd love to use the descriptions in those letters for her book."

"That is, if you and your mother are willing," Wesley said. "I know they must be very personal and hold a great deal of emotional attachment."

Nathan's expression grew pensive. "I'm not sure. You're right about the attachment. Every year on the anniversary of his death, she brings them out and reads through them. She says it's like she can hear him talking to her."

Lucie said, "You're blessed, Nathan. We have nothing from our father but bank statements, memos, business correspondence, and invoices. Cold and distant."

"Pretty much describes his personality," Wesley said.

"Not always," Lucie countered. "I think it was the wealth that changed him. So much money. It became like a game to him."

"She's right," Wesley said to Nathan. "I think once the fun of chasing strikes was gone, he became bored. Running a business presented no challenge. No fun."

"I'm sure you've wondered what he might have been like had there been no strikes," Nathan offered. "No gushers. No mansions. No millions."

Wesley pushed back his chair and drained the last of the lemonade. "Funny you should say that. It's only been recently that that exact thought has come to mind. I think that's why he became enamored with stocks. It, too, became a game."

"Mother would have been different as well," Lucie said. "She was more affected by the wealth than Dad. She came from poverty, and was clearly smitten with her position of social standing and power."

"So, she overplayed it at every juncture," Wesley put in. "I mean, the two of us weren't allowed to play with other children in the neighborhood. Riffraff she called them."

Now Lucie laughed. "Goodness mercy. I'd almost forgotten that." She stood to her feet and started stacking the plates. "Nathan, I'm so sorry. How we must be boring you to tears with our maudlin recollections."

"Not at all, Lucie. I like getting to know people. We're all products of our histories. I sure enough learned that as I met other hoboes out there riding the rails. Each one had a story. And a history."

Both men began helping clear the table, carrying things to the kitchen, for which Lucie was grateful since Siegrid was gone.

Once the dishes were washed up and put away, Nathan took his leave.

"Hey, we can sit out here and have a cup of coffee," Wesley said. It was clear he didn't want the evening to end.

"Tomorrow's the day I meet with Trent in Tulsa to talk about designing his signs. After all the excitement of this day, I need a good night's sleep."

"You have a ride to Tulsa?"

"Trent insisted on coming to get me."

"Whoa." Jabbing his thumb at Nathan, he said to Lucie. "Check this out, Sis. The owner of the entire company is coming to fetch the new guy."

The comment made their visitor blush, which he tried to hide. Sensing it, Lucie jumped in. "You know, I never did learn how the plane ride went."

The three of them were walking Nathan out the side gate and down the driveway to the road.

Quickening his step, he said over his shoulder, "All I can tell you is I never used the barf bag."

Lucie had to laugh at that.

"Hey," Wesley called after him. "You coming to the dance Saturday night?"

Nathan turned around, walking backward asked, "What dance?"

"There's a flyer posted in our store window. Take a look as you pass by. All the details there."

Nathan's answer was a little salute and a smile. He turned around and was gone.

Chapter 20

JULY 1933, TULSA, OKLAHOMA; RED FORK, OKLAHOMA

J ust the thought of riding all the way to Tulsa with Trent Calvert made Nathan nervous as a cat. He was certain he'd be stammering, stuttering, and mumbling all over his words.

As it had been with his first plane ride, all the worries were for naught. Trent was as easy-going and down-to-earth as many of the men Nathan had met in the hobo jungles.

Trent had just learned from Lucie the news about their fathers knowing one another. He seemed to be quite taken with that discovery. In fact, he wanted to know more details. As the dusty miles flew by, Nathan was chatting freely, without a thought that this man was, no doubt, a millionaire many times over.

When the conversation turned to the Pattons, he echoed what Wesley had said about Henry Patton being overtaken with greed, allowing the money to affect his decisions rather than common sense.

Trent, it appeared to Nathan, was grounded firmly in common sense. He touched briefly on his beginnings in oil—a miracle of being in the right place at the right time—and his goal to always reinvest in the business and to take care of his employees.

"To this day, we have yet to let even one employee go," he said around the ever-present pipe clenched between his teeth. "I gathered them in a meeting shortly after the crash, and together we made plans of how to cut back expenses." He went on to explain how Okesa's loyal employees agreed to share assignments and working hours. In the field, the men alternated days of work, so at least they could earn something, as opposed to those lining up at the soup kitchens around the country.

"Or eating Mulligan stew in a hobo jungle."

Trent glanced over at him and smiled. "Or that." Continuing, he said, "Some of our equipment we held together with baling wire, and out on the derricks, at night, they even started using one or two light bulbs rather than a whole string of lights. I continue to be amazed at the ingenuity of our people."

Clearly, the manner in which Trent Calvert ran his business, and how Henry Patton had run his business were polar opposite. From what Nathan derived from Wesley and Lucie, their father paid little or no attention to his workers.

The Okesa offices, located in the Philtower Building, surprised Nathan by the low-key, informal appearance. It seemed Trent had no taste for flair or opulence. Clarette had already arrived and sat waiting in the conference room with her notebook open, ready to work.

Time flew by as cups of coffee were filled and re-filled, and ideas tossed around regarding the look, feel, and tone of the road signs. At no point did Nathan feel out of place. His ideas, especially when it came to color combinations and font styles, were readily accepted. By the time they finished, the designs were well established. Each sign would carry the Okesa logo and a short message announcing that a well-stocked filling station was just a few miles ahead.

Trent handed Nathan an envelope. "We've not talked about your fees yet. We can do that later, so this check is to retain your services. And pay for the materials to get you started."

Now Nathan did stammer a little as he thanked Trent.

"We thank *you*," Trent said, "I believe this can be the beginning of a strong relationship. It stands to reason that eye-catching signs will affect the Red Fork station, and if so, we'll use the idea around other of our locations."

To which Nathan could only nod. He was overwhelmed.

It was Clarette who drove him back to Red Fork late in the afternoon. She, too, had heard the story about the two fathers having known one another. Nathan soon learned that among their little *clan,* there were very few secrets. However, she didn't know about his mother's stash of cards and letters. When he brought it up, she nearly drove clean off the road.

"Your father, while working in the oil fields during the boom, wrote letters about it?"

"And cards. Lots of postcards."

"With details."

Nathan had to smile about her growing excitement. "Very detailed. My father was quite articulate when it came to writing. My mother and I often thought if it hadn't been for the accident, he could have been a talented author."

"Your mother... What's her name?"

"Lovina."

"I'm sure Lovina is very protective of all that correspondence. Now that he's gone."

Nathan nodded. "Yes. She is."

"But do you think she'd let us use them? The content? The details that have to do with life and work during those years. What it was *really* like. This would be on-the-scene reports. Not old memories."

"Wesley and Lucie already asked me the same thing. I just don't know."

"Well, what if we paid for her train ticket? To come for a visit?" She glanced over at him now. "How long since you've seen her?"

He was quiet for a moment. "Over a year. About a year and a half, I guess."

The thought of having his mother come to Red Fork was a little confusing. He, of course, wanted to see her. But Red Fork was where her beloved husband was nearly killed in a raging fire. And did eventually die due to the after effects.

"I don't know," he said again.

"Could you ask and see?"

Nathan understood Clarette's being excited to get her hands on such valid resource material. But this was his family. He wanted more than anything to protect his mother.

As they entered Red Fork, Clarette drove through Main Street and turned off to get to Third Street and pulled into the driveway at Ma Powell's house.

Nathan still had not answered her last question. "Thank you very much for the ride. And for your ideas and support at the meeting."

"I think it worked out well. You're a talented young man. And I know Trent's thankful to have you on board."

Standing outside the car now, he leaned down and peered in the window at Clarette. "And about the other. All I can say is I'll pray about it, and if I feel a peace about it, I'll contact Mother and see what she thinks."

Clarette smiled. "You sound like Erik. I swear, that man's a prayer machine. But yes, that sounds like a good plan. I'll patiently wait to hear back from you. Well, maybe not *patiently*, but I will wait."

Nathan gave her a nod and headed toward the back of the house to his private entrance.

Lucie had pulled four or five outfits from the oaken chifforobe in her bedroom, and had them spread across her bed. She was in a perfect tizzy trying to choose which one to wear to the dance.

"This is so silly," she chided herself as she plopped down on the bed after flinging a skirt out of her way. "I've gone to these dances every month since I moved to Red Fork, and never cared a whit what I wore."

Siegrid called from her room down the hall. "Lucie? Are you talking to me?"

"I'm muttering to myself."

"Are you ready yet?"

At that, Lucie fell backward on the bed and heaved a deep sigh. "Nowhere near. How about you?"

"Close. What's going on with you?"

"I have no idea. Come help me."

When Siegrid appeared in her doorway, Lucie sat up, looked at her friend, then rolled her eyes. Siegrid's dusky-rose, puff-sleeved dress fit snug at her tiny waist and fell into a generous skirt that was guaranteed to swirl during a square dance. That girl would look stunning in a flour sack. And her flaxen curls—definitely her crowning glory. It just wasn't fair.

"What's wrong?" Siegrid asked. "Should I change? Is it too fussy?"

Lucie had to laugh. "No, my friend. Not too fussy. You look like a million bucks."

Walking over to where Lucie was sitting, still in her under-slip, her hair in pin curls, Siegrid picked up one of the skirts. "Can't make up your mind?"

"Siegrid, I've been to these dances, and never cared what I wore…"

"Um. And tonight?"

"It's different."

"Because a certain someone will be there?"

Folding her hands in her lap, Lucie nodded, feeling her face warming up. And not just because of the heat. "Does it show?"

"A little. But don't worry about it. Just enjoy the time."

Siegrid walked to the chifforobe and started breezing through all that was hanging there. "A dress. You need a dress. Flinging all over the place in a square dance, your blouse will come untucked and tend to appear a bit sloppy."

Now Lucie was on her feet. "I hadn't thought about that."

"Here." Siegrid pulled out the blue crepe with the ruffled cap sleeves. As with Siegrid's, the skirt was full and flowy. "What about this?"

Lucie had to laugh. "You'll never believe this, but I had so many expensive, luxurious clothes in my closets before we moved here, that I packed a lot of them away. I was afraid the people of Red Fork might think I was showing off. I've taken great effort to dress down."

"That makes sense, I guess. But the trial's over. By this time, no one thinks you're showing off." She took the blue dress off the hanger and handed it to Lucie and set about hanging all the skirts and blouses back up in the chifforobe. "And if that's how they think, they've got the problem. Not you."

Lucie pulled the dress over her head, and while she fitted the belt and fastened it, Siegrid was pulling bobby pins out of her hair and tossing them on the vanity. After the curls were all free, Lucie sat down on the upholstered vanity bench and ran a brush through her hair.

Looking at her reflection in the large round mirror, she sighed. She turned around to Siegrid. "Your curls are all natural, aren't they? No pin curls for you."

"Curly yes. Sometimes when it rains it's almost kinky."

"And the color. You'd put Jean Harlowe to shame."

"That's not always a blessing."

"No? Why? It's the perfect shade of blonde."

"Guys at school seemed to assume I was of the Harlowe persona."

"And that is?"

"Oh, you know. *The Blonde Bombshell.*"

The thought of that misrepresentation set Lucie to giggling. If there was one thing Siegrid was not, it would be a bombshell. So quiet. So gentle. So innocent.

Finishing her own hair with a flip of the hairbrush, Lucie asked, "How did you clear up the confusion."

"One good slap across the face did the job pretty well."

"You didn't."

"Oh, but I did. The cad deserved it. After that, word spread and I was safe."

"Maybe you were the bombshell after all," Lucie said. "Just not the type they had you pegged for."

Laying the hairbrush on the vanity, Lucie stood up, stepped back and turning around a couple of times, she nodded at her reflection. "Not too bad, I guess. Thanks for suggesting the dress."

"You look gorgeous. Now come on."

By the time they left the house to walk together to the VFW Hall, Lucie felt a little better. This queasy feeling in the stomach was something new to her.

Wesley was already on location helping set up. The Okesa Filling Station always teamed up with Sam Peterson, the grocer, to fill a washtub with chunks of ice in which to chill bottles of soda pop. A Mason jar sat on a table beside the tub for whatever a person could afford. Penny. Nickle. Dime. It didn't matter on dance night.

Lucie had asked Wesley to please protect Siegrid tonight against the onslaught of a few of the local yokels who often ogled at her when they came into the store. Or when she and Siegrid ate lunch at Annie's. He promised he would.

A full block before they reached the hall, they could hear the musicians tuning up. The street out front was filled with an array of dusty ancient cars and trucks. Very few new vehicles appeared in Red Fork these days. Several wagons with horses—a few with mules—hitched to them, parked along the street as well.

Approaching the door, they could see the expansive hall was already filled with people. From the old to the young, everyone loved dance night. For one evening they could kick up their heels and forget their troubles.

Lucie saw him the moment she was inside. He was off to the side, standing by the soda-pop-filled washtub, talking with Wesley. Her awareness of him was breath-stealing.

His expression brightened when he looked over and saw her. Or did she just imagine it? At that very moment, a few ladies from the church gathered around her and Siegrid to welcome them, making small talk about the weather, about business, about who most recently had given up and abandoned their farm. They blocked her view of Nathan. She didn't want to appear forward by trying to look past them. She just waited, smiling and nodding as the ladies talked.

Presently, Gus Wilton fired up his fiddle with a jig tune guaranteed to set every foot a-tapping. Luther Cavanaugh abandoned his bank president role on dance night. As dance caller, he could spit out those calls faster than an auctioneer. Rounding out the stage band, Hans Cormick played a lively harmonica, and Isaac Yates kept a strong beat blowing into a stone jug.

"Grab your partner, gather in," Luther called to the crowd. "We're gonna pound this floor till the roof caves in." And the vibrant, lively fiddle picked up the beat.

Suddenly, there he was. Standing beside her holding out his hand and looking at her with those soft hazel eyes. "Will you be my dance partner?" Nathan asked in a quiet, polite tone.

Lucie could never remember ever being tongue-tied in her life, but now her heart was in her mouth. All she could do was smile and nod.

She placed her hand in his and felt a thrill go all through her. Walking out on the floor, they joined other couples to make a square. Since she knew most everyone in town, she knew all their partners in the square. She tried to ignore their *knowing* smiles. Small town busybodies always think they know more than they actually do.

Luther began the call, and they were off...

Join hands, circle to the left, that riverboat's awaitin',
All aboard it's time to go.
We're churnin' muddy water, Hold it steady as we go.
Allemande left the corner girl, turn a right hand around your partner,
Men star left and turn it once around that town,
You star promenade that girl around.

Nathan knew all the moves and never missed a beat.

Lucie's feet were flying, her skirt whirling, and every time there was a swing, or promenade, Nathan's hand rested on her waist, he was looking directly into her eyes and smiling.

Four ladies chain now, go straight across that river,
We're dancin' on the levee,
Chain 'em back and watch 'em go.
Now put the ladies back-to-back, men go round that outside track now.
Get back home, Do Paso.

The hall reverberated with boots, brogans, and high heels hitting the wooden floor in rhythm, the calls sounding out at breakneck speed, the music pounding with liveliness.

Don't you hear that whistle blow?
Now corner box the gnat, then, you dosido an' then you
Left allemande new corner, come home, promenade.

Ya promenade 'er, it's up the river we go.

I see that riverboat, so ...

Bow to your partner, corners, all, as up the river we go.

Lucie wasn't sure at what point her nervousness left. Maybe it was by the third or fourth dance. The farmers smelled like farmers, but Nathan offered a woodsy cologne fragrance, an aroma she was certain she'd never forget.

Later in the evening, Luther and his musicians called for a break. Not letting go of her hand, Nathan led her over to where the soda pop was iced down.

"Your favorite?"

Lucie looked to see if there was an orange Nehi. Spotting one beneath the surface of the icy water, she pointed. "Orange."

Now he had to release her hand, leaving it with an empty sensation. Pulling out the dripping bottle, he grabbed a church key lying on the table, popped open the bottle and handed it to her. He plunged his hand back in and pulled out an RC Cola. He swiped the drips from the bottle and flicked them at her, making her laugh.

"Ah. Cool," she said. She felt as hot and sweaty as everyone in the room looked.

After opening his bottle and dropping coins into the Mason jar, he nodded toward the side door. "Let's get some air."

He led the way out the door. It wasn't much cooler outside, but quieter. Except for the soft cry of the hooty owls, chirping crickets, cicadas, and vibrations of the tree frogs. An occasional whicker of one of the horses floated back from the street. A dog barked in the distance. The moon shone through the trees as the two of them walked away from the noise. The VFW hall, a free-standing building set off from Main Street, was bordered by the city park with the grade school building situated on the far side.

The bandstand with its pointy roof sat in the midst, surrounded by swing sets, a tall wavy slippery slide, and a well-used, paint-chipped wooden merry-go-round. Here and there, park benches sat invitingly under the shade trees. Flower beds that perhaps thrived last spring, gave off a sad wilted look in the summer heat.

"You're a natural at square dancing," he commented. Leading the way to one of the benches, he motioned her toward it.

Thankful to be off her feet, she was ready to sit down. Nathan seated himself beside her, but not too close.

"Looks must be deceiving," she commented with a laugh. "I knew nothing about square dancing before moving here."

"Well, then. You're a quick study."

"Maybe that's it. Or a forced study. Wesley insisted we attend every month. As part of our role in Red Fork public relations." She turned to look at him. His dark curls clung to his sweaty forehead. He swiped at his forehead with his sleeve. "You're not too shabby yourself, you know. You seemed to know every dance."

"Contrary to your upbringing, Miss Patton," he said with a grin, "square dancing was all we did back in Ulen, Indiana. Population five hundred."

"Ah yes," she said with a deep sigh and an exaggerated wave of her hand. "The Formal Grand Cotillion before the queen of England—or was that the Shah of Iran—was absolutely remarkable. All the avant-garde attended. Such an affair."

"Touché."

She could tell he had embarrassed himself. She set about to release him. "You have to remember, I was just a little kid who lived like a songbird in a cage. I actually wasn't allowed to do much of anything that might have been thought of as fun."

He gave a soft chuckle. "If that were me, I guess I'd be in a hurry to learn to square dance as well."

"And I was. Thankful for the excuse. The intoxicating music. The rhythm. How can a person not dance when Gus sets that bow to his fiddle?"

"That's some real talent on that stage." Nathan drained the last of his cola and laid the bottle in the grass by his feet.

"You should have heard them when Manny was still here. He played a mean washboard. That man was born with rhythm in every bone in his body."

"With the thimbles and everything?"

"And everything.

"Would have loved to have heard that. So, what happened to Manny?"

"Foreclosure. The family left for California a few weeks ago."

"He lost his place?"

"Lost it all. House, barn, outbuildings, acres of farmland. All the farm animals."

Nathan was quiet a moment. "It's heartbreaking. It seems to be happening everywhere."

"Luther did all he could to prevent it. But in the end..." She let the sentence drop. She had loved Manny and his wife and kids, and cried when they left.

"Luther seems to be a fair man. Not many bankers are."

"Trent attests to that fact. He said any bank that didn't have a run after the crash must have been doing something right."

"That's good to know. Looks like I'll be needing to set up an account. But I wanted to be sure it's in the best place."

Lucie brightened. "Really, Nathan? That's such great news. I mean, just a few weeks ago..." Now she'd stumbled into a trap. Embarrassed she tried to right herself.

Nathan reach over and took her hand. "I know, Lucie. Just few weeks ago, I was a dirty hobo, hopping freights with nowhere to go. And now look..."

Just then Gus's fiddle was whipsawing once again and people were shouting to "git on back in here."

Nathan, still holding her hand, pulled her to her feet. "Hear that? Time to *git*."

"Oops. Don't forget the pop bottles."

Releasing her hand, he picked up the bottles off the ground and they hurried back across the park. Entering the hall once again, she told him, "When you hear *Oh Johnny Oh,* you'll know that's the last dance."

Placing his hand on her waist and guiding her into a group to make a four square, he whispered, "I hope that's hours from now."

If anyone else attended the dance that night, Lucie wasn't aware. It was just her and Nathan. It was close to midnight when she recognized the first chords of *Oh Johnny Oh.* Even the little kids loved the simple steps of this circle dance.

The whole town joined in. The circle encompassed the entire hall. As dancers moved from one partner to the next, it took many repeats to get back to your own.

All join hands and you circle the ring
Stop where you are. Give your honey a swing
Swing that little girl behind you
Now, swing your own. If she hollers swing her harder!
Now, you allemande left with your corner girl
and do-si-do with your own
Now, you all promenade with that sweet corner maid
singing' Oh, Johnny, Oh, Johnny, Oh!

When Lucie came to Rand, as always, his face grew red as he put his arms around her to the "give your honey a swing" part. Most anything could make Rand blush. Then her ornery brother swung her so hard she nearly fell to the floor, with him laughing at the sheer fun of it all. Every farmer with calloused hands, every young stud eyeing all the girls, the shop keepers, and the grandpops. All the way around the circle. And all Lucie wanted was to be near Nathan.

What in heaven's name had gotten into her?

As the last strains of the music faded away, families gathered their children, picking sleeping infants up off the floor, and filing out to the street for the journey back to their farms and ranches. Town folk strolled down Main Street toward their homes. Nathan had committed to help Wesley return cases of pop bottles back to the store.

In his polite manner, he told her good-night and thanked her for being his partner.

She and Siegrid strolled back to the house, each lost in thought. Sleep was a long time coming as Lucie lay in her bed watching the moonlight stream in. The train whistle sounded through the still night air and into her open bedroom window. The clink and clank of the cars hitting and moving as it make its quick stop. The trains on which Nathan had spent so many months, had now brought him here to Red Fork. In her mind, she played and replayed the entire evening.

She'd never liked a fellow before in her life. But she was sure she liked Nathan. But did that mean anything? After all, who else would he have spent the evening with? Was she mistaking his attentions? That was it. He kindly extended friendship. That's it. After all, she'd fed him that day in the backyard. He now felt he owed her a favor.

Later, she heard Wesley come in. The sounds of him moving around were comforting. It was all she could do to keep from flying down the stairs to ask his opinion in this whole confusing mess. But that was silly. What could he say? He might even laugh at her, and she surely wasn't ready for that.

Chapter 21

JULY 1933, RED FORK, OKLAHOMA

"Don't you dare go to sleep until you hear the news," Wesley had told Lucie in his most firm, older-brother tone. "I'll call you as soon as I can."

Of course, he needed the money. No paying passenger could he refuse. That meant he was headed to Artie's, and to his faithful Blue Bolt. The plan was to pick up passengers in Oklahoma City and take them to refineries near the coast in Texas. Most likely, he'd be in the air when the news of Wiley Post's landing came through.

Wesley's stern warning came to Lucie as he had backed out of their driveway earlier that afternoon. She and Siegrid were outside seeing him off. Lucie had come home from the store for a quick lunch, and Siegrid was taking a break from her canning chores in the kitchen.

Ever since the famous pilot had taken off eight days before, bound for his round-the-world solo junket, Wesley had had the radio turned on, catching every bit of news. The radio in the living room was always blaring. Now he'd started taking the smaller Philco from room to room. He even had it sitting on the linen cabinet in the bathroom while he was shaving.

"You're going to electrocute yourself," she warned him as she walked by the open door. She'd read somewhere that water was a prime conductor for electricity. She certainly wouldn't have trusted an electrical appliance anywhere near a drop of water.

"To hear about my hero? My oh my. Oh, what a way to die."

She laughed and shook her head at that remark. Her brother was truly enamored with Wiley Post exploits. And most recently, he and Artie had installed new instruments in the Blue Bolt. Night flying and navigating blinding rainstorms now became a reality.

His comment after the installation and a few night flying test runs was, "Look at me. I'm catching up with old Wiley."

And now that the landing in New York City was expected that night, the chance of him being near a radio was slim. And he was not too happy about it. Throughout the day, newscasters reported that crowds of thousands were gathering in the city to welcome home the conquering aviator.

At breakfast that morning, Wesley pored over the *Tulsa World* as he ate, intent on not missing one little detail. "Mark my word, Sis. Today, July 22, 1933, is a date that will become even more historical than Lindy's landing in Paris in twenty-seven."

Secretly, she wished he could be home to hear it all for himself. But business at the filling station and the store had become steadily slower as the economy continued to suffer. His passenger service brought in the needed income.

She and Siegrid decided they would station themselves in the upstairs screened-in porch to keep their vigil. It was a Saturday night, so at least they didn't have to open the store the next morning. And church didn't start until eleven.

Saturdays were the busiest days at the store, and she and Rand had kept up a steady pace throughout the day. Meanwhile Siegrid slaved away in the steamy kitchen canning tomatoes. Rows of Mason jars, filled to the brim with the crimson fruit, bore testimony to her work. Both ladies were weary, but yet excited.

"When I was a little girl, living out in the woods," Siegrid was saying, "I would have never in my wildest imagination thought that one day I could sit at home and hear people talking in New York City."

"I guess there was no radio in your home?"

Siegrid shook her head. "Never even saw one until after Papa died and Mama, Vega, and I went to live with Pastor and Edith Stedman. She smiled at the memory. "Vega and I sat on the living room floor and stared at that big box with the sound coming out it. They had to laugh at us. But as I remember, Mama was pretty taken with it as well."

The Philco now sat on a small table situated between two large rattan chairs, into which Lucie had stacked the red and yellow flowered chintz pillows. Just another of the few items she and Wesley had whisked away before the auction. It'd been so difficult to decide what to take. The attorneys had severely limited them in what they could claim as theirs. And since they had no idea where they would end up, the decisions were even more difficult.

While Siegrid set up two oscillating fans, Lucie strung out an extension cord to connect the radio. They'd already filled a crockery bowl with popcorn, and a pitcher of iced lemonade and glasses were stationed nearby. The landing wasn't expected until about midnight. It looked to be a long night.

The large, upper-story, screened-in porch had become Lucie's favorite spot in the entire place. While the upstairs rooms were quite warm, the porch caught every little breeze that filtered through the shade trees. And with the added fans, became comfortable. She loved how the night noises wafted through the screens.

They promised to keep one another awake, because the rattan chairs were quite comfy. The two of them seldom ran out of things to talk about and their ongoing conversation paused only when a new announcement came over the airwaves. The most recent report came from Edmonton in Canada. That meant Post still had a couple thousand miles to go before putting the *Winnie Mae* on the ground in New York.

The crockery bowl was now empty. The lemonade pitcher was as well.

Lucie stood to her feet. "I think coffee would be a good idea about now."

"Here, I'll help you take those things."

"No. Stay where you are and listen. I'll only be a minute."

It was as she coming back up the stairs, carrying the tray loaded with the percolator and cups, Siegrid started yelling. "Hurry. Oh hurry Lucie. He's coming in!"

"Already? Oh my gosh, come help me. I almost tripped on the landing, you startled me so."

Siegrid cranked up the volume, then came to Lucie's rescue.

The need for coffee had fled as they listened. The announcer was yelling into his microphone. Loud cheering could be heard in the background.

The announcer described how shocked they were saying, "He just dropped out of the sky." They hadn't expected the last leg of his flight to be so quick. But a tailwind, along with good weather, aided his speed.

Now Post's every movement was followed, almost like the play-by-play of a baseball game. By the time they had him at the hotel with his wife, they were still reporting his every word.

In the midst of the excitement, the phone in Wesley's office was ringing.

"I bet that's Wesley checking in."

Both jumped up and ran down the stairs.

Lucie no sooner had the receiver in her hand she heard Wesley's voice shouting on the other end.

"He did it, Lucie. He did it! I got to hear every detail. On a radio. Here at this airport here in Texas. They said I could stay right here by the radio and listen till he arrived. Wasn't that swell of them? Lucie, he did it. Seven days, eighteen hours, and forty-nine minutes. Who would have ever dreamed? Lucie? You there? Say something."

By now both she and Siegrid were laughing. Lucie had the receiver away from her ear and both could hear every word.

"Say something? You crazy man. I can't get a word in edgewise. But I'm very happy for you, that you got to hear the moment it happened. I know it was important to you."

"Important? What an understatement. It's historic, Lucie. Absolutely historic. He did what no other person in the whole world has ever done."

At least now he'd stopped shouting. His voice resumed a bit of normalcy. Continuing, he added, "You know what this is going to do for my business, and every other pilot like me? The trust in airplane travel will grow. People will see that it's super safe. It's a great day, Lucie. A great day. My hero did it."

"We need to sign off, Wesley. I know this is costing you."

She noted he hadn't reversed the charges.

"Hey, it's another one of those miracles God keeps pouring out. My passengers knew how excited I was and offered to foot the bill." He paused a minute. "Is Siegrid there?"

"Right by my side, listening to every high-volume word."

"Tell her I said hello."

"Tell her yourself."

She handed off the phone to Siegrid. She was curious, but couldn't hear what he said. She thought it a little odd that he wanted to say something to Siegrid, but maybe he was just being polite.

They no longer wanted the coffee, but Lucie wasn't about to waste it. It was too precious. Between the two of them, they cleared everything from the screened-in porch. Back in the kitchen, Lucie removed the grounds from the percolator, then placed it on the counter. She'd heat it up for breakfast.

After all the excitement and the hard day's work, Lucie fell into a deep sleep.

Chapter 22

AUGUST, 1933, HOLLYWOOD, CALIFORNIA

The two hundred dollars had disappeared. Just like that. Poof. Because if she even thought about attending the Hollywood parties, Sadella would need a new dress. Actually, she'd need a couple of dresses. Shoes and bag to match of course. Once those were purchased, she was almost broke. Again. But at least now she could accept Denby's invitations to the parties and make a suitable showing. Looking presentable changed her attitude and her demeanor. Her confidence soared. In Hollywood, the key to success was being seen. Recognized. Often.

The parties usually took place at an elegant mansion of the most famous stars. Sadella was confident one day she'd be living in similar opulence. Opulence that would put the Tulsa Patton Mansion to shame. Each star-owned mansion boasted sunken living rooms, five or six bedrooms, bathrooms with golden spigots, outdoor courtyards, formal gardens, gazebos, and a luxurious pool complete with multi-colored lights. Toward the end of most any party someone would either fall, jump, or be shoved into the pool. Sadella made sure she was nowhere near the pool. She also made sure she never touched a drop of alcohol. Getting tipsy fit nowhere in her big plans. Staying cool-headed did.

Furtively ascending the back stairs with one of the high-ranking producers, also was not in her plans. She'd heard the talk among the Jarrell House girls, which of the up-and-coming stars made their entrance into stardom with such shenanigans. Sadella's strategy would be to arrive at the pinnacle based solely on her own acting talent.

Effortlessly moving among the party-goers, she talked to anyone and every-one. It was easy for her to broach most any subject. Stepping into a group, no matter what they were discussing, she chimed in. No one appeared to resent her intrusion, nor did they talk down to her. Her sensation of actually belonging grew with each succeeding party.

While her acceptance at parties felt within her grasp, the possibility of col-lecting the remainder of the promised one thousand dollars from Reznick for getting Siegrid to Hollywood, seemed more and more remote. She'd spent hours mulling over ideas in an attempt to come up with a workable plan. It was pretty obvious her younger siblings hated her, but Siegrid was unaware and innocent. Sadella needed a way to bypass Wesley and Lucie to make her plan work.

Then it happened. Or at least a hint of a possibility happened. It was at Carole Lombard's house on a Saturday night. Carole was famous among the stars for hosting some of the most expansive, wild parties. Denby had driven her there. He'd become Sadella's so-called date for the parties. After all, no one in Hollywood would dream of walking into a party solo. They entered together, but seldom stayed together. Unless married, couples rarely remained together throughout the evening. And sometimes even the marrieds went their own separate ways.

When they pulled up in front of Carole's white stucco house with the stately pale-blue brick trim, it was obvious the party was at full tilt. Expensive auto-mobiles lined the narrow street in front and the side streets as well.

For some odd reason, she and Denby hung closer than usual for the first part of the evening, enjoying the table laden with the most expensive cheeses, fruits, cold cuts, and tiny sandwiches. Massive, imaginative ice carvings served as table centerpieces. Both of them navigated to the food. Rarely were there sit-down banquets. Sadella knew she'd be in heaven at a banquet. So much food.

As they were filling their plates, a fellow she didn't know came up to Denby. "Hey there, Baer. I just heard the good news." Giving Denby a hearty slap on the shoulder, which nearly knocked the overflowing plate from his hand, he went on. "Congratulations. When's it scheduled? When're you headed east?"

Denby calmly scooped up caviar with a heart-shaped cracker. "I've been told Hollywood is a regular telegraph system. Now I believe it." Chomping down on the cracker, he allowed for a pregnant pause.

It was obvious the intruder was hungrier for Denby's answer than for the food spread out on the table. Sadella looked at Denby's expression to see if this was good news or bad. It surprised her that if he had good news, he'd not shared it with her. They'd become quite close in the past few weeks. Close friends—which was the most she wanted or allowed.

"If it's any of your business, which it's not..." Denby began, then stopped. His next item from his plate was a small sandwich trimmed in the shape of a diamond. He downed it in one bite.

"Come on, pal. It's already being talked about." The man now tried the nonchalance pose and turned to the table and grabbed a similar small sandwich from the platter. "We're your best fans."

"You know how it is, Kris. We're the last to know. The word is rehearsals start in September."

"It'll be getting cold in New York. You'll miss the California flowers and sunshine."

"Maybe." Taking Sadella's arm he steered her away from the table. "Hey, I think they're dancing out on the veranda."

Sadella wasn't ready to leave the food, but she let herself be taken out to the veranda, where indeed they were playing a waltz. It was too early for the jazz numbers. Those usually started when party-goers were too soused to care what they looked like as they maneuvered the tricky jitterbug steps.

Denby led her to an upholstered couch situated against the far wall of the veranda. He set about finishing off the food on his plate.

"So," she ventured, "it's none of the business of the guy named Kris. How about me? Is it none of my business? You're going to New York? Broadway?"

Denby nodded. "I really wasn't ready to tell anyone out here."

She knew he referred to the Hollywood crowd, some of whom could be cutting, cruel, and vicious. Jealousy ruled.

"It's a major role. My agent's been working overtime to convince them to take me on. And it finally happened." He turned to her now. "I planned to tell you when the schedules were firmed up."

Sadella's mind was whirling. Her date. Her ticket to all the parties. She knew of no one who could step into that role. September—a few short weeks away. But then, another thought hit her. Tulsa. The train to New York would go through Tulsa. And Red Fork. What if...?

Laying his plate on the floor beside the couch, he reached out and took her hand. "Hey girl. Where'd you go? Are you upset that I didn't tell you sooner?"

"What? Oh no. I know you. Your intentions were good. I understand."

What if Denby could make a layover in Red Fork? At her request *visit* her family. He could take Siegrid aside and drop hints about coming to Hollywood. Explain to her that she already had an entrance to stardom. Could it work?

"Well then, if you're not mad at me, let's dance."

For the remainder of the evening, Sadella worked the idea over and over in her head. What to say. How to ask him. How to broach the subject. She knew he liked her, but this was a lot to ask. She'd be receiving eight-hundred dollars upon delivery. Why not offer him part of the take?

Late that evening, as Denby dropped her off at Jarrell house, he let her know that he would miss her terribly while in New York. When he leaned over to kiss her good-night, she offered him her cheek.

She could tell he was miffed, but that was of no concern to Sadella. Romancing had no place in her plans. She made a fuss of over-thanking him for the evening, in an attempt to make up for withholding the kiss. She was in a hurry to get alone and think. This was a great idea, but she needed time to cook it to perfection.

That night the nightmare of Jasper being dragged away haunted her once again. When Clarice mentioned it the next day, asking "Who's Jasper?" Sadella played dumb and said she had no idea. "You know how dreams are," she quipped and the subject was dropped. But the nightmare never went away.

Chapter 23

AUGUST, 1933, RED FORK, OKLAHOMA

Nathan had to laugh at himself. He simply assumed he'd be the one out in the blazing sun digging holes in the hard ground along the roadside to install his signs. Thankfully, he was wrong.

Once he had a half dozen signs all painted and readied, he telephoned Trent to let him know.

"That's great news," came Trent's friendly voice over the staticky line. "I'll send the crew with the drilling equipment out there tomorrow morning. They'll get them set in no time. Where should I tell them to meet you? And what time? I figured you'd want to watch them set up. Am I right?"

Equipment? Well of course. After all, this was an oil drilling outfit. The Okesa Oil and Gas Company would have all sorts and sizes of drills. The joke was on him.

"That's a big affirmative, Trent. I do want to see them go up. Have them meet me at the barber shop. How about seven?"

"Done. I'll send along a Kodak and extra rolls of film. I'll need you to take pictures of the process and the signs in place."

Nathan couldn't help but wish Clarette would be on the scene. She was the professional photographer. But if Trent thought the Kodak shots would be sufficient, who was he to quibble with the boss?

It was a crew of three who parked a beat-up, rusty truck in front of the barber shop the next morning. It looked to have survived many miles of travel out across the prairie going from one drilling site to the next. On both doors the words *Okesa Oil and Gas Company* were painted in what was once cobalt blue, now faded.

The first thought to cross Nathan's mind was to refresh those faded words. With a quick followup realization that the truck was too old and battered to warrant such attention. His time was better spent taking care of roadside signs for Okesa.

Earlier that morning, Nathan had walked over to Wade's house where Wade assisted him in loading the signs in Wade's car to transport them to the barber shop. Wade had kindly continued to allow Nathan to use his garage as a workshop.

At the barber shop, they carefully unloaded the signs and propped them against the brick front. The signs caused no little stir among the local business owners and a few early shoppers. From inside the shop, Nathan sensed the buzz as townspeople gawked and commented to one another. He knew that, even as a newcomer, he was gaining the respect of the townspeople.

The moment the truck pulled up, he was out the door of the shop. As he approached, the man nearest the passenger door jumped out and offered his hand and doffed a stained Homberg. "Howdy, Nathan. I'm Hobson, but you can call me Hobs." Turning to the other two, he said, "There, making a wild attempt at driving sits old Merle. He don't gots no nickname cause Merle already sounds like a gal." Then snickered at his own joke.

Merle, who showed signs of gray in what straggled bits of hair peeked from beneath his cloth newsboy's cap, gave a wave of his hand. "Aw don't listen to Hobs. He's always running off at the mouth."

Sitting by Merle was a thin guy who didn't look like he could handle a day's work. His battered Panama hat sat on the back of his head. He stretched out his hand. "And I'm Erwin, but please don't call me *Er...* "

At that, Nathan had to laugh. As he returned the handshake it surprised him that it was a stronger grip than he expected. "Glad to meet you. All of you."

"I guess them's the signs," Merle said pointing.

Nathan gave a nod.

"Hobs," Merle directed as though he were team captain, "give Nathan a hand and get 'em loaded so's we can get this job done before noon heat."

After the signs were loaded, Nathan started to jump up into the truck bed, but Hobs moved him out of the way. Waving to the truck cab he said, "Go ahead, I'll take the rear compartment."

Immediately Nathan attempted to protest. Riding in a truck bed was child's play compared to a rattling, empty freight car. "Aw no. I can..."

But before he could finish the sentence Hobs had swung a leg up and was over the side of the truck bed, settling in. That finished the matter.

As soon as he'd crawled in and slammed the door, which didn't fit quite right, Erwin gave Nathan's ribs a jab. "This is just for today," he said, "'cuz you're the guest." Giving a raspy laugh, he added, "Enjoy it. Probably won't last long."

That comment sounded to Nathan as if he were now part of the crew. He liked that thought. Just then, Merle tossed over something at Nathan which he barely caught. It was the Kodak.

"It's loaded," Merle informed him. "Extra rolls there in the glovebox. Boss says you need it."

With a slight shrug, Nathan retorted, "I guess so."

Thankfully, he'd grown up around cameras, so he at least knew how to change out the film and aim the thing.

"And one more thing," Merle said. "The boys here said you'd probably be green enough to be bareheaded." He reached behind the seat and pulled out a Panama hat nearly as worn as Erwin's. "Take this. Don't aim to have you dying of heat stroke."

They were so right. He'd needed a hat, but hadn't time or money as yet to get one. And this one fit. He didn't let himself think what a filthy head it might have sat on previously.

As they headed out of Red Fork, Erwin unfolded a yellowed section map. Nathan could see several spots marked with red ink.

Pointing with a skinny, nicotine-stained finger, Erwin said, "Right here's where Boss says we plant them signs you painted."

"Right fine a idea." Merle said, "Road signs to pull them travelers to the filling station." Peering around Erwin, he asked Nathan, "That yore idea?"

"Oh no. Not mine alone. It was a collaboration."

Erwin looked over at him. "A colla.... What?"

"Collaboration. Several people sharing ideas. Then we came up with the plan."

"Oh sure nuf. I gots it. A few heads together is better than one."

"That's how it works," Nathan agreed. Then he added, "Isn't this a little out of your line? Aren't you used to giant oil rigs?"

"Sure that," Merle replied. "But we'd do most anything Boss asks. He's determined to keep us all on the payroll."

Erwin nodded his agreement. "Even bust holes in this godforsaken rock-hard, dry Okie dirt to set signs."

"Even that," Merle said.

When Trent said *equipment* Nathan envisioned a generator, belts, drill bits, and the works. Not at all. At the first site, Merle gunned the old truck bouncing down though the bar ditch and up the other side, almost throwing Hobs out of the back. He was swearing loudly.

"If I'd knowed you's gonna jump the ditch," he hollered, "I'da hopped out first." He was alongside the truck now, talking through the rolled-down window and rubbing his backside. Merle's loud guffaws tended only to heat Hobs up a few degrees. But all was forgotten as the work commenced.

The drilling apparatus needed no motor. Just a wooden tripod, a height above the men's heads. Once they selected the exact spot, between the road and the edge of a field replete with drought-ridden corn stalks, they assembled the tripod. In its center was fastened a study metal pole with a large drill bit at the bottom. A crossbar situated mid-way on the pole, allowed for two of the men to turn the drill. Simple, yet effective. Nathan was amazed at how quickly the holes were drilled and the first sign set up.

From a small tank in the truck bed, Erwin drew water into a bucket. He then added dry concrete and stirred the mixture with a stick. With skillful moves he packed the concrete around the base to stabilize the legs of the sign.

Standing back to survey his work, he waved his trowel in the air. "There now. That oughta hold up against them mean old Okie winds."

"Nothing to say that our drillin' wasn't better than your cementin'," Merle said. "So quit your dreamy-eyed wallering and help get this stuff loaded."

From one site to the next they went, the men drilling, setting the signs, and Erwin filling in with the concrete. All the time snipping at one another. But it was obvious to Nathan, there was no rancor. By the time they finished and were headed back into town, Nathan had filled two whole rolls of film. The event had been chronicled.

Lucie and Siegrid cleared the table while the others sat talking around the dining room table. Once again, they'd served dinner in the dining room to make room for the guests. It wasn't just a company dinner. Trent had dubbed it an official business meeting. Even Nathan was invited. Well, he had to be there since it had to do with the marketing idea that included his signs. As usual, Lucie was secretly pleased that she got to be in his company once more.

Erik and Clarette were seated to her left, Siegrid to her right, which allowed Trent, Wesley, and Nathan to be directly across from her. When she dared to glance his way, her eyes connected with Nathan's and the sensation bewildered her.

He'd asked her to go with him to the picture show one evening the week before. Since it was a week night, the theater wasn't packed like on a Saturday night.

Lucie felt the whole town was on observation alert as they walked together from Cairn Cottage to the Roxy. The town was dark when they emerged from the theater having watched little Shirley Temple tap dancing her way to stardom.

Nathan never took hold of her hand, although she wished he would. Then chided herself for thinking such a thing. They'd known one another such a short time, they were still strangers. During the day, her thoughts often drifted toward him. She'd recall clever things he said. And remember the sound of his voice—a voice she was coming to enjoy more each time she was near him.

Their business dinner had involved batting around ideas for capitalizing on the signs. Rand and Everett had no interest at all in such a boring conversation. They were heading for the woods. But Erik made them take Jacie with them. They weren't too happy about the babysitting—which seemed to always happen—but they weren't offered a choice in the matter.

"Just having the signs parked along the road isn't enough," Trent was saying as he pulled out his pipe and began filling it.

Wesley spoke up. "Really? I don't get it. I've seen the signs and I think they're swell. I bet they'll compel every driver to stop at our place."

"That's the point, Wesley. We need to measure the marketing."

Lucie and Siegrid returned to the table with pots of coffee and were filling mugs. "Measure the market," Lucie said. "Of course. That makes perfect sense. You probably measure the marketing for Sparkie the Space Boy."

Trent held out his mug and after it was filled and he took a sip he said, "You can bet your boots we do. We know our listening audience and we know that the parents

listen to Sparkie as much as the kids. Otherwise, we'd take a different tack."

"But you can't measure who reacts to a sign," Wesley commented. He was always the practical one.

"Sure, you can. When they come to the store, and get gas or supplies, just ask," Trent said, waving his pipe at them.

"What about giving something free if they say they stopped because of the sign." This was Nathan's input.

Trent smiled. "That might work."

Clarette said, "But then everyone in town would come get gas or a can of beans, and say they saw the sign just to get a giveaway."

"Here's how I envision it." It was Nathan again. Holding up his hands, he gestured his words. "You have big signs posted both outside and inside the store. It can say something like, *Did you see our roadside sign? Mention it and receive your gift.* Beneath this sign is a large sheet of lined paper. At the top it says, *Sign here to receive your gift.* That way no one can keep coming in just to get the gift. We have their signatures."

Erik laughed his booming laugh. "Ingenious," he said.

"I like it," Trent agreed.

"And the gift?" Clarette asked. "What's the gift?"

Trent drained his coffee and held out his mug for yet another refill. "At first I was thinking a Baby Ruth. It's everyone's favorite candy bar. But then if there are several youngsters that wouldn't be fair."

"Chewing gum," Lucie ventured, happy to have the chance to contribute. "A pack of chewing gum."

Nathan glanced over at her and smiled, making her face grow hot. "Make it Chiclets," he said. "More pieces to share."

Trent slapped the table, startling all of them. "Now that's what I call a marketing strategy." Looking around the table at each of them, he added, "Y'all make a powerful team. If this idea is successful here, we'll replicate it."

Turning to Clarette, Trent asked, "How's the researching coming along for the book?"

Even though he had no involvement with the publishing of the book, Trent was definitely planning to cash in on the advertising and Okesa would be fully behind it with endorsements.

Smiling broadly, Clarette announced that the elderly citizens of Red Fork were a treasure trove of information and wanted nothing more than to tell endless back-to-back stories. "I've learned one thing. Get them isolated. Only interview one at a time. In a group, it's a madhouse as they talk over one another.

It does help as they remind one another of some forgotten little detail, but extremely difficult to take notes and keep up."

The remark brought laughter around the table.

"Yeah, them old boys love to outtalk each other," Erik added.

Just then, Nathan spoke up. "I have news about my mother."

That captured their attention. The room went quiet.

"Good news, I hope," Clarette said almost in a whisper. Ever since she'd learned about the letters that Andy Anderson had penned all those years ago, Lucie knew she was keen to use them in her book. She'd heard Clarette express her interest more than once.

From his pocket Nathan drew out a letter, removed it from the envelope and read:

I've been thinking about what you said about your father's letters. And of course, you are quite perceptive when you said they are precious to me. To us. As I've prayed about this, it occurred to me that such letters are not only filled with love and sweet sentiments, they are also filled with history and if it's possible for them to be used to enlighten others, then I agree to share them. Please tell Mrs. Torsten I am at her service.

As he folded the letter and returned it to the envelope, a collective sigh of relief sounded around the table.

"What a kind, gentle spirit she has," Clarette said. "I so look forward to meeting her. She is coming here. Isn't she? I mean, the letters are so connected to her..."

Nathan smiled. "I've promised her the letters would never leave her possession. So, yes. She's agreed to come. I'm sending the train tickets next week."

Nathan's news seemed to crown the evening as they pushed back chairs and made ready to make their departure. And at the perfect moment, Everett and Rand came in with a jar filled with lighting bugs, and a coffee can containing three small snakes, which they swore were not harmful. Sigrid asked to see. As she peered into the can, she confirmed. "Safe," she said.

Clarette was backing away. "Harmless or not, just keep them far away from me."

"But Mother," Everett protested, "you should see the beautiful markings."

"I'll take your word for it," she said as she took a very dirty Jacie up in her arms.

"Rand knows how to find them," Everett explained to anyone who would listen to him. "And he's teaching me."

Siegrid stepped over and put her arm around his shoulder. In a fake whisper, she said, "Next time you come, Everett, I'll teach you to gig frogs."

Everett's eye lit up. "True enough? Hey everyone! Did you hear that? Gigging frogs."

Shaking her head and moving toward the front door, Clarette said, "We heard. We all heard."

"Can I? Can we? Next time. Will you let me?"

His excited voice was fading as his mother guided him out onto the porch.

Lucie was laughing. "Oh Siegrid. You may be on his mama's bad side."

"We'll spare her the gory details," Siegrid said, trying not to laugh.

After the guests had left, Siegrid was in the kitchen washing up the last of the dishes, Wesley, Nathan, and Lucie were left sitting on the front porch steps talking.

"I've been wanting to ask something of the two of you," Nathan was saying.

Lucie, thankful for the evening darkness, couldn't see his face, sparing her the frustration of what his laughing eyes did to her.

"Ask away," Wesley said.

"I'm creating more signs for Trent, and he told me the other day, our next stop is in Vinita."

"His filling station in Vinita is a major one," Wesley said, "so that makes sense."

"I know your mother is in the... the facility there." He stopped a minute as though he was struggling with what to say next. "May I... Well, would it be all right with the two of you if I paid her a visit?"

"Mother?" His shock at the idea was apparent. "You want to visit Trevalene? For heaven's sake why? She doesn't know anyone. She just sits there."

Lucie was speechless. What was this fellow thinking?

"I know all that," Nathan said, his voice soft. "You know, I spent years by my father's side as he suffered all the effects from his massive burns. I watched closely how he responded to different sounds, people, events, just things around him." He paused again. Wesley and Lucie waited, not wanting to interrupt his thoughts. "I mean, it can't hurt. And I'll be right there in the town. Close."

"Lucie?" Wesley wanted to know her reaction.

"This is very kind. And he's right, Wesley. What could it hurt? And he knows what it's like..." She turned to her brother, seeing his outline against the golden light coming from the front door. His face was shaded, but she knew he was smiling. "You're okay with it, aren't you?" "Yep. I think it's wonderful. After all, we're the only two people interacting with her beside the staff there." Wesley reached over and placed his hand on Nathan's shoulder. "Thanks friend. We're grateful."

Chapter 24

SEPTEMBER, 1933, VINITA, OKLAHOMA; RED FORK, OKLAHOMA

Thirty dollars. Only thirty dollars for the old jalopy, but it least it ran. When Trent told Nathan he'd found an automobile for him, Nathan was elated. When he first laid eyes on the thing, he wasn't too sure.

"Wish I could do better by you, pal," Trent said. They were standing in the parking lot adjacent the Philtower building looking it over. "One of my roustabouts located it in Pawnee. Just sitting there in a farmer's yard. The farmer needed a few dollars much more than he needed that old Dodge. "You can pay it out a little at a time. I trust you."

Chances were the little Dodge Coupe was once red. Now mostly rust. But at least it wasn't open top; he'd be protected from the elements. That would mean the wind mostly, since it seldom rained these days.

Trent invited him to take it for a spin.

"Crank?" Nathan asked.

Shaking his head, Trent replied, "Surprise. Self-starter. Just mash that thing down."

It took a few tries for Nathan to adjust the throttle to the just-right position. But eventually he got the hang of it. As Trent said, he mashed his foot hard on the starter and it sprang to life. The gears were fairly smooth. "I had one of the fellows grease it up for you," Trent told him.

Before Nathan had gone even a few blocks around downtown Tulsa, he knew he and this car would become great friends. He was able to give Trent five dollars as a down payment, and he was off.

That had been the Saturday previous, and now it was early Monday morning as he drove north toward Vinita. The sun was barely peeping its rosy head over the horizon far across the prairie. The dust boiled up around him as the Coupe chugged along. Having his own transportation spelled a new sense of freedom and independence. This beat riding in the Okesa truck all hollow.

In his pocket he'd tucked away the letter of introduction he was to hand to the front desk at the hospital. Lucie had handed it to him the day before as they stood together outside the church after service. The relentless midday sun beat down, even as they stood in the shade of the towering catalpa tree. Her lavender dress perfectly fit her tiny frame, the skirt swirling slightly in the hot wind. Her lavender cocked beret, with the slightest veil that came barely to her eyebrows, completed the outfit.

Being near Lucie unnerved him so, he always felt he blathered his words rather than speaking clearly. His mind knew what he wanted to say, but the words got stuck.

She had handed him the letter sealed in a blue envelope. She was thanking him once again for his kindness. For a brief moment, she held his hand as she pressed the letter into his palm. And there it was again. That jolt of electricity from the scarcest touch.

"Thanks for trusting me," came his quiet reply.

As he turned to go, she said, "Please come by for dinner and let us know how it goes. Wednesday maybe? Wesley's due back then."

He nodded and gave a wave as he walked away.

The night of the square dance, he had seemed to be able to converse in an almost sane manner with her. But the more he grew to know her, the more time he spent in her presence, the more bumfuzzled he seemed to become.

Checking his map, he saw the point where he was to meet his three sign-posting pals on the highway just outside Vinita. He spotted the truck ahead of him and pulled off. In their boisterous manner, they greeted Nathan. Shaking his hand, slapping him on the shoulder and thanking him.

"If it t'wern't fer you," Hobs said, "we wouldn't have this gig."

"Glad I could be of service," Nathan said as he stepped to his car and started pulling signs out of the trunk.

They'd already hauled out the drilling rig, had it set up ready to drill.

"How many ya got?" Merle asked.

"Six."

"Guess Boss wants three on one side of town and three on the other," Erwin ventured.

"Gets 'em a-comin' and a-going'," Hobs said as he began turning the vise to cut into the hard, dry prairie. "Good thinking." Then he added, "This may take a couple of us. Like drilling through a layer of shale."

"Wish we had enough water to soften it up," Nathan said as he watched them strain and sweat to break through the hardened dirt.

"Cain't do that," Hobs said. "That wet stuff we gots is for our dry palates, and the cement, not this stupid Okie red dirt."

Nathan spelled them a bit taking his turn at the drill. He didn't mind the hard work at all. The joy of seeing his signs set into their places filled him with a sense of satisfaction, and a feeling of accomplishment. He wasn't sure how he'd come to be so blessed, but his heart was filled with thanksgiving to God.

The relentless sun was straight up in the sky by the time they accomplished the mission and all six signs were in place.

"They's a nifty little café in town." Hobs jabbed a thumb in the direction where the town of Vinita lay behind them. "My stomach's complaining so's I can hardly think straight. Let's go grab a sandwich."

"I'm all aboard with that," Merle agreed. "Anderson? You comin' with us?"

Nathan shook his head. "I have an appointment to keep."

"Back in Tulsa? Then you shore enuf need food," Hobs said draining a tin cup of water he'd filled from their water tank in the truck bed. Refilling it, he handed it to Nathan.

"Not in Tulsa."

"You gots a appointment in Vinita?" Erwin said. "The onliest thing that's in this burg is that place out there for crazy folk."

Nathan took a minute to drink the water, refreshing his parched throat. Then he said, "Yeah. Well. That's where I'm going."

Silence hung in the hot still air for a moment.

"You know somebody there?" Merle asked.

"I don't really know her. But I'm going to soon." He wasn't sure how much to reveal. This was Lucie and Wesley's business. "It's the mother of someone I know and I offered to stop in and visit."

The truck was loaded and the men were piling in.

"Good luck to you," Merle said. "Seems a kind gesture on your part."

Nathan shrugged. "We'll see."

The truck started up and over the noise, Erwin yelled, "All's I can say is you is missing out on some scrumptious biscuits and gravy."

Nathan laughed as he watched the truck bounce wild across the ditch, up onto the highway and drove off leaving a cloud of dust in their wake.

Tooling up the long drive to the complex, Nathan was astounded at the massive size of the place. Nothing had prepared him for a small city plunked right out here on the Oklahoma prairie. Cows grazed in a nearby pasture, clucking chickens ran free, healthy gardens appeared to be well-watered.

"Must have a deep well around here someplace," he muttered gazing up at the silver water tower reflecting the mid-day sun.

Driving further he saw two shiny red fire trucks ensconced within an efficient-appearing fire department garage. Of course, firemen and trucks would be a necessity this far from town.

Following signs that spelled *Office*, he drove right up to a three-story brick building, parked his coupe and made his way up the steep stone steps to a wide covered veranda. Pushing against the tremors of anxiety shaking his insides, for the millionth time, he doubted this decision. Such a formidable place. Whatever made him think this was a good idea? Pausing at the door, he sucked in a deep breath before pushing it open. The antiseptic smells hit him and in a moment waves of nausea swept over him.

Hospital smells always triggered memories of the many trips to the hospital they made with his father.

"How can we help you?" asked the lady dressed in white sitting at the front desk. Her voice was kind and worked to snap him out of his stupor.

A panicked thought hit him. The letter. What had he done with Lucie's letter? Oh yes. He'd taken the time to fold it up and tuck it into his wallet for safe keeping. He'd almost forgotten.

Mumbling a bit, he crossed the wide entryway to the desk all the while digging for his wallet and pulling out the folded letter.

Struggling to keep his voice steady, he said, "I have… It's a letter… My friends asked me to visit their mother."

He unfolded the letter and laid it out for the lady to see. Picking it up and reading it, her eyes brightened. "What a gracious thing to do. For them and you." Looking at the letter and back up at Nathan, she said, "So you're Nathan?"

He nodded, still fighting to get his stomach settled down.

Pulling out a bulging notebook, she paged through it. Finding what she was looking for, she said, "Ah. This is perfect. Lunch is just over and Trevalene can be brought to the visiting room." Closing the notebook, she added, "I'll call for an attendant who'll show you the way." She paused, then added, "She gets so few visitors. Thank you for doing this."

"You're welcome."

"The attendant's name is Milton. He'll meet you out there on the front veranda."

Nathan nodded, thanked her and headed outside, thankful for fresh air. Even if it was hot air, it had no trace of antiseptic to it.

Milton was a lanky fellow with an open, cheerful face. Nathan couldn't imagine being cheerful working in a place like this. Could there really be so many crazies in this world?

Walking across the property, they passed several of the large brick buildings before entering one and walked down a long hall that led to a vast, open room, quite obviously the visiting room.

The room was faced on one whole side with tall windows letting in plenty of light. Because the room faced north, graced with towering oaks just outside giving shade, along with whirring fans placed about the room, they had defeated the heat somewhat.

Trying not to stare at the patients, Nathan followed Milton across the room to where a woman was seated in a chair that resembled nothing more than a baby's high chair with a tray fastened to the arms of the chair.

Trevalene's graying hair hung in unkempt tangles and the print dress hung about her thin frame. As she sat there, she ran her hands over the tray repeatedly. Nonstop. Nathan recalled times when his father, during times of most intense stress would sit in the middle of his bed, fold his arms across his chest and rock. And rock. Ceaselessly. Those were the most difficult times for Nathan and his mother.

In a rather loud voice Milton looked at the notes in his hand. "Miss Trevalene, you have a visitor. This is Nathan. He knows your son and daughter." He set about pulling up a chair positioned for Nathan to sit right in front of her. Once Milton left, Nathan moved the chair around a bit to the side. Now he could talk to her and not look directly at her. It seemed easier somehow.

After clearing his throat a couple of times, he croaked out, "Hello Mrs. Patton. You don't know me." He shifted in his chair. Trevalene stared straight ahead, her hands gliding across the tray. Slowly. Methodically.

He started again. "I know you don't know me, but I sort of know you. You see, I know your two children, Wesley and Lucie." He paused. He could clearly watch her face for any response. "I live in Red Fork where they live. I've spent time with them. I've even had dinner at their house on occasion."

Nothing. He continued. "And you're never gonna believe this, but my father, Andy Anderson, worked with your husband, Henry, back during the big rush in the oil fields." Again, he paused and watched. "My father wrote letters home to my mother in Indiana. That's where I'm from—Indiana. That's where I grew up. Until I left to ride the rails because my mother had to close her photography studio. She's a professional photographer, you see. And she takes good care of Uncle Sacha."

Now he was just yammering. That wasn't going to get anywhere. "In my father's letters he talked about Henry. And he also talked about his partner, E.V. Harland. Isn't that an amazing coincidence? Almost unbelievable. Wouldn't you agree?"

The hands continued their repetitive swiping of the tray. The eyes holding that blank stare.

Again, clearing his throat, he said, "Mrs. Patton, I want you to know that I kinda have a thing for your daughter. For Lucie. I don't have anyone else I can tell that to, but I want you to know. At this time in my life, I have nothing at all to offer her. So, I just gotta bide my time. For God's timing." Shifting in his chair again, he added, "But I don't mind waiting. I mean, she's certainly worth the wait. I just hope no other fellow comes along and sweeps her away. Not many fellows in Red Fork, you understand. I don't think I need to worry. But I can only hope she'll be patient as well."

Another pause. A little longer this time. He had thought if anything might trigger a response, him talking about Lucie would do it. Nothing. "She's about the cutest little thing I ever did see. Smart too. A hard worker. Gollee, that gal can work. She's caring and considerate. When I try to talk to her I get all choked up. My old stomach does flip-flops.

"So you see, Mrs. Patton, my big predicament is that I don't know whether to let her know. Or not. Do I ask her to wait for me? Or not?"

If Nathan had not been watching so closely, he surely would have missed it. But for a split second the hands were still, and the head, crowned with a tangled mass of greying hair, gave a slight nod. Barely perceptible, but he saw it. And he knew he saw it. Gathering all his courage, he placed his hand on her thin shoulder.

"Thank you, Mrs. Patton. Thank you so very much. I receive that."

The hands resumed their methodical swiping.

Taking a large feed sack, Nathan had created an interwoven rope drawstring at the open end. This he strung from a tree limb at the hobo jungle. Strung it high enough to keep out the critters. Although an aggressive coon could probably rip it apart, as yet, that hadn't happened.

Once a week he walked through densest section of the timber, on the far side of the creek bed, avoiding the road. In his arms he carried a package holding a few items. Coffee. Dried beef. A few apples. Beans. Not much. They couldn't carry much and they didn't need much. Seldom would they ever stay more than one night.

One particular day, the sound of approaching footsteps through the under-brush startled him. He figured a lone hobo was looking for a spot to settle. Not wanting to embarrass the fellow, he stole away out of sight. He remembered the stigma all too well.

Kneeling down behind a large stone-shelf outcropping, he waited. He heard the sound of the person taking down the feed sack. This made him doubly pleased that he just filled it.

Unable to resist his curiosity, he ventured to slowly move to where he could barely see. Still not wanting to disturb the traveler. Stunned beyond belief he saw it was Lucie. She had to stretch as high as she could reach, and finally resorted to pulling over a fruit crate to stand on. Taking down the bag, she pulled it open, picked up her cloth-wrapped treasure and tucked it down into the bag. Nathan could only guess. Cornbread? Biscuits? Pound cake?

That task completed, she proceeded to pull out a handful of clothespins from her pocket and clip them to the rope that was strung between the trees. Clothespins. Who but a kind-hearted human being would think to provide clothespins? Wet clothes dried much more quickly pegged than draped.

What a kind, selfless, and very courageous gesture. His heart pounded so he thought he would keel over right there in the dirt. If ever he thought he loved this girl, all doubt had been obliterated.

Until she left, he sat there motionless, not daring to breathe. Just soaking in the image of her climbing up on the precarious, flimsy crate and placing her gift in the sack. He'd once been that lost and wandering hobo, so grateful for any small gesture of kindness. It was almost as if she'd given this gift directly to him. With the back of his hand, he wiped away his tears.

Chapter 25

SEPTEMBER, 1933, RED FORK, OKLAHOMA

D enby leaned back in the overstuffed leather chair and stretched his long legs out as best he could. At the moment, he was alone in the club car, and even with the windows open and the air blowing in, he was constantly wiping sweat from his face with his handkerchief. Loosening his tie helped some. His suit coat hung from the coatrack in the corner. Shoving his Homburg down over his eyes, he attempted to catch a nap before anyone could come barging in with an attempt to make conversation. He was definitely not in a mood to talk.

On the table beside him lay the thick, bound play script in which he was due to star in a major role in a few short weeks. Nearly all his lines had been committed to memory. He'd been told many times that he was genius when it came to memorizing lines. However, the dimwitted Hollywood producers failed to take notice. So far, at least. But he wasn't done with his drive to be featured on the movie marquees. Not by a longshot.

The nap he so longed for eluded him. On long train excursions, sleep was the best way to speed up the long, boring hours. It was the dread he suffered that prevented sleep. The closer to Oklahoma, the more the dread grew. He had no desire to stop in a no-account, backwoods burg called Red Fork. And then attempt to inconspicuously woo a beautiful young damsel to consider coming to Hollywood. Just thinking about how preposterous such an assignment could be, he almost laughed right out loud. He'd heard those Okies were armed with shotguns.

Spending his growing up years in the Lower East Side of Manhattan, then moving up to better digs after getting his break in vaudeville as a teen, he had never in his entire life stepped foot in a small town. And he wasn't looking forward to it now.

If it weren't for Sadella, he'd ride right on through to New York. But then... He had to confess, he'd been fascinated with her from the first moment he met her on the set at Starline. Although at twenty-eight she was several years older than he, it seemed not to matter. They'd been paired in a couple of walk-on parts, and he realized right away that she needed him as an escort for the myriad of star-studded Hollywood parties. He was more than happy to agree. She was a real looker and he liked having her on his arm.

He admired her brassy attitude. More than once, he'd witnessed how she covertly weaseled her way into fortuitous positions. Especially, making headway with Mr. Reznick, whom she easily addressed by his first name. No one else in the studio that he knew of, would dare such a stunt.

Denby hadn't the heart to tell Sadella that she had little to no chance of a starlet role at her age. The ingénues who snagged those roles had already been in the moving pictures since they were nineteen or twenty. The studios kept them on because they were ticket-sellers with thousands of adoring fans. Their faces decorated the covers of movie magazines, and shone forth in the newsreels.

It somewhat saddened him that she clung to the idea that this ploy might work in her favor. She hadn't yet grasped how ruthless the industry could be. While she was dreaming of getting on Reznick's good side to get a starring role, all the old guy wanted was a new starlet. Once he had that starlet in his grasp, he'd drop Sadella like a hot potato. Denby sensed it coming clear as a bell. Poor Sadella even thought he was doing this favor for her because she promised to pay him. Oh, her foolish mind. He agreed simply because he wanted to help her as much as possible. Speaking of *good sides*, that's where he wanted to be with Sadella.

He was still alone in the club car. Pulling off his hat, he stood to his feet and stretched. He must be losing his mind.

Following Sadella's instructions to him before he'd left Hollywood, Denby debarked in Tulsa, secured a hotel room, and hailed a taxi for Red Fork. Tulsa was nothing to write home about. Sitting in the front seat with the cabbie, Denby remarked, "I thought Tulsa was supposed to be the Oil Capital of the World."

"Yup. You got it. That's us." He chewed the end of a matchstick which seemed to be splintering as he spoke. His yellow cabbie hat sat perched on the side of his head with the bill sitting cock-eyed.

"Looks like it's a bit low on oil." Denby meant it as a joke. The cabbie wasn't amused.

"Don't know where you're from mister, but our people are in a world of hurt right now. Tulsa's doing a mite better than other places I know of."

Denby wondered what other places this Okie might know of, but didn't address it.

The cabbie added, "I'm right pleasured to have this fare. Don't think I'm not. But I'd be grateful if you didn't bad mouth my home town."

"You're right. I apologize."

"The oil rush started right here in this area. Maybe you didn't know, but the oil and gas from this old Okie dirt supplies most of the nation. In fact, the place you're headed to—why that was the first gusher."

"Red Fork?"

"Red Fork." Swerving the automobile to miss deep chugholes, he almost knocked Denby over, making him cling for dear life. "None of my business, Mister, but why's a fancy dude like you going there? Nothing there to speak of."

"Just a quick visit. A friend of mine asked me to stop and pay her respects to some of her family."

"You from California?"

Denby nodded. "I am."

"Must be the Pattons then."

"It is at that. How'd you know?"

"Most everybody in these parts know that Miss Sadella hit out for Hollywood almost before her daddy was cold in the ground." The matchstick moved around as he talked. "You gotta know the Pattons was famous folk during the high-rollin' money days. Built that big old mansion across from all his shiny refineries. Then come along the crash. So old Henry just up and cashes out with a bullet to his noggin." The cabbie shook his head. "Funny how it affects folks. To have money. Then not. They can't deal with it."

Denby never remembered Sadella saying anything about her father committing suicide. But then, it wasn't as if they talked about anything of any depth or importance. Just small talk.

"Almost there," the cabbie said. "Where'd you want let out? At their filling station?"

He took a paper from his shirt pocket. "There's a house at the edge of town..."

"The kids' house. Know right where it is. Cairn Cottage they call it. Nice little place."

Red Fork, to Denby, looked like a back-lot movie set. Unreal. He could almost wish Mr. Reznick were here with him. And the house.... Even more. Two-story white rock with a large screened-in porch extending the breadth of the second story. Beneath that, a wide veranda graced the front, inviting any tired visitor to sit a spell in the several rocking chairs placed about. A white picket-fence enclosed the front yard, which was suffering in the summer heat, with only a few patches of green.

"This is it," the cabbie announced as he pulled into the drive. "Am I supposed to wait?"

Denby was staring, transfixed. "Wait? Oh no thanks. I'll probably be here most of the day. I'll telephone if I need you later." Pulling out his money clip, he glanced at the meter and drew out the needed bills. "Keep the change."

With a wide smile, the cabbie replied, "You betcha. Glad to be of service."

After reaching into the back seat for his hat and jacket, he stood at the side gate as the cab drove out in a cloud of dust. Dust, he began to realize was a steady reality in Red Fork, Oklahoma.

At that moment, the screen door opened. And there she was. Tall, slender, and if possible, even more stunningly beautiful than the snapshots Sadella had shown him. Even in the unflattering house dress covered with a flower-print bib apron, he could imagine her dressed in Hollywood finery. She had the potential to outshine even Mary Pickford. Maybe Sadella was right after all. In his mind, he was already cashing in on an equal finder's fee. Past anything Sadella could offer him.

Letting the screen door slam, Siegrid walked out onto the porch wiping her hands on a feed-sack cup towel. Now he could see she was barefoot. "I saw the taxi cab pull up. Not many strangers come up this way in a cab. Mostly they come up from the creek, hungry and looking for a handout." She slung the towel over her shoulder. "You don't much look like you're needing a handout."

Denby hadn't moved from his spot at the gate.

"If you're a salesman," she said, "we're not buying. And if you're from the government, you need to talk to Wesley or Lucie."

Looking down at the latch on the gate, he said, "Can I come in? I'll explain."

"I guess so. You look harmless enough." She shrugged and then smiled. "But these days, who can tell."

Lifting the latch and opening the gate, Denby swore to himself that any moment Mickey Rooney in his Andy Hardy role would come dancing out the front door and Judy Garland would join him and they'd burst into song.

"This is the Patton residence isn't it? Cairn Cottage?"

Siegrid nodded. "And who's asking?"

"My name is Denby Baer." He brushed the brim of his Homburg with his fingertips, hoping it was a friendly gesture. "I'm a friend of Sadella Patton. I'm on my way to New York and Sadella asked that I stop in and pay my respects."

Now Siegrid broke into a wide smile. "Sadella? Wow. You're from Hollywood? Well now, why didn't you say so sooner?" She waved him up onto the porch and reached out to shake his hand. "Welcome to Red Fork and Cairn Cottage." Pulling out one of the chairs by the table, she waved for him to sit. Which he did.

"I'd invite you inside, but I don't think Wesley'd like that with him not being here. Wait a minute here and I'll fix you a glass of lemonade. Then I'll walk you down to the store. Wesley's home today. I'll telephone and tell them." She was talking as she walked inside letting the screen door slam.

With Wesley and Lucie duly informed, after Denby had downed the glass of cold lemonade, the two walked to the store. Siegrid moved with such an easy grace, Denby had a difficult time believing she'd grown up out in the sticks with a bootlegger as a father. At least that was the most he'd learned from Sadella's telling.

Dressed in his serge slacks, white shirt, tie loosened against the blistering heat, and his spectator wingtips, he felt quite out of place. He'd shoved his hat back, but was still thankful for the bit of shade it offered.

The store sat back away from the street with two red gasoline pumps stationed in front. No curbing, but a gravel driveway allowed the automobiles to pull up to the pumps. The large sign read: *Okesa Oil and Gasoline Station.* In the window was a likeness of the Spaceboy Sparkie and his Spacedog Sport. He'd heard the Saturday morning radio show many times—whether he wanted to or not. Did this company have something to do with the nationally-known, popular kids' program?

A feed store sat next door to the filling station. Between the buildings, Denby could see out back where a horse-drawn wagon sat, with men loading feed sacks. Again, he felt he should hurry over to wardrobe and don his costume to play a part. Was this place real?

Denby wasn't sure what he expected, but the overwhelming friendliness was definitely not it. Before he knew it, cute little Lucie with the bright eyes, curly hair, and turned-up nose was standing on a small stool so she could stand tall enough to reach the wall telephone, calling friends in Tulsa to come to dinner that night.

"Because we have a guest here all the way from California." Then she added, "He knows Sadella."

As she was putting through the telephone calls, Wesley was making friendly conversation and offering him a cold bottle of Royal Crown dripping wet from the pop cooler.

It was the Torstens who ended up driving Denby back to his hotel that night—after an evening the likes of which he'd never experienced before in his life. Not one person even remotely resembled what he'd heard from Sadella. He expected a group of country bumpkins. He never remembered her speaking of any of them without disdain in her voice.

Seated at the dinner table next to the novelist, Clarette, he was drawn deep into conversation about the most recent plays opening on Broadway. She knew every single theater. As well as their locations. Her husband, Erik, Denby learned, served as editor of a national oil and gas magazine. Wesley, he learned (only by happenstance because none of them were braggarts—unlike every human being in Hollywood), flew his own airplane carting oil company moguls around the country. Not a single person he knew in Hollywood could fly an airplane.

"Uncle Wesley flew with Wiley Post!" This announcement from Clarette and Erik's son, Everett.

That grabbed Denby's attention. Post was world famous. He asked, and then was regaled with the story of how Wesley's first plane ride as a young boy was with Wiley Post.

"But then, that's not all," Everett added, seemingly enjoying knowing the whole story. "Once Mr. Post learned how that lit Uncle Wesley's fire about flying, he came right to Artie's airport in Jenks."

The story had to pause as about three different people around the table explained about Artie and what and where was Jenks, Oklahoma.

Then they let Everett finish the story. "And you will never in a million years guess who came with him?" Without taking a breath, he almost shouted: "Will Rogers!"

One of the twin girls piped up in her soft little voice, "And we all went out there to meet them both."

On and on it went. He learned that Wesley now flew Nathan Anderson—another friend that had been invited to dinner—out to California to paint airplanes.

"Paint airplanes?" Denby was confused.

Now Nathan spoke up. "The numbers. Sometime logos. At Luscombe mostly." In a humble manner, he added, "Only a couple times so far."

"But he's good," Wesley said. "They like his work."

The young man painted airplanes at Luscombe. In California. Denby's mind went whirling. It seemed unending. He learned that Siegrid's older sister, Tessa, and her husband Gaven, were both college graduates, now teaching at Lee School in Tulsa. Siegrid herself could boast of two-years of college.

Not country bumpkins, my dear Sadella. Not by a long shot.

Add to all that, prayers. Praying. And talk about answered prayers. He'd never heard any group of people refer to God so much. Almost every other sentence was giving *glory to God*. Whatever that meant. Denby wasn't really sure. But he had to admit, he wasn't put off.

It was well after midnight when the Torstens pulled up in front of the hotel to let him out, all thanking him profusely for stopping on his way to New York to spend the evening with them.

Tulsa had rolled up the sidewalks hours ago, and all was quiet and still. Even with the sun down, the air hung heavy with Oklahoma heat—which Denby was certain he'd never get accustomed to. Erik stepped out onto the sidewalk to shake Denby's hand. The Swede was a big guy with strong hands and a quiet demeanor. As they were saying their good-byes, Jacie leaned half her body out the back window.

"Mr. Denby. I have a bye-hug for you."

The invitation startled him. He'd never been around kids all that much.

"Mama says you live hundreds of miles away and I might never see you again for the rest of my whole, live-long life."

Stepping over to the outstretched arms, Denby allowed them to be wrapped around his neck. And it was soft and sweet.

Reaching across her he shook Everett's hand.

"Thank you, Jacie, Everett. I'm glad I got to meet you." Turning toward the hotel steps, he waved and added, "All of you."

Scenes of the evening ran through is head as he later stood at his hotel room window looking at the deserted streets of Tulsa. While each moment had been amazing past belief, it was the time alone with Siegrid that topped it with a flourish.

The dinner table was laden with some of the most wonderful food he'd ever tasted, but it was the frog legs that fascinated him. He had to know—what does it take to catch a frog? And how could they be so big? He thought frogs were little things.

As the womenfolk cleared the table, it was Siegrid's invitation that she show him a frog gig and maybe even see a bullfrog. The creatures could certainly be heard with their raspy croaking.

As Siegrid led the way along the cool creek amidst the thick wooded area, it was then that he told her.

"I'm here on a mission, Siegrid," he said, "and it has to do with you."

She stopped stone still with the frog gig in her hand—a menacing weapon if ever he'd seen one. "Me? Why that's ridiculous. You don't even know me."

He then pulled out the envelope that had been burning a hole in his pocket for all these miles, and all these hours.

"Siegrid, your photo has been seen by Myron Reznick, head of Starline Productions Studio. It was a snapshot that Lucie sent to Sadella. When Reznick saw it, he told Sadella that he wanted to make you a movie star."

Denby realized at the moment, he'd almost stopped breathing. Either she'd laugh and push away the idea as ludicrous. Or she'd warm up to it. To his surprise, it was the latter. *Well*, he was thinking, *after all, what young, red-blooded American girl didn't dream of being on the silver screen?*

First, of course, she wanted assurance that what he was saying was real. In the envelope was the short note of invitation on Reznick's studio letterhead and signed by Myron himself. A note from Sadella. And then, in a smaller envelope, money for a train ticket. Denby had slipped a few extra bills in as well, knowing she would need money once she arrived. He gave her the number of the theater in New York. "Call me anytime," he said. "Someone there will get hold of me."

Sadella's note warned Siegrid not to tell anyone her plans, because, as the note read, "None of them trust me. They will try to stop you, and that could ruin your chances at stardom."

Denby caught the early train the next morning. Watching out the window as the small Red Fork station whisked by and faded into the distance, it dawned on him that his life had been filled with actors, actresses, playwrights, producers, directors, and scores of wannabes. He couldn't remember being surrounded by so many down-to-earth, genuine, kind-hearted people in one place. He liked them. He really liked them. He knew he'd love to visit again. But once they learned the reason for his visit, they'd probably never welcome him back. Ever.

Chapter 26

October, 1933, Red Fork, Oklahoma

Everyone loved Lovina Anderson. Lucie especially. Even at a first casual glance, anyone would know Lovina and Nathan were mother and son. That same swarthy complexion, the hazel eyes, and dark curly hair. Even their mannerism and soft way of speaking.

Lovina's plan was to stay for only a few days as she was continuing to care for her elderly Uncle Sacha and didn't want to leave him in the care of others for very long. Mrs. Powell kindly allowed Lovina to stay in Nathan's room, and Nathan took to the sofa in her living room.

Clarette was there almost the minute Lovina arrived on the scene. Between Nathan wanting time with his mother, and Clarette wanting to get every possible historic detail in a few short days, Lucie had precious little time with Lovina.

Lucie surprised herself as she realized she wanted time to ask Lovina all about Nathan. What was he like as a little boy? Ornery? Obedient? Creative? Teasing? Fun-loving? She wanted to know all about him.

The confusion inside her was frustrating beyond words. Certain moments, the way Nathan looked at her, when he didn't think she knew he was looking, she felt he cared about her. Other times, it was almost as if he avoided her. Unless he had left behind a sweetheart in Indiana, she was fairly sure there was no other girl in his life. If he did care, and if he was serious about her, she wished he'd come out and say so. The not knowing was driving her a little batty.

She scolded herself for even allowing the confusion, and then she would tell herself that she'd simply stop thinking about him. But then, without fail, there he'd be once again. Right in front of her. Those eyes. Those curls. That smile. The gentle voice. His eagerness to always bring out his Bible and share a verse. And her heart pounded inside her—it was embarrassing.

The plan was to use Cairn Cottage as *research headquarters,* as Clarette called it. With the dining room table cleared, they spread out the letters which Lovina had kept in perfect order according to dates. Both Wesley and Lucie were amazed at how often Andy Anderson spoke about Henry Patton. And Lovina's eyes fairly glowed as she grasped the import of this connection.

"Only the Lord could have created such a rendezvous," she said as she looked around the table at each of them. Her words tinged with a heavy French accent, in Lucie's mind, made her even more endearing.

What Clarette looked for was descriptions of Red Fork, the melee of the early day rush. And there was plenty. Descriptions of where they slept—under wagons, in old sheds, out on the ground. The details of what they ate and how they hired and paid their roustabouts. Borrowed money. Went without. On and on. She took copious notes as Lovina read aloud the parts of letters she was willing to share.

Clarette could barely contain her excitement. "This is exactly what I needed," she told Lovina. "I've interviewed many of the old timers around here, but their memories sometimes fail them. And other times, they just try to out-talk one another. But this..." She waved her hand over the letters and postcards strewn out over the table. "...this is immediate. As it happened. With this added, I'll have the manuscript ready for the publishers in no time."

Siegrid and Rand were kind enough to mind the store so Wesley and Lucie were free to entertain Lovina, and also to listen in on the contents of the letters. Nathan, of course, was there as well.

At one point, Lovina surprised them by asking, "How far to the oil field? And where was the fire? I want to see it." Pointing to her camera which she'd placed on top of the sideboard, "I'd like to photograph."

Nathan in his quiet voice said, "Are you sure, Mother?"

She nodded. "Very sure now. A few years ago, perhaps not. But now. Oui. I'm well enough." Then she added, "You may not have known, but Andy would never have been injured, had he not gone into the fire to save someone. Someone who had fallen."

Silence fell over the room. No one spoke. No one had known. Not even Nathan. After a few moments, Clarette asked, "Do you know the man's name? The one he saved?"

"Just that he was a close friend of Henry's partner. The man named Harland."

Wesley and Lucie exchanged glances.

"I have here a letter from Mr. Harland in which he thanks Andy." She reached out to place it in Wesley's outstretched hand. "I never contacted him again, but always wondered how his friend fared." As Wesley read the letter, she added, "Perhaps I could meet him?"

Lucie knew what Wesley was thinking. She had the same thoughts running through her head. E.V. Harland had wanted nothing to do with the Pattons following Shelby's death.

"Tell you what," Wesley was saying, "Nathan, why don't you drive your mother to the site. That would seem to be a private family moment. While you're away, Lucie and I will contact E.V., and see what can be arranged."

Wesley sat at the desk in his office holding the phone. Lucie paced as she waited. She couldn't believe for a second that E.V. would give them the time of day.

Clicking the receiver Wesley gave the operator the number of the Harland Oil Company office. Lucie could tell the secretary came on the line. Wesley gave his name, and after a few short minutes, he was informed that E.V. would not take his call. Wesley sucked in a deep breath, looked over at his sister, and took a new tack.

"Please, ma'am, I know E.V. doesn't want to talk to me, but would you please tell him that this has to do with a man by the name of Andy Anderson. I think he will recognize that name. Mr. Anderson's widow is visiting here at our home in Red Fork. She would very much like to meet Mr. Harland. I think he will agree to that."

That turned the tide.

E.V. still would not talk to Wesley, but by way of the secretary invited them to his office later that afternoon.

"How about three?" Wesley said. Then, "Three it is. The conference room. Fifth floor. Got it. Thank you." Before hanging up, he added, "Please thank Mr. Harland."

Replacing the receiver on the hook, Wesley sank back into his creaking wooden office chair, and dramatically wiped his brow. "Whew."

Also breathless, Lucie asked, "Do you think his invitation includes us? You and me?"

"My sweet sister, this is an open door. And we're going to walk through it." Standing to his feet, he said, "If he doesn't want us there, he can throw us out."

Lucie couldn't recall the last time she'd seen E.V. Harland. Her memories of him were vague. She'd been so little. Of course, E.V. and Flora attended the formal dinners that Trevalene put on. She and Wesley would lie on their stomachs on the wide landing at the top of the staircase and watch as the guests arrived all decked out in their finery until Chloe, their nanny, chased them off to bed.

So when E.V. walked into the conference room after keeping them waiting for nearly twenty minutes, she could hardly believe it was the same person. The years had not been kind to him. The eyes sad and empty, his skin sallow, his frame lean, his step halting. Not even the tailored suit, silk tie, shiny shoes, and diamond watch could mask the decline. Round glasses did nothing more than magnify the sadness in his eyes.

The offices of the Harland Oil Company were as pretentious as the Okesa Oil and Gas Company's offices were unpretentious. In the front lobby, long rows of brass chandeliers lent the ceiling a golden glow. Intricately designed marble floors and carved marble columns, stained-glass windows, along with works of art mounted in giant gilded frames and well-appointed artifacts, created the instant impression of extravagant wealth.

But, as Lucie thought to herself looking at this worn-out man, nothing can buy health or happiness. E.V. surprised her by his ability to look them in the eyes and shake hands all round as Wesley made the introductions.

Taking in the sight of Wesley and Lucie, he said, "You two Pattons have done well." He paused, then added, "In spite of it all."

Prior to the visit, they'd filled Lovina in on the incident with Sadella and Shelby and the anger and bitterness which had resulted. She had carefully sorted out the letters that mentioned E.V. by name. As they sat around the highly-polished walnut conference table, she read them aloud. As he listened, they could see E.V. almost visibly retreating into a cloud of memory that seemed to overwhelm him.

"So long ago," he said, his voice barely above a whisper. "So long ago." His hands were clasped together on the table in front of him now in a rocking motion. "We were an unbeatable team. Yessir. We were. So close. Relied on each other. Andy was the one who kept everyone laughing. A good man. He was a good man."

E.V. looked over at Lovina and repeated. "Your husband was a good man." She nodded, but no one spoke. It was as though they were each one respectfully waiting. Allowing him time. Space.

"The fires. Always there were fires. If not from the carelessness of handling the nitrogen, then lightning. Or in this case, from the pockets of natural gas. Just without any warning, would burst into flame." At this the wrinkled hands unclasped and he made circles in the air.

"It was Andy and my man, Murray. I'd told them to not to be going down to the creek. Pockets of gas would hang there. But it was hot and they just wanted to cool off."

At that moment, a wizened, unsmiling lady knocked at the door and at his bidding entered, carrying a silver tray with a large pitcher of ice water and glasses.

"Shall I pour?" she asked as though it were fine wine.

Lucie quickly stood up. While thankful for a cold drink, she resented the intrusion. It was an emotional moment for Lovina. "Let me do it."

The lady gave a surprised look and quickly left.

Nodding to E.V., Lucie said, "Go on."

As he continued with the story, she filled each tall glass, handing one to each person at the table.

"I wasn't there, you see," he went on. "I only know what was told me by those two and the other men. Flames erupted, the two ran but Murray fell. Andy stopped in his tracks, ran back into the fire to drag Murray out. Everything was a tinderbox. Dry as it is right now." He waved toward the open windows. "Andy could have kept running. He would have been safe..." E.V.'s low, shaky voice trailed off.

"Did Murray live?" Nathan wanted to know.

E.V. nodded. "Scarred of course, but just passed a few years ago." Looking across the table at Nathan, he asked, "And your father?"

"He suffered a great deal. He died five years ago."

E.V. pulled a handkerchief from his pocket, took off his glasses and began to clean them. Stalling apparently. "Guess we shoulda kept up with Andy. So much happening around that time. It was a wild time. Lots of mishaps, accidents, and men getting hurt."

Lucie glanced at her brother. She knew what he was thinking. That was many years ago. So much could have been done for the Andersons. Andy saved a life, for heaven's sake. How could they have just let it go?

Replacing the glasses on his nose and adjusting them, and looking at no one in particular, he said, "Then Henry and me had that falling out."

Wesley dared step in. "Falling out?"

"That sister of yours. She out there in Hollywood? Trying to be some high falutin' movie star?"

Lucie didn't trust herself to speak. Wesley just nodded.

"That's what people are saying. Didn't know if it was true." More long pauses. No one knew what to say. "I warned Shelby. Told him to stay clean away from her. Course, he didn't listen. Kept hanging around with her."

E.V. stood now. Lucie wondered if he was going to walk out. Instead, he stepped over to the windows. "I told him. I said, 'Shelby, if you go out with her again, I will disown you. You will have nothing.' Then I said…" At this his voice broke and they could barely make out the words. "Then I said, 'Shelby if you choose to waste your time with that floozy, then you are no longer my son. Just don't come back here.'" His shoulders shook as he added, "That was the night he died."

Lucie truly thought the man was going to fall out on the floor. Wesley got to his feet, gently took E.V. by the shoulders and guided him back to his chair. Softly, he said, "It's all right now. Everything's all right."

"It's not all right. I've bottled up the hate for her, but it was me. It was all my fault. I let Shelby have anything and everything he wanted. Never told him no. I created the wild playboy he became."

Looking up at Wesley, he said, "Then I turned my hate on Henry and Trevalene. And you two as well. And it's eating me alive." Cradling his face in his hands, he said, "And that's not all. The day before Henry killed himself, he called me."

Lucie caught her breath. She hadn't known that her father talked to anyone prior to his suicide. "What did he say?" she asked.

Shaking his head, E.V. said, "We'll never know. I refused his call."

It was all Lucie could do to keep from screaming and running from the room. Who knew how things might have changed if her father's old friend had been willing to talk to him? Perhaps Henry just needed to talk things out. Now she wished she'd never stepped foot in this room.

Nathan spoke up. "Sir, why are you choosing to hold all of this inside you? It's ruining your life."

E.V. once again removed his glasses, laid them on the table and wiped his eyes with the monogramed handkerchief. "What am I supposed to do? None of the hateful things I did can ever be changed."

Now Lovina chimed in. "Not changed, Mr. Harland. But forgiven. Just ask the Lord to take it away. The Bible says He's faithful and just to forgive."

"He'd never forgive me. I'm a hopeless case."

"If Jesus forgave those who crucified Him, He'll forgive you. Just ask him." This from Nathan.

Wesley, still standing by where E.V. sat, looked at the others and nodded toward the door. It was time to leave. This appointment was over. They stood to go.

"Thank you for your time, monsieur," Lovina said. E.V. didn't even look up as she added, "Your son is gone. My husband is gone. Mr. Patton is gone. But you... you still have a life. A life in which you can do much good. If you chose to do so."

They left him sitting there in his pain.

The Torstens and the MacIntyres had all piled into Eric's car to come gather at the Red Fork train station the next morning to see Lovina off. They'd all fallen in love with her. Everyone was talking over one another, letting her know she was welcome to come back anytime. To come and stay longer. Fanning herself with her hand, she laughingly promised to do so just as soon as it cooled down some. If it ever did.

She fussed over Nathan, reminding him how proud she was of him. Giving him hugs, kissing his cheek and in general embarrassing him in front of everyone.

And then she was gone. Lucie felt her absence immediately. She knew Nathan must have felt it even more. She stepped over to him and said, "You are one blessed fellow to have such a special mother."

He surprised her by reaching out to take her hand. "I know, Lucie. I know. But thank you for making her feel so welcome. And so loved."

Chapter 27

October, 1933, Jenks, Oklahoma; Red Fork, Oklahoma

Wesley couldn't hide much from Artie. The two of them had known each other too long for that. Artie knew almost the minute Wesley walked into the hangar that something was terribly wrong.

The wide hangar doors were closed against a cold wind that was sweeping down from the north. In August, Wesley had wondered if he'd ever don a jacket again, but now his flight jacket was zipped up tight and the lamb's wool collar turned up. Artie had heard him drive up and was walking across the hangar to meet him at the side door.

"You don't have any gigs. What're you doing...?" Looking at Wesley's face, he said, "Let me get you some coffee and let's talk."

Together they walked to Artie's office where Artie rinsed out mugs and filled each with some of the worst-tasting coffee ever. Anyone who ever visited the hangar swore to the fact.

Settling into his office chair, propping his booted feet on his cluttered desk, Artie said, "Okay. Out with it. Who died?"

Wesley pulled off his jacket and sat in the chair opposite, sipped the hot coffee and grimaced. "It's Siegrid. She's gone."

"Siegrid left? Back to Glennpool? Back to teaching?"

"That would be minor. This is major."

"I'm listening."

"Remember that actor dude? The one Sadella told to stop by and say hello to her *family*." The last word filled with derision. "I should have known better."

"Denby whatshisname...?"

"Yeah. Him." Taking another sip of the nasty coffee he set the mug on the desk and leaned forward. "You ready for this? You're never in a million years gonna believe it."

"Well, from what I've known about Sadella, I probably would."

"Under the guise of wanting to know about gigging frogs, he and Siegrid went out to the creek, which gave him the chance to hand off two letters to her. One was an invitation from the head of the movie studio where Sadella hangs out waiting for her golden opportunity."

Artie, sensing Wesley's anger rising said, "Take a breath."

"It seems in a letter Lucie sent to Sadella, she enclosed photographs of her and Siegrid. This movie producer happened to see them..." He paused. Looking at Artie, he added, "You know how good looking she is."

Artie only nodded.

"The letter, signed by this guy stated he wanted to make Siegrid a movie star. Then another letter from Sadella instructed Siegrid not to tell us, because we would stop her and ruin her chances. In that letter was money for a train ticket."

"And Siegrid took the bait?"

"She did. I was on that New Mexico flight, Lucie at the store. Siegrid packed her things, left a note and hopped the train to California."

"None of my business, but what did she say in the note?"

"Not too much. Mainly that this was a chance of a lifetime, and she couldn't let it pass her by." He paused letting the anger cool a bit. "She explained about the letters from the head of the studio and the one from Sadella."

"And your first reaction? Kill the Denby dude? Or go after the girl?"

"The latter. It was all I could do not to jump in the Blue Bolt and go bring her home. Lucie absolutely forbade me."

Artie leaned back in his chair. "So. Tell me. Why hadn't you told her?"

"Told her?"

"That you're in love with her, you empty-headed numbskull."

Wesley shrugged. "I was waiting for the right time."

Artie picked up a shop rag, wadded it up and threw it at his young friend. "And tell me just exactly when the right time was going to be?"

Catching the rag, he shook his head and said, "Artie, I really don't know. She's so sweet. So good. So beautiful. She takes my breath away. Sometimes I can't even carry on a normal conversation with her. It's crazy. Never felt like this before in my entire life."

Artie chuckled.

"I'm in misery, and you're laughing at me." He threw the rag back, and it hit Artie square in the head. "This isn't funny."

"Her leaving—now that's not funny. You sick with love—now that's funny. Does Lucie know?"

"She does now."

"You can't tell me she didn't suspect."

Wesley nodded. "You're right about that."

"Now what?"

"That's what I came all the way out here to ask you. What should I do? I love her. I want to marry her. And she's chasing after some silly dream."

"Maybe silly to you, but quite obviously, not silly to her. You gotta admit, she's every bit as beautiful as any of those so-called stars whose names are up in lights." Artie drained the last of his coffee. "Maybe she can't act. That would end it."

Wesley shook his head. "She's graceful. Moves like a dancer. Contained. No fluttering like so many females I've met. I'm willing to bet, she'll wow them all with her acting."

Artie stood and took his mug to the sink. "My advice? Wait. Hard as it may be. Just wait. If she's yours, God'll bring her back to you. And if she's not, then you don't want her anyway."

"Ouch."

"You're a big boy. You can handle this. And maybe it's all the better that she doesn't know your feelings for her. That way, at this point, she's fully free to make her own decisions." Leaning back against the counter, he added, "Just please. Promise me. Never take that Blue Bolt up in the air when you're this outta sorts. Promise?"

Letting loose a deep sigh, he said, "I promise."

Chapter 28

OCTOBER, 1933, HOLLYWOOD, CALIFORNIA

I f ever Sadella's acting talents were needed, it was at this very moment. Clarice was practically bouncing off the walls with excitement.

"RKO," she said again. She'd already repeated it a half dozen times. "He was from RKO. We—me and Royce... You know Royce. I've been telling you about Royce, the soda jerk. He and I made up this wordplay—kinda like Abbot and Costello." Making sure she had Sadella's full attention, she paused a minute. "You remember me telling about that?"

Sadella nodded as she continued hanging up her clean dresses in the chifforobe. She'd just carried them from the Chinese laundry down the street. With Denby in New York, she was hoofing it everywhere. She sure missed his being available take her wherever she needed to go. She steeled herself against what she was hearing. Clarice getting *discovered*. And by a guy from RKO, no less.

"He heard us. It's really funny. I'll have to have Royce come over some night and we'll go through it for you and all the girls. Anyway, we do it to make the customers laugh. And this guy wanted my attention at the cigar counter." She paused at the mirror and adjusted her curls.

"I knew he wasn't wanting any cigars."

"And how did you know that?" Sadella couldn't help asking.

"Oh Sadella. You coming from money, you know men rolling in dough don't buy their cigars at the drug store. He'd be at the tobacconist's on Wilshire or someplace like that." She sat down on their bed and flopped backward. "I was shaking like a little kitten. I knew he wanted to talk to me. RKO. He was a director from RKO."

Sitting up again, she pushed her hair out of her face and went on. Sadella bit the inside of her cheek to keep from screaming.

"They're looking for a comedienne for a small part in their next picture. He'd heard me and Royce and said he loved how I was so quick with my lines. Plus, he said we were really, truly funny."

Leaping to her feet she whirled around three full dance turns, because, of course, Clarice hadn't dropped out of dance lessons like Sadella had. "In the morning. Eight o'clock in the morning. I've already charted it out on the bus schedule."

She came up behind Sadella and surprised her by grabbing her and whirling her around in a couple of turns. "I know you're thrilled for me. It's because of you that I'm here. Now the door's open, and I'm walking through it."

That had been a week ago, and Clarice most certainly did get the part. She was up every morning, catching the bus to the studio. Coming home every evening still in makeup, exclaiming over the day's work.

And then there was Siegrid. If Clarice was disgusting, Siegrid was twice as disgusting. Never had Sadella seen more fuss and bother over a newcomer to the studio. Myron made sure the studio paid for Siegrid's rent at the Studio Club. In spite of the fact that she was insanely envious, Sadella was thankful Siegrid wasn't living at the Jarrell House. If she did, Sadella was certain she would have to strangle the freshly-arrived-in-Hollywood ingenue.

Denby was away. No parts were coming her way. She was drowning in jealousy to the point of outright anger. The eight hundred dollars she so coveted from Myron, had disappeared within a few weeks. She still wasn't even sure where it all went. She'd tried to wire some of it to Denby, and he told her to keep it That he didn't need it. Rather than being thankful, to her it felt like a rebuff. How could anyone not need money? Was he pushing her away? She had no one to take her to the parties. Nothing was turning out right. Clarice kept telling her to just go downtown and grab a part time job.

"That's what I did, and look how it turned out for me," Clarice would say. Now she was getting some pretty substantial paychecks.

A part time job? Sadella had never had to take a job in her entire life. Jobs were for *other people*. Definitely not for her.

Then, as if things could get no worse, she learned through the grapevine that Denby was paid a sizeable sum—much more than her measly thousand—as a finder's fee for convincing Siegrid to come to Hollywood. How dare they? It had all been *her* idea. Well, not *really* her idea. She just *happened* to have the photo that Myron just *happened* to see. But it had all been her plan. She was the one who should have had the finder's fee. It was all so wrong. So wrong.

Then she met Lisandro.

Chapter 29

NOVEMBER, 1933, RED FORK, OKLAHOMA

"Jorgenson? They changed her name to Jorgenson? Siegrid Jorgenson?"

Wesley had just come in from an overnight gig he'd taken to the Gulf coast ferrying two Getty executives. The flights were fewer now so they were pinching pennies as the economy seemed to worsen with each passing day.

Lucie climbed down from the ladder where she'd been lining up Prince Albert cans of tobacco on a higher shelf. The store was cold with only the coal-burning stove situated in the center of the store to heat the place. Rubbing her hands together, she said, "Her postcard that came yesterday gave the warning. I guess the studio bigwigs felt Jurgen was too similar to the Jergens hand lotion."

Lucie hated how dismal Wesley's countenance was these days. He was absolutely no fun. She wondered how he interacted with his clients. Hopefully, he was congenial enough to keep them on tab. They couldn't afford to lose any of them.

He laid his hat on the counter and unwrapped the scarf from around his neck. "Jorgenson. Her name's not Jorgenson."

"I don't guess we have much say." Moving an orange crate out of her way, she came around from behind the counter. "I have to admit, she looks good on the screen."

Wesley muttered something she couldn't quite catch, so she went on, "She had quite a few lines. A couple of close ups. And her name on the credits. You want to go see it tonight? I don't mind seeing it again."

He shook his head. "Thanks, but no. I'm tired. If you're okay for the rest of the day, I'm headed to the house."

She definitely wasn't okay, no more than he was okay. After the door closed behind him, Lucie looked around. Never had she been so weary of the store and all the work that went with it. Last month they barely broke even. Trent was such a strong encourager telling her that the road signs were working wonders. The list on the counter of travelers who stopped by because of Nathan's signs continued to grow. They'd had to order another case of Chicklets gum to give away.

Also, the October Sparkie giveaway had been a hit. On the Saturday before Halloween, they handed out cardboard masks of Spaceboy Sparkie or his Spacedog Sport—they could choose. By Halloween night, nearly every kid in Red Fork had carefully cut out their masks, cut out the eye-holes, and attached string on each side and proudly donned their Sparkie and Sport likenesses. All up and down Main Street, business owners handed out candy. Some of the children could be heard singing the theme song,

Spaceboy Sparkie and his Spacedog Sport
Zooming out to their Jupiter Port

Still and yet, it was tough going for the *Okesa Oil and Gasoline Station*. Their dream—hers and Wesley's—was a filling station. A real, honest-to-goodness, free-standing filling station. No more cans of green beans, packages of crackers, and glass jars filled with candy. The store part of their enterprise put them in direct competition with Peterson's grocery store. Neither Wesley nor Lucie liked that. In such a small town, it didn't seem fair. Trent agreed, but at the moment there was nothing anyone could do about it.

All across the nation, free-standing stations were popping up. Hardly any—except the most back-woodsy locations—were pumps just stuck out in front of a general store. That was so out of date.

Lucie had clipped a photo of an updated, modern filling station from one of Erik's Oil and Gas magazines. The photo was posted in her bedroom where she could look at it and dream about it every day. Sooner or later, it would happen.

Glancing at the clock she was thankful it was nearly time to lock up and go home. They'd hired Rand's mother, Oney, to help out at the house. They couldn't pay her much, but at least Lucie didn't have do the washing. Of all the household chores, she hated laundry the most. Oney would have their supper ready, for that Lucie was thankful.

As she was locking the door, she heard Nathan's Coupe drive up. No matter when, no matter where, the moment Nathan was in her midst, her heart would not stop pounding. Smiling at him, she called out, "Sorry Mister, we're closed. No gas today."

He'd rolled down his window. "That wind picked up. It's pretty chilly. Thought you might want a ride home."

"And an invitation to supper? I think Oney made chicken pot pie."

"Sounds like a fair exchange to me. Hop in."

Nathan had invited her to go with him to the picture show a couple weeks prior. He always invited her to the monthly square dances at the VFW Hall. The invitations were polite and intentional. He never took it for granted that she would go. That part of him touched her deeply. To anyone else it might be a small thing, but to her it was special, and she cherished each time he invited her. One evening before the cold set in, he'd asked her to take a walk. Sometimes if he stayed for supper, they would sit on the porch and talk. That he cared, was blatantly obvious, but never had he ever spoken his feelings aloud to her. Sometimes she just wanted to take him by the shoulders and shake the words out of him.

Patiently, she waited.

Chapter 30

DECEMBER, 1933, RED FORK, OKLAHOMA

Nathan was well aware that it pleased Wesley and Lucie when he voluntarily traveled to Vinita a couple of times a month to see Trevalene. During his visits, he talked to her about Lovina coming. About Clarette's book, which was now at the publishers. As he talked, he carefully watched her expressions. He was more than confident that she heard and comprehended. He, of course, had no authority to talk with the doctors, but on one occasion, he visited with one of the workers to ask about her responses. He agreed with Nathan. He, too, could see her expression changing as he spoke with her.

Now, the first week in December, Christmas decorations had transformed the visiting room into a much more cheerful place. He was told that a Christmas party was set for the Sunday afternoon before Christmas.

"It's almost Christmas, Trevalene," he said, as he sat in front of her. "I'm told there's going to be a Christmas party here."

The eyes never wavered. The hands moved slowly, steadily across the lap tray of her chair.

"I bet you used to give some of the best parties in all of Tulsa. Maybe all of Tulsa county. Am I right?"

Still no response.

"I know Wesley and Lucie will want to join in the celebration. I'd like to come with them. Would that be okay with you?"

It happened so quick he barely caught it. But her eyes glanced at him. And she gave the briefest nod.

It took his breath away. Stopping for just a moment, he continued as though it were the most normal moment in the world. "Well, that's just great, Trevalene. You are so kind. I'm glad you want me to be with your family. Thank you so much."

The Christmas spirit seemed to waft through all of Red Fork. For a time, the townspeople could forget the hard times. In the center of town where Main Street intersected with Pickard Avenue, the town fathers had wired up a phonograph player and a loudspeaker, blasting Christmas songs into the very air they breathed. Everyone seemed filled with the joy of the season. All except Wesley Patton who was gruff as an old bear.

The Saturday Giveaway Days were wild at the store. It was moments like this that Lucie missed Siegrid terribly. She'd always been right there to help. And having taught school, she was great with the children.

Lucie wasn't sure how the word got out but Red Fork's younger generation found out that a plastic, cellophane-wrapped replica of the spaceship *Carina* was the prize for December. It was probably Rand. He had trouble keeping things to himself. The noisy, laughter-filled line formed early. The weather was balmy, making it feel more like spring than Christmas—an added blessing. With no frigid wind blowing, all could be handled from the front porch of the store with the children lining up in the driveway.

They'd had trouble previously with the youngsters saying they wanted two, sometimes three more prizes, for other siblings. Wesley, who wasn't as gentle with the kids, but was a great lawgiver, put his foot down. The only way a child could receive an extra toy was for a parent to come and verify that there truly were other siblings.

By now, both Wesley and Lucie knew most of the families. And of course, Rand knew all of them by name. The problem had lessened, but they still had their guard up. The worst would be to run out of stock and some might not get a toy at all. Which would break Lucie's heart. With the economy in the mess it was in, many of the children had no toys of their own.

Right in the midst of the commotion, Lucie heard Nathan say, "Lucie, I hear the telephone."

She looked up from the box from which she was carefully taking out the cellophane-wrapped toys one at a time. "Mercy me. Not now."

"Go ahead." Nathan came up on the porch from his post of navigating the line. "I can do this."

Wesley and Rand were at the end of the line in an attempt to bring the littlest ones to the front.

"Thanks." Lucie went inside, grabbed the receiver from the wall phone. "Hello. Okesa Filling Station. Lucie speaking."

The operator's voice came on the line. "Will you accept a collect call from Siegrid Jurgen?"

Lucie nearly dropped the receiver. "Yes, we will. I mean, yes, but please Operator, wait just a minute. Please. Can you hold the line?"

The operator couldn't keep the amusement from her voice. "Of course. Party in California, please hold."

"Yes. I'll wait."

Lucie, hearing Siegrid's voice was moved to tears. Laying the receiver on the phone-book tray, she ran out on the porch. "Wesley," she called out, "come quick. It's Siegrid on the telephone. Hurry."

"Take over, Rand," he said as he ran toward the store.

As they huddled together in front of the hand-crank phone, Lucie held the receiver between them. "We're ready now, Operator. We accept the charges for this call," she said.

"Siegrid. Oh Siegrid. It's so good to hear your voice," Lucie said. "How are you? I saw your picture. You're so good. Are you just loving it?"

Wesley shook Lucie's arm. "Will you let her talk?" Then into the mouthpiece he said in a shaky voice, "Hello Siegrid."

"I'm so sorry to bother you two. I miss you so much. Thank you for paying for the call."

Her voice was strained. Lucie could tell something was wrong. "We're here Siegrid. Did you call to tell us something?"

The line went silent. Lucie thought for a brief moment that her friend had just hung up. Then she said with a sob catching in her voice, "I don't know what to do. I just don't know what to do."

Wesley's face was grief-filled. "Siegrid, what do you mean? What's going on? Are you all right?"

"They... they... it's the bigwigs in the studio. They want me to do things." She choked on another deep sob. "Things I don't want to do. Would never do."

"You mean in the movies?" Wesley asked.

"No," came the simple answer.

Now Wesley was fuming. "Where's Sadella? Is she not there to help you? To safeguard?"

"South America. She left for South America right after Thanksgiving."

"South America?" Lucie silently mouthed the words.

"A Latino actor named Lisandro convinced her she was a great actress and could have greater success away from Hollywood. So, she left with him."

"Where's that Denby guy?" Wesley wanted to know.

"Still in New York." Another pause. "They're threatening to kick me out of the place where I'm staying if I don't..."

"What?" Wesley practically yelled into the phone. "Why those..."

Lucie just knew the next words were going to be a string of curse words. She touched his shoulder.

"Siegrid, listen to me. Pack your things. Take a cab to the Burbank Airport. I'll be there in a few hours."

"I can't leave, Wesley. They have me under contract."

"We'll worry about that later. I can tell them right where to put their precious little contract. Right now, you go pack."

Now Lucie spoke up. "Siegrid, we want you here. Here with us."

"I know. I know that now. And I want to be there. I've grown to despise this place."

The moment they hung up, Wesley telephoned Artie. Filled him in and told him to get the Blue Bolt ready.

"You know this is on your penny," Artie warned. "She could get a flight out from there. A lot cheaper."

"I would hock everything I own, Artie. I'm gonna go get my girl."

As soon as Wesley left, Lucie rang up Tessa to give her the good news. Her sister was coming home. Home for Christmas!

Nathan was surprised when Wesley said, "Come on, Anderson. We're headed to Hollywood. I need a co-pilot."

Of course, he didn't need a co-pilot. Never needed a co-pilot. Maybe he was so worked up, he just needed someone to talk to.

Leaving poor Lucie in the lurch, with only Rand to help her finish out the Giveaway Day activities, within the hour they were on the road to Jenks to Artie's and the Blue Bolt.

Nathan was surprised because the two of them had had sharp words a few days prior. Lucie, Nathan was sure, was totally unaware that her brother had gone off on him. He'd pulled into Okesa to get gas and it was Wesley who came out. They started out gabbing like usual, then all of a sudden, Wesley asked—more like demanded—to know what Nathan's intentions were toward his sister.

At first, he had no idea how to answer. He'd sort of been wondering the same thing himself, but to have Wesley come at him was a shocker. Before it was over, Wesley accused him of just *stringing her along.*

Struggling to keep his temper, Nathan ended up saying it was his business and for Wesley to stay out of it. Naturally, Wesley came back with the fact that he was only watching for his sister's good.

It was all Nathan could do to keep from making a snide remark about the fact that Wesley was sore because he hadn't looked well after his own love affair. Later, he was glad he held his tongue. It was clear Wesley was hurting much more than he'd been letting on.

Nathan guessed if being hopelessly in love with a girl, but having nothing in the world to offer her, if that could be labeled as *stringing her along*, he would have to plead guilty as charged.

When Wesley called him out to be his *co-pilot*, Nathan took it to be a quasi-apology for the previous angry words. And he gladly accepted. Other than hating to leave Lucie on Giveaway Day, Nathan relished the opportunity to once again go up in the Blue Bolt. And it looked like a second chance for Wesley with his girl.

Cleared for landing, they taxied past the impressive white Burbank terminal capped by a roof of red tiles, all shiny and new in the California sunshine. Once the Blue Bolt was secured and out of the way they entered in the cool interior.

Nathan couldn't help but wonder what might happen if Siegrid were not there waiting. He envisioned an angry young man combing Hollywood searching for her, and ready to take care of anyone who might have prevented her leaving.

It took a minute because she had situated herself off in a corner alone, two suitcases at her feet.

"There she is," Nathan said.

"I see."

She looked up at them through red-rimmed eyes. She didn't even stand up but remained sitting there. Nathan had never seen a more distraught person. He stood back as Wesley went to her, sat down beside her and took her in his arms.

She leaned into his shoulder sobbing. He was rocking her and assuring her that everything was all right. "You're safe now. You're going home."

"I'm so ashamed," Nathan could hear her soft voice saying. "It's nothing like I thought. It's so... it's all so ugly. Under all the glitter, just ugly. I should never have..."

"Shhh. It's all over now." Wesley pulled out his handkerchief and handed it to her. He held her from him for a moment so he could look at her as she wiped the tears from her face. "Siegrid Jurgen, I love you. I've been a miserable mess ever since you left. I want you to come home and be my wife. Will you marry me?"

"But I'm such a dunce. How could you ever...?"

"You're not a dunce. You tried something and learned it wasn't for you. That's it. But if you are a dunce, you're the most beautiful, most wonderful dunce I've ever met in my life."

Now she was crying again. But she was nodding with her head once again buried in his shoulder. It was the strangest marriage proposal ever.

Nathan kept checking his watch. They had no plans to stop over. It was a touch-and-go mission. Grab her and get back home. He gave a little wave to get Wesley's attention and pointed to his watch. Wesley stood and pulled Siegrid to her feet.

"Nathan old buddy, would you grab her bags?"

Giving a short laugh, he strode over and grabbed her suitcases, most thankful that he was now the *old buddy*. Laying his hand on Siegrid's arm, he said, "It's all okay. We're just thankful you're safe."

She nodded and gave a soft thank you.

Minutes dragged by as Lucie waited for word. Rand was such a trooper. He loved the Saturday matinees and especially on the Giveaway Days, he nearly always followed the kids down to the movie house. But today, such a thing wasn't even mentioned. He stayed by her side.

It was around three when Wesley's telegram was delivered. It simply said:

CARGO SAFE STOP RETURNING NOW STOP ARTIE'S BY 9

Now she could breathe easier. Terrible thoughts had been racing through her head ever since Siegrid's call. How ruthless were those Hollywood kingpins anyway? Would they have prevented her leaving?

"Rand, would you go tell your mother to fix something extra special for supper tonight? We're celebrating Siegrid's homecoming. Tell her it has to be something easy to keep in the warming oven. We may be eating late."

"Sure will. Be back in a whipstitch."

It was Saturday. Their busiest day of the week. The day the farmers and ranchers came in for groceries, feed, and supplies. They had to stay open until at least six.

It was nearly six when the telephone rang. She was in the middle of figuring a ticket and making change, so it took a minute before she could run catch it. The customer left, the store was empty, so near time to locking the doors.

"Lucie? It's Artie. The Blue Bolt has crashed."

Chapter 31

December, 1933, Oklahoma City, Oklahoma; Red Fork, Oklahoma

Lucie froze. She wasn't sure she was hearing the words. Her mind refused to receive it.

"In a field just this side of Oklahoma City."

Her mouth went dry. She couldn't speak.

"Lucie? You there? Lucie, listen. I got it through the dispatch."

"Hurt? Are they hurt?" she managed to say. What she meant was, *Are they alive?*

"We need to get over there fast."

He was talking over her. "Is anyone hurt?" she asked again, practically yelling into the telephone.

"They were all taken to the hospital in Oklahoma City, but nothing serious. Now stop talking and get yourself here. Pronto!"

Who to call? Who? Her mind was rattled. She was pacing behind the store counter. *Stop*, she told herself. *Just stop. Breathe. Think.*

Tessa and Gaven? No. It would take too long for them to get from Tulsa, then they still had to drive to Jenks. Wade. Wade would do it.

Returning to the telephone she spun the crank and gave the operator Wade's number. Relating the news of the crash and her need to get to Jenks, his reply was, "Grab your hat and coat. I'll be right there."

While waiting for Wade, she telephoned Tessa to let her know. "Be praying," she said. "Artie's taking me to them."

When she and Wade arrived at Artie's they saw he already had the *de Havilland Dragon* on the runway. The *Red Dragon*, as Artie called it, his newest acquisition was on the block for re-sale. He'd only had it up a few times. The logical choice since it seated six. Under her breath, Lucie praised God he'd not yet sold it. Thanking Wade profusely, she ran toward where Ralph stood by waiting to assist her up into the cabin.

"We're all praying," Wade yelled after her.

Lucie had only been up in a plane one other time in her life, but it was smaller. The Red Dragon was huge. Taxiing down the runway, Artie explained that this small runway wasn't really built for craft this large. She stopped breathing until they were in the air.

"What happened to our beloved Blue Bolt?" she wanted to know. "Malfunction?"

Artie shook his head. "Wind shear. Practically ripped the tail off. Luckily it was over an open space. Pasture land. Wesley skillfully brought it down, but with a hard landing. Knocked Nathan clean out. Injured his ankle as well, so Wesley said. They were x-raying it when Wesley called me from the hospital."

They were alive. That was all that mattered to Lucie. It would be later when the dollar signs would begin racking up in her brain. She saw no way they could ever afford to have the Blue Bolt repaired and back in the air. And in the meantime, no income from commissioned flights.

Wesley demanded to see Nathan, even though his head was throbbing with pain. He remembered was the terrifying sensation of the plane whipping out of control and his yelling that he was taking it down. He remembered the loud noise of the crash, then nothing.

The nurse finally resigned to his demands, just to calm him down. Now that Lucie and Artie had arrived, Wesley felt renewed and was able to push through the pain.

In Nathan's room, he said to the still form lying there, "Nathan? Can you hear me? Nathan, it's Wesley. Look at me."

The eyes fluttered a bit, then opened. In a softer tone, Wesley said to someone, "This is the first he's opened his eyes since we brought him in. Like me, he slammed his head pretty hard."

Nathan could feel a face close to his, and could hear Wesley's voice faintly in the distance. "Someone's here to see you, buddy."

Forcing his eyes to open, there was Lucie's sweet face within inches of his.

"Lucie." He reached up to touch her. Barely above a whisper, his words halting, he said, "Lucie... I love you."

Now she was closer. "I know," she said. "I've been waiting forever to hear you tell me." Leaning closer she kissed his forehead. "I've loved you since I fed you cornbread under the King Oak."

"As the plane went down, my last thought was of you. What if I'd lost my chance?"

"Chance?"

"Please, Lucie. Marry me. Soon. I don't want to live one more day without you."

Now Wesley spoke up. "Not sure there's a preacher hanging out at the hospital just waiting for these types of occasions, pal. How about we wait till we get you home?"

Nathan peered around Lucie at his friend. "Always the logical one. Except when it's about your girl."

Forgetting his throbbing head, Nathan pulled Lucie to him, kissing her full on the mouth as he'd been longing to do for months. And heard her say, "I'm yours, Nathan Anderson. Forever yours."

He wanted to add that he had nothing to offer her, but when Lucie wouldn't stop kissing him, he guessed it could wait. Then he realized she already knew that. And it simply didn't matter.

Lucie's joy bubbled over as they flew home. The four of them together. Flying in the Red Dragon as though they were royalty. Siegrid and Wesley had come out of the crash with only bruises and scratches—plus Wesley's bad bump on the head. They'd been checked over and were fine. Nathan also with a whack on the head and his bummed-up ankle. It could have been so much worse. *A miracle*, they kept saying.

"I'll have a plane like this someday," Wesley said as he leaned back in the plush cushioned seat. Situated around a small table, they could have been relaxing at a local restaurant.

"You should be up here with me learning to fly the thing," Artie said from the cockpit.

"Please, Artie. Promise me you won't sell it till I get the chance to take it up at least one time."

"When the right buyer comes along, it's gone. We gotta get the cash together to get poor Blue Bolt's tail and nose repaired."

"Don't remind me," Wesley replied with a groan.

"But this was all my fault," Siegrid spoke up. Snuggled up against Wesley, she'd been quiet the whole time—except when, at the hospital she and Lucie were hugging and squealing as they were reunited.

"Siegrid," Nathan said, "if it took a nasty bump on my head to bring me to my senses, then I thank you from the bottom of my heart. I'd go through it again in a split second."

"That blow on the head may have knocked some sense into you, but you were blathering on about nothing before you came to," Wesley told him.

"Oh no. What was I saying? Was it incriminating?"

"It was hard to hear. Hard to make out. Crazy stuff. Something about a Santa suit. You kept repeating about a Santa suit."

Now Nathan sat up too quick, and his hand flew to his head. "Oh. Ow. Still hurts."

"The doctor said for you to take it easy," Lucie told him. "And to stay awake for several hours. You may have had a concussion."

"But tomorrow. Tomorrow afternoon's the Christmas party at the hospital. Trevalene's expecting us. All of us." He looked around at them. "We have to be there."

Wesley was shaking his head. "What does that have to do with a Santa suit? I'm lost."

Nathan eased back into his seat again. The throbbing wasn't easing up.

"The last time I visited her, she was mumbling. Most of the time, I couldn't make out anything. Just incoherent mumbling."

"Mother actually tried to talk?" Lucie looked over at Wesley. "That's amazing." They'd been waiting for so long for a glimmer of hope that one day she might be well. To return to awareness and normalcy.

"I still thought she was babbling," Nathan continued, "but then a few words came clear. I scarcely paid any attention. I wasn't going to even mention it to you. But now I guess I have. So. Did you ever have a Santa suit?"

Lucie couldn't help but laugh. "Oh yes we did. One year, Mother coerced Daddy into wearing a Santa suit for the party at the Rotary Club Christmas party. Remember, Wesley?"

"How could I forget? He was furious. Swore he'd never do it again. And I mean he *swore*."

Nathan, deep in thought said, "Maybe she wants me to wear the Santa suit to the party."

"No," Wesley countered. "Probably not. I'm willing to bet that thing is long gone. I bet Dad threw it in the furnace."

Still thinking, Nathan asked, "Is there a green wardrobe trunk?"

"Oh," Wesley said, "that's the other thing you were muttering. You kept saying, *green wardrobe trunk.*"

"Well? *Is* there a green wardrobe trunk? Somewhere?" Nathan wanted to know. "That's the other thing Trevalene said. I couldn't make that up."

"Mother made coherent word combinations," Lucie said, barely above a whisper. "That's beyond belief." Turning to Nathan and kissing his cheek, she said, "You have such a gift. And yes, we *do* have a green wardrobe trunk. Isn't it in the attic with the others, Wesley?"

"Before the auction, we took out as much as we were allowed. Among which were several trunks from the Patton mansion attic. First thing on the agenda when we get back to the house—we go up to the attic, dig into the green wardrobe trunk, and see if there's a Santa suit."

Lucie said, "And if there is?"

"Then perhaps our mother has not completely lost all her faculties after all."

Upon landing in Jenks, Artie and Wesley took care of the Red Dragon, with all of them repeatedly thanking Artie for ferrying them to Oklahoma City and back. What a blessing it had been.

Nathan's ankle, badly sprained, but not broken, had him limping. They'd done a great job of wrapping it at the hospital. Lucie was more than happy to let him lean on her as they made their way to where Wesley had left his car that morning.

Back at the house, Lucie couldn't help but watch Siegrid's reaction at returning home. Their prodigal-come-home walked around the kitchen as in a daze, touching everything.

Wesley had been smart enough to grab her suitcases from the plane before they were all carted by ambulance to the hospital. Now he set them down beside the kitchen table. Lucie watched as he gathered his bride-to-be in his arms and held her. "Welcome home," he whispered into her hair.

"It truly is," she answered. "I had to leave to know. To really know. This is my home. My real true home."

"The cooking and cleaning in your absence I didn't mind," Lucie put in. "But gee whiz I surely hated doing the books again. Numbers give me a stomach ache."

"What I want to know is who's going to carry me to the attic?" Nathan said from where he'd seated himself on a kitchen chair. "Or do I have to crawl?"

Wesley shrugged. "Sounds like a good idea to me. Knees work good on stairs. And since you were the message bearer, you have to be witness."

Nathan was still a bit woozy from the pain medication, but he said the pain in his head had eased some. They let him go first up the stairs and gave assistance when he flagged a little.

The air in the attic was cold and still. Wesley reached up and pulled the chains on two separate hanging bulbs, illuminating the low-hung room.

He turned to Lucie and said, "It seems like ages ago that we brought all this stuff in here. At the time, it felt like the end of the world."

"And it was more like the beginning," she replied. Stepping over to the far wall under the eaves, she motioned to where four trunks were situated. "There it is. The green wardrobe trunk."

"So, there really *is* a green trunk." Nathan's voice held a sense of wonderment. "That's unbelievable."

"Wouldn't you know it'd be on the bottom," Wesley said. He stepped forward and pulled the other trunks down off the green one. Then dragged the green one to the center of the room under one of the lights, stirring up dust as it moved.

"It's not locked is it?" Lucie wanted to know.

Wesley knelt down in front of it and pushed two bronze latches which flew open. "Nope. Not locked."

Carefully nursing his ankle, Nathan had settled himself cross-legged on the floor.

"The floor's so dirty," Lucie said to him.

He shrugged. "These clothes have come through a plane crash so I guess it's okay."

She had to laugh at that. Stepping around him, she peered into the trunk, wondering what old memories might be buried there. Meanwhile, Wesley was digging and pulling items out and laying them on the floor. Old books. Photo albums. Cast off clothes. Cigar boxes filled with mementoes and keepsakes.

"Oh my gosh," Lucie said. "I see the red. There it is."

"I see it too. I can't believe this. Mother was right," Wesley said. He dug down and pulled to yank out the Santa suit. But it wouldn't come free. Removing a few more items above it, he said, "Something's holding it. Something's wrapped up in it."

"Let me see." Lucie knelt down beside her brother. She reached down and said, "It's hard." Gently pulling the Santa suit, she let out a shriek and nearly fell over backward. "No! This is impossible!" she cried out. "She would never..."

Now Wesley saw it as well.

"What?" Nathan asked. "You two are white as sheets."

Fully unwrapping the object, Lucie lifted it for all to see.

"It's the Qing Dynasty vase."

"What does it mean?" Siegrid whispered.

Wesley looked up at her with tears in his eyes. "It means, my darling, we're not poor anymore."

"And mother knew all along. She did this," Lucie whispered. "For years it was locked in the wall safe in her dressing room. As far as we know, it's a priceless artifact."

Silence hung heavy in the room as they tried to absorb the significance of the discovery. Then Nathan looked over at Lucie. "Then Henry didn't know..."

"That's what just came to me," she answered.

"And me," Wesley said. "If he'd known it was in their possession, he would never have pulled that trigger."

Lucie began to weep. Nathan pulled her into his arms and let her cry.

With a catch in his voice, Wesley reasoned, "Perhaps Mother was going to surprise him. Maybe after the auction?"

Siegrid, who had been silent up until this point, barely above a whisper, said, "It's no wonder the woman lost all reason. First her being the one to find him. That would have been enough to destroy the strongest person. But then knowing she could have prevented it..."

"Maybe some things are best left unknown." This from Wesley who stood to his feet, and lifted the priceless object above his head. "In a miracle moment, God allowed her to come back to reality. And I'm thanking God for it."

Lucie, drying her eyes with the handkerchief Nathan handed her, said, "And thanking Nathan as well." Then, "And please, big brother, don't you dare drop that thing!"

Chapter 32

February, 1934, Red Fork, Oklahoma

The cold February air resounded with sounds of hammering, sawing, crowbars ripping out old wood, and shouts from the men as they worked all around outside and inside Cairn Cottage. The lower level porch was now screened-in, matching the one above.

A full kitchen had been installed upstairs, and an outside staircase added.

"Covered stairs," Lucie had insisted. "So that during an ice storm, the stairs are free of ice."

"If moisture ever falls from the skies again," Nathan had added.

There'd still been precious little rain, and the ranchers and farmers were suffering.

They'd returned from the cool air of the Colorado Rockies two days earlier. Wesley had known the perfect location for their honeymoon. A hunting lodge nestled in the foothills, overlooking a clear mountain lake, and surrounded by small individual log cabins. Before the Crash, he'd many times flown oil moguls to the lodge on elk-hunting expeditions. Now, the place wasn't as busy, the owners welcomed the foursome with open arms and treated them like royalty, making sure they had the best pick of the cabins.

Wesley warned that in February they could get caught in a snowstorm and be snowed in for days. Nathan, with eyes glowing, replied, "Sign me up!"

There'd been no storm, just soft, light snow sifting down the entire time, enthralling them as it gave off diamond-like glittering in the bright noonday sunshine. Learning to walk with unwieldy snowshoes, they trekked deep into the woods, and up and down hills, with much laughter and silliness. And, of course, inevitable snowball fights. The blistering heat of the past Oklahoma summer faded from their memories.

Snuggled in Nathan's arms in front of a roaring fire, Lucie's heart filled to overflowing with joy and peace. Never in all her life had she experienced such a sense of belonging. A sense of being treasured. His gentleness and respect continually amazed her.

Their double-wedding had drawn the attention of the entire town of Red Fork. Who'd ever heard of a double wedding? Lucie had to laugh as she listened to the chatter among the townsfolk. Keeping the affair small, they'd invited only their closest friends to be in attendance, followed by a reception in the church basement. As Wesley said, "If we opened it to the whole town, they'd turn it into an event to top all events."

Lucie agreed. That wasn't what she wanted. Plus the fact that luggage belonging to all four was packed and loaded in Wesley's Hudson—ready to head to Jenks and the Blue Bolt.

The wedding plan was super simple with Clarette and Erik as matron-of-honor and best man for Lucie and Nathan. Tessa and Gaven standing up for Siegrid and Wesley. Pastor Levinson seemed to be having more fun than anyone and was more jovial than Lucie had ever seen him. He was heard to comment several times that he was the only preacher he'd ever known to conduct a double wedding. He seemed to be more than excited to accept the honor.

But the surprise came as they exited the church following the reception, to find a large crowd of their fellow townspeople ready to cheer and throw rice. Which was quite an honor knowing how tight food budgets were for these families. That rice could have been dinner.

Shortly after the four of them set their wedding date, a friendly discussion had ensued. They knew they wanted Cairn Cottage to be their home. How could they make that happen?

"Simple," Wesley told them. "We'll create a full apartment upstairs."

Then—which couple would live where?

"Lucie loves the upstairs screened-in porch," Siegrid said.

"That's easy, we'll screen in the downstairs porch as well." Again, Wesley's logic.

Each one insisted they cared not who lived where. They literally ended up taking a broom straw and breaking it in half. "Shorter one lives upstairs," Lucie announced. They were sitting together drinking coffee in the kitchen making plans. And then, she drew the shorter straw. Secretly she was pleased. It meant she wound up with the newer kitchen. But still, it just didn't matter. They were all together.

The outbuilding behind Cairn Cottage had been cleaned out and expanded to house Nathan's sign-painting shop on one side, and Lovina's photography studio on the other. She and Uncle Sacha had moved from Indiana early in January. Nathan had located a small house to rent not far from Ma Powell's. Now his family was all safely settled into Red Fork. Nathan was sure Uncle Sacha would live to be a hundred.

At the State Hospital Christmas party, the sight of a Santa on crutches, had brought smiles and laughter to many of the hospital residents, and all the workers as well. The foursome brought with them gifts of candies and nuts and fruit. Of course, they couldn't serve everyone, but worked with officials to serve those who would be in the visiting room at the same time as Trevalene.

It was a great disappointment to Lucie that Trevalene never again spoke a coherent word after clearly saying to Nathan the words *Santa suit*, and *green wardrobe trunk*. The perfect combination to lead them to the priceless treasure. Lucie kept close watch all during the party, saying softly to her mother that Nathan was wearing the Santa suit hoping against hope that it would trigger a reaction. But nothing. No response. It was as though Trevalene's mission had been completed.

On New Year's Day, Lucie received the call from Vinita saying that Trevalene had passed away peacefully in the night. She simply went to sleep and never woke up to see 1934.

The night of the Qing vase discovery, they immediately called Luther Cavanaugh out of bed, telling him he needed to meet them at the bank. By then, it was well after midnight. They didn't tell him why, because telephone operators were known for having big ears and for spreading rumors. The president of the Red Fork bank was the only other person who knew what had been discovered. He opened the vault and the vase was secured.

The four of them talked it over and made the decision that they would tell no one else. The following week, Mr. Cavanaugh had called Lloyd's of London and within a few short weeks an auction had been scheduled. Even in the midst of a world-wide economic depression, many museums, and not a few wealthy individuals, showed interest.

Packed in sawdust and old newspapers, tucked neatly into a fruit crate, the precious vase flew from Artie's in Jenks, Oklahoma, to New York City in the now-fully-repaired Blue Bolt. Nathan accompanied Wesley on the trip. Both had to agree it was an emotional moment signing the papers to seal the transaction.

They were all pleased it went to a museum, because, as Wesley said, "It's be buried long enough. Others need to enjoy its beauty."

Most of the proceeds from the sale went into two separate trust accounts for both couples and their subsequent families. At first Nathan protested, saying the money wasn't his. But Wesley informed him that, first of all, if it hadn't been for him, the thing might have stayed in the trunk for another decade. And secondly, he was now most definitely a part of the Patton family. Like it or not.

That settled it.

The whole town turned out for the ribbon-cutting. The grand opening for the Okesa Filling Station happened two weeks after the Valentine's Day double wedding.

Lucie, along with her husband, her brother, and her sister-in-law, stood in front of the free-standing white structure with the massive sign above it boasting *Okesa Oil and Gasoline Station*. On the pillars supporting the overhang were painted the words *Oil* on one, and *Gas* on the other. And of course, it was Lucie's talented husband who did the painting. The wide overhang allowed vehicles to drive beneath, protected from the weather, to receive service. The glass globes atop the three new red gasoline pumps sparkled as they reflected the Oklahoma sunlight.

As she looked out over the crowd, it pleased her that these people were now her friends and neighbors. Then she noticed, off to the side, there stood E.V. Harland, hat held low in his hands. Their eyes met. He nodded to her and gave a little salute. She nodded back and smiled. A rift healed. It felt good.

Most of the stock in the store had been sold for pennies on the dollar to Sam Peterson, who was thrilled with the windfall. Tearing down the old store, and building the new filling station gave work to many men in the community, as had the work on Cairn Cottage. Some said that Wesley and Lucie had turned the Patton bad luck to good, and brought it over to Red Fork. Lucie wasn't a bit sorry to see the old store go by the wayside.

Music from the local square-dance band filled the air with foot-tapping songs to celebrate the filling station grand opening. It had turned out to be a community holiday. The mayor made a speech. Pastor Levinson prayed over the new business. A glossy red ribbon stretched from pump to pump and tied with large bows. The four of them stood together, with Trent alongside. And each with scissors in hand, cut the ribbon.

Suddenly without warning, Rand, who was standing nearby, broke into song...

Spaceboy Sparkie and his Spacedog Sport

Zooming out to their Jupiter Port

Now his voice grew louder and he was waving his arms, directing his self-made choir. And the whole town chimed in...

There goes Carina – careening through space

on a race

to save the cosmos.

Gus caught the melody on his fiddle, and almost within seconds Hans joined in on the harmonica. Then, over the sound of the whole town repeatedly singing the jingle, Luther broke in and was heard to shout, "Grab your partner. Form a circle. Time for *Oh Johnny Oh!*"

Lucie looked over at her husband. "Nathan. It's a street dance."

"Well of course. Isn't that what these crazy little backwoods, oil-patch towns are all about?"

Grabbing hands and laughing, they joined the wild and raucous circle of dancers as the music blared forth up and down Red Fork Main Street.

Epilogue

Clarette Torsten's historical account of the early days of the oil rush in Red Fork opened with the account of Donly "Andy" Anderson saving a fellow worker from the flames of a natural gas fire. Thanks to Lovina, Clarette had access to the graphic details. The book went on to pay homage to the many men and women who literally gave birth to the Oklahoma oil industry. Among others, the names of Henry Patton and E.V. Harland were included, describing the vital roles they had played.

The book enjoyed brisk sales. Widespread advertising in the *Oil and Gas Reporter* plus the already-established name of author, Clarette Torsten, helped to boost the sales. The royalties poured in, making no small waves with her editors at the publishing house in New York.

To the everlasting joy of all the folks who called Red Fork their home, she titled the book...

Red Fork Roots

Norma Jean Lutz Bio

Norma Jean Lutz's writing career began professionally in 1977 when she enrolled in a writing correspondence course. Since then, she has had over 250 short stories and articles published in both secular and Christian publications. The full-time writer is also the author of over 50 published books under her own name and many ghostwritten books. Her books have been favorably reviewed in *Affair de Coeur, Coffee Time Romance, Romance Reader at Heart, and The Romance Studio* magazines, and her short fiction has garnered a number of first prizes in local writing contests.

Norma Jean is the founder of the Professionalism In Writing School, which was held annually in Tulsa for fourteen years. This writers' conference, which closed its doors in 1996, gave many writers their start in the publishing world.

A gifted teacher, Norma Jean has taught a variety of writing courses at local colleges and community schools, and is a frequent speaker at writers' seminars around the country. For eight years, she taught on staff for the Institute of Children's Literature. She has served as artist-in-residence at grade schools, and for two years taught a staff development workshop for language arts teachers in schools in Northeastern Oklahoma.

As a writer who loves writing for teens, and hanging out with teens, Norma Jean has launched the **Clean Teen Reads** website and blog. Lots of fun stuff for teens! Check it out here:

www.CleanTeenReads.net

The Site for Teens Who Love Books and Stories

Also by

Other Titles by Norma Jean Lutz

Titles Featured HERE https://njnotations.shopify.com
The Tulsa Series
#1 Tulsa Tempest (Christian historical romance)
#2 Tulsa Turning (Christian historical romance)
#3 Tulsa Trespass (Christian historical romance)
#4 Return to Tulsa (Christian historical romance)
The Norma Jean Lutz Classic Collection
Flower in the Hills (a sweet teen romance)
Tiger Beetle at Kendallwood (a sweet teen romance)
Rockin' into Romance (a sweet teen romance)
Oklahoma Exile (a sweet teen romance)
Forever is Over (a pre-teen novel about friendship)
Lingering Dreams (a sweet teen romance)
Teen Coming-of-Age Action Adventure Novels
Brought To You By The Color Drab
A Noble Cause: An Honorable Man Will Uphold a Noble Cause

20th Century Inspirational Historical Romance

Cater to a Whim

The Winning Heart